The bitterness in his voi
wrap her arms around him and hold him close to ease some of the vast pain of betrayal.

"I'm so sorry that happened," she murmured. "But at least you learned you had good friends you could count on."

Wes somehow managed a rusty laugh. "Are you always such an optimist, Mrs. Haynes?"

"Oh, no," she assured him. "Far from it. I've just learned the value of good friends over the years. I would have been lost without them."

He gave her a searching look and she wondered how much truth she had revealed with her words. She wanted to tell him what had happened with Aaron but now wasn't the time, after he had unburdened himself about something much darker from his own history.

She couldn't think of anything else to say and realized they had been standing for a long moment, gazing at each other silently.

He was an extraordinarily good-looking man. Once a woman could see beyond his intimidating size and fierce features, she began to notice other things. The softness of his mouth. The firm line of his jaw. Those intense blue eyes fringed with long, dark eyelashes.

Dear Reader,

What an honor it is to be part of Harlequin's 75th anniversary celebration. No other publisher has so consistently been focused on stories of people opening their hearts to love, despite all the many obstacles they may face. For decades, Harlequin has been gracing bookshelves around the world with enchanting stories filled with swoon-worthy heroes and captivating heroines. I'm delighted to play a small part in remembering all the things that make Harlequin books so special—the promise of love, the thrill of unexpected twists and the satisfaction of happily ever after.

The anniversary celebration seemed a perfect chance for me to finish off my Women of Brambleberry House series. Through the six books in the series, I have come to adore this rambling old house by the seashore. Returning to it feels like coming home for me and I hope my readers feel the same. I have loved revisiting old friends and making new ones!

It's also a great pleasure to me that my novella *A Mother's Hope*, written several years ago, was chosen to be included in this book. That story is dear to my heart and I'm so happy to see it reach a wider audience than the first time it was published in a Mother's Day anthology.

Thank you for being part of this incredible journey, and here's to many more years of shared stories, cherished moments and the enduring power of love.

All my very best,

RaeAnne

A BEACH HOUSE BEGINNING

RAEANNE THAYNE

ISBN-13: 978-1-335-40192-2

Harlequin Enterprises ULC
22 Adelaide St. West, 41st Floor
Toronto, Ontario M5H 4E3, Canada
www.Harlequin.com

Printed in U.S.A.

New York Times bestselling author **RaeAnne Thayne** finds inspiration in the beautiful northern Utah mountains, where she lives with her family. Her books have won numerous honors, including six RITA® Award nominations from Romance Writers of America and Career Achievement and Romance Pioneer Awards from *RT Book Reviews*. She loves to hear from readers and can be reached through her website at raeannethayne.com.

Books by RaeAnne Thayne

Harlequin Special Edition

The Women of Brambleberry House

A Soldier's Secret
His Second-Chance Family
The Daddy Makeover
A Soldier's Return

A Beach House Beginning

The Cowboys of Cold Creek

A Cold Creek Christmas Surprise
The Christmas Ranch
A Cold Creek Christmas Story
The Holiday Gift
The Rancher's Christmas Song

Canary Street Press

The Cliff House
The Sea Glass Cottage
Christmas at Holiday House
The Path to Sunshine Cove

Visit the Author Profile page
at Harlequin.com for more titles.

To all the hundreds of people at Harlequin
who work with such passion and heart to get our books
into the hands of our amazing readers. Thank you!

CONTENTS

A BEACH HOUSE BEGINNING

Chapter One

"Jenna? Are you still there?"

Jenna Haynes slowly lowered herself to one of the kitchen chairs of her apartment on the second floor of Brambleberry House. Her cell phone nearly slipped from fingers that suddenly trembled.

"I…yes. I'm here." Her voice sounded hollow, thready.

"I know this must be coming as a shock to you." Angela Terry, the prosecuting attorney who had worked on the Oregon part of her case, spoke in a low, calming voice. "Believe me, we were all stunned, too. I never expected this. I'm sorry to call you so early but I wanted to reach out to you as soon as we heard the news."

"Thank you. I appreciate that."

"Seriously, what a shock. It's so hard to believe, when Barker was only halfway through his sentence. Who expects a guy in the prime of his life to go to sleep in his cell one night and never wake up? You know what they say. Karma drives a big bus and she knows everybody's address."

Jenna didn't know how to answer, still trying to process the stunning news that the man she had feared for three years was truly gone.

On the heels of her shock came an overwhelming relief. A man was dead. She couldn't forget that. Still, the man had made her life a nightmare for a long time.

"You're…you're positive he's dead?"

"The warden called me to confirm it himself, as soon as the medical examiner determined it was from natural causes. An aneurysm."

"An aneurysm? Seriously?"

"That's what the warden said. Who knows, Barker might have had a brain anomaly all along. What else would cause a decorated police officer to go off the rails like he did and spend years stalking, threatening and finally attacking you and others?"

Jenna fought down an instinctive shiver as the terrifying events of two years earlier crawled out from the lockbox of memories where she tried to store them for safekeeping.

Dead. The boogeyman who had haunted her nightmares for so long was gone.

She still couldn't quite believe it, even hearing it from a woman she trusted and admired, a woman who had fought hard to make sure Aaron Barker would remain behind bars for the maximum allowable sentence, which had been entirely too short a time as far as Jenna was concerned.

Jenna didn't know how she was supposed to feel, now that she knew he couldn't get out in a few years to pick up where he left off.

"I hope I didn't wake you, but I wanted you to know as soon as possible."

The concern in her voice warmed Jenna. Angela had been an unending source of calm and comfort, even during the most stressful of times during the trial.

"No. I'm glad you called. I appreciate it."

Slowly, her brain seemed to reengage and she remembered the polite niceties she owed this woman who had fought with such fierce determination for her.

"You didn't wake me," she assured Angela. "I have school this morning."

"Oh good. I was hoping I didn't catch you while you were sleeping in on your first day of summer vacation or something."

"One more week for that," Jenna answered. "I'm just fixing breakfast for Addie."

"How is my little buddy? Tell her we need to get together soon for a *Mario Kart* rematch. No way can I let a seven-year-old get the better of me."

"Eight. She turned eight last month."

"Already? Dang. I can't believe I missed her birthday. I'll have to send her something."

"You don't have to do that, Angela. You've done so much already for us. I can never thank you enough for everything. I mean that."

"Well, we still need to get together and catch up. It's been too long."

"Yes. I would love that. I'll only be working part-time at the gift shop this summer so my schedule is much more flexible than during the school year."

"We'll do it. We can have Rosa join us. I'll set up a text string and we can work out details."

"Thank you for telling me about Aaron."

"I know you had been worrying about his possible release next year," the other woman said, her voice gentle. "I hope that knowing he can't ever bother you again goes a little way toward taking a weight off your heart."

"It does. I can't even tell you how much."

They spoke for a few more moments before ending the call with promises to make plans later in the summer.

Jenna set her phone on the table slowly, released a heavy sigh and then covered her face with her hands.

Dead.

She didn't quite know how to react.

Since the arrest and conviction eighteen months ago of the man who had tormented her for years, she had been bracing herself for the moment when he might be released, when she might have to pick up her daughter again and flee.

She had hated the idea of it.

Brambleberry House, this beautiful rambling beach house on the dramatic coastline of northern Oregon, had become a haven for them. She had finally begun to rebuild her life here, to feel safe again and…happy.

Lurking at the edge of her consciousness, though, like the dark, far-off blur of an impending storm, was the grim realization that someday she might have to leave everything once more and start again somewhere else.

Now she didn't have to.

She wiped away tears she hadn't even realized were coursing down her cheeks.

He was gone. They were free.

"What's wrong, Mom?"

She turned to find her daughter in the doorway, wearing shorts, a ruffled T-shirt and a frown.

Jenna gave a laugh and reached for Addie, pulling her into a tight hug.

"Nothing's wrong. Everything is terrific. Really terrific."

Her perceptive child wasn't fooled. She eased away, narrowing her gaze. "What's going on?"

Jenna didn't want to talk about Aaron Barker. She didn't want Addie to have to think about the man who had threatened them both, who had completely upended their lives simply because he couldn't have what he wanted.

"Nothing." She gave a reassuring smile. "I'm just happy, that's all. It's a beautiful day, school will be out next week and summer is right around the corner. Now hurry and finish your breakfast so we can get to school. I could use your help carrying the cupcakes for my class."

Addie still didn't look convinced. Sometimes she seemed

far too wise for her eight years on the earth. Apparently she decided not to push the matter.

"Can I have one of the cupcakes? You said I could when we were frosting them last night."

The cupcakes were a treat for her class, a reward for everyone meeting their reading goals for the year.

Jenna pointed to the counter, at a covered container near the microwave. "I've got two there for us. I was going to save them for dessert later tonight after dinner, but I suddenly feel like celebrating. Let's have a cupcake."

Addie's eyes widened with shock and then delight. She reached for the container and pulled out one of the chocolate cupcakes, biting into it quickly as if afraid Jenna would change her mind.

"You still have to eat your egg bites and your cantaloupe," Jenna warned.

"I don't care. Cupcakes for breakfast is the best idea ever."

She couldn't disagree, Jenna thought as she finished hers, as well as her own healthier breakfast. Still, the call was at the forefront of her thoughts as she hurried through the rest of her preparations for the school day.

Twenty minutes later, she juggled her laptop bag, a box of cupcakes and a stack of math papers she had graded the evening before.

She couldn't help humming a song as she walked out of her apartment, Addie right behind her.

A man stood on the landing outside her apartment, hand on the banister. He was big, dark, muscular, wearing a leather jacket and carrying a motorcycle helmet under his arm.

For one ridiculous moment, her heart skipped a beat, as it always did when she saw her new upstairs neighbor. Her song died and she immediately felt foolish.

"Morning," he said, voice gruff.

"Um. Hi."

"You've got your arms full. Can I help you carry something?"

"No. I've got it," she said, her voice more clipped than she intended.

His eyes darkened slightly at her abrupt tone. Something flickered in his expression, something hard and dangerous, but he merely nodded and gestured for them to go ahead of him down the stairs.

Did he guess she was afraid of him? Jenna had tried to hide it, but she strongly suspected she hadn't been very successful.

"Come on, Addie."

Her daughter, who seemed to have none of Jenna's instinctive fear of big, tough, ruthless-looking men with more ink than charm, smiled and waved at him.

"Bye, Mr. Calhoun. I hope you have a happy day."

He looked nonplussed. "Thanks. Same to you."

Jenna led their little procession down the central staircase of Brambleberry House, which featured private entrances to the three apartments, one on each floor.

As she hurried outside, she couldn't help wondering again what Rosa Galvez Townsend had been thinking to rent the space to this man.

She had heard the rumors about Wes Calhoun. He had a daughter who attended her school, and while Brielle was a grade older and wasn't in Jenna's class, the girl's teacher was one of Jenna's closest friends.

Teachers gossip as much as, if not more than, other populations. As soon as Wes Calhoun rode into town on his motorcycle, leather jacket, tattoos and all, Jenna had learned he was an ex-con only released a few months earlier from prison in the Chicago area.

Learning he would be her new upstairs neighbor had been unsettling and upsetting.

Rosa—who functioned as landlady for her aunt Anna and Anna's friend Sage, owners of the house—assured her he was a friend of Wyatt, Rosa's husband, and perfectly harmless. He had been wrongfully convicted three years earlier and had been completely cleared, his record expunged.

That didn't set her mind at ease. At all. She would have found the man intimidating even if she hadn't known he was only a few months out of prison.

She hurried Addie to her small SUV, loaded the cupcakes into the cargo area and made sure Addie was safely belted into the back.

As she slid behind the wheel, Jenna watched Wes climb onto his sleek, black, death trap of a motorcycle parked beside her and fasten his helmet.

While he started up the bike, he didn't go anywhere, just waited, boots on the driveway. He was waiting for her, she realized.

Aware of his gaze on her, steely and unflinching, she turned the key in the ignition.

Instead of purring to life, the car only gave an ominous click.

She tried it a second time, with the same results, then a third.

No. Oh no. This wasn't happening. She was already running late.

Normally she and Addie could ride bikes the mile and a half to the school, but not when she had two dozen cupcakes to deliver!

Hoping against hope, she tried it a few more times, with the same futile click.

"What's wrong?" Addie asked.

"I'm not sure. The car isn't starting, for some reason."

A sudden knock at her window made her jump. Without power, she couldn't lower the window, so she opened the door a crack.

"Having trouble?" Wes Calhoun looked at her with concern.

She wanted to tell him no, that she was a strong, independent woman who could handle her own problems. But what she knew about cars could probably fit inside one spark plug. If cars even had spark plugs anymore, which she suspected they didn't.

"You could say that. It won't start. I'm not getting anything but clicks."

"Sounds like it might be your battery. Do you know how old it is?"

"No. I bought the car used two years ago. It was three years old then. I have no idea how old the battery is. I do know I haven't replaced it."

"Pop the hood and I'll take a look at it."

"You don't have to do that. I can call road service."

He gave her a long look. "You seemed in a hurry this morning. Do you have time to wait for road service? If it's your battery, I can give you a jump and get you on the road in only a few minutes."

She glanced at her watch. The phone call with Angela had thrown off her whole morning schedule. She was already going to be late, without adding in a potentially long wait for road service.

"Thank you. I would appreciate a jump, if you don't mind. Can you jump a car with a motorcycle, though?"

"I don't know. I've never tried. I was talking about my truck."

He had an old blue pickup truck, she knew. He drove that on the frequent days of rain along the Oregon Coast.

"Right."

"Let's take a look first under the hood. Can you pop it for me?"

She fumbled beneath the steering wheel to find the right lever that would release the hood, then climbed out just as Wes was taking off his leather jacket and setting it on the seat of his motorcycle.

The plain black T-shirt he wore underneath showed off muscular biceps and the tattoos that adorned them.

As he bent over the engine, worn jeans hugging his behind, his T-shirt rode up slightly, revealing a few inches of his muscular back. Her stomach tingled and Jenna swallowed and looked away, appalled at herself for having an instinctive reaction to a man who left her so jumpy.

"Yep. Looks like you need a new battery. I'll give you a quick jump so you can make it to work. If you want, I can pick up another battery and put it in for you this evening."

Jenna tried not to gape at him. Why was he being so nice to her, when she hadn't exactly thrown out the welcome mat for him?

"I…that would be very kind. Thank you."

"Give me a second to pull my truck around."

"What's wrong with the car? Is it broken?" Addie asked from the back seat after Wes moved to his pickup truck and climbed inside, then started doing multiple-point turns to put it in position for jumper cables to reach her battery from his.

"The battery is dead. Our nice neighbor Mr. Calhoun is going to try to help us get it started."

"I can't be late today. I have to give my book report first thing."

"Hopefully we can still make it in time," she answered, as Wes turned off his truck and released the hood latch, then climbed out, rummaged behind the seats for some jumper cables and started hooking things up.

"What do I need to do?" she asked, feeling awkward and clueless. She had needed to have a vehicle jumped a few times before, early in her marriage, but Ryan had always taken care of those kind of things for her. She should have paid more attention to the process.

"Nothing yet. I'll tell you when to try starting it again."

He hooked up the cables, then fired up his truck before

coming back to her car. "Okay. Let's give it a go and see what happens."

Mentally crossing her fingers, she pushed the ignition button. To her vast relief, the engine turned for a second or two, then burst into life.

"Yay!" Addie exclaimed. "Does that mean we don't have to walk to school?"

"We would have found a ride somehow," Jenna assured her. "But it looks like we've been rescued, thanks to Mr. Calhoun."

"Thanks, Mr. Calhoun. I have to give a report this morning on a book about bees and didn't want to be late."

"You're very welcome. You can call me Wes, by the way. You don't have to call me Mr. Calhoun."

Her daughter beamed at him, unfazed by that hard, unsmiling face. "Thanks, Wes."

"You can as well," he said to Jenna. Their gazes met and she couldn't help noticing how long his dark eyelashes were, an odd contrast to the hard planes of his features.

"Thank you, Wes," she forced herself to say. "I really appreciate the help."

"It was no problem. I'll grab a battery for you today. Do you have jumper cables, in case your car doesn't start after you're done at school today?"

She was relieved she could answer in the affirmative. "Yes. I have an emergency kit in back with flares, a flashlight and a blanket, along with a few tools and jumper cables."

"Good. With any luck, you might not need them."

"Thanks again for all your help."

He shrugged. "It's the kind of thing neighbors do for each other, right?"

His words filled her with guilt. She hadn't been very neighborly in the two weeks since he had moved in. She hadn't taken any goodies over to welcome him and did little more than nod politely in passing.

Was he being ironic? Had he noticed how she went out of her way to avoid him whenever possible?

She hoped he didn't notice how her face flushed with heat as she mustered a smile that faded quickly as she backed out of the driveway and turned in the direction of school.

Wes watched his pretty neighbor maneuver her little blue SUV onto the road toward the elementary school.

When he was certain her vehicle wasn't going to conk out on the road, he returned his pickup to its customary spot and climbed back onto his Harley.

It might be easier to take the truck today but he was in the mood for a bike ride, which was just about the only thing that could do anything at all to calm his restlessness.

That was an odd turn for his morning to take, but he was happy to help out, even if Jenna Haynes looked at him out of those big blue eyes like she was afraid he was about to drag her by her hair up the stairs to his apartment and lock her in his sex dungeon.

He might have found her skittishness a little amusing if he hadn't spent the past three years in company with people capable of that and so much worse.

It still burned under his skin how she and others considered him. An ex-con. Not an innocent man wrongfully convicted because of a betrayal but someone who had probably been exactly where he belonged. Even if he hadn't done the particular crime that had put him behind bars, he was no doubt guilty of *something*, right?

He hated it, that pearl-clutching, self-righteous, condemnatory attitude he had encountered since his release. After two months on the outside, he was still trying to adjust to the knowledge that his slate would never be wiped completely clean, no matter how many neighborly things he did.

He couldn't be bothered by what Jenna Haynes thought of

him. What anybody thought of him. He had clung to sanity in prison by remembering that he was not the man others saw when they looked at him.

He lifted his face to the sun for just a moment before shoving on his helmet. He couldn't get enough of feeling the warmth of it on his face or smelling air scented with spring and the sea.

Clutch your pearls all you want, Ms. Haynes, he thought. *I'm alive and free. That's enough for today.*

He drove his bike through light traffic to Cannon Beach Car and Bike Repair, the garage where he had been lucky to find a job after showing up in town with mainly his bike, his truck and the small settlement he had received from the state of Illinois.

He had just parked the bike and was taking off his helmet when a tall, dark-haired and very pregnant woman climbed out of a silver sedan and hurried over to him.

Wes sighed and braced himself, not at all in the mood to have a confrontation with his ex-wife that morning. Though they had a generally friendly relationship, he couldn't imagine why she would show up unless she was mad about something. Not when she could have called or texted for anything benign.

"There you are," Lacey exclaimed. "I thought you started work at eight."

He looked at his watch that read eight oh five. "I had a neighbor with a dead battery. It took me a minute to get the car started. What's up? Have you been waiting for me? You could have called."

"I know. But I had to run next door anyway to pick up something at the hardware store after I dropped off Brielle at school, so I figured I would stop here first to talk to you while I was out."

He really hoped she wasn't about to tell him her husband had been transferred again, after only being moved here a year ago to become manager of a chain department store in a nearby town.

Wes liked it here in Cannon Beach. He liked running on the beach in the mornings and sitting in the gardens of Brambleberry House in the evenings to watch the sun slide into the water.

He liked his job, too. He had worked in a neighborhood auto mechanic shop all through high school and summers during college and definitely knew his way around an engine, motorcycle or car.

Did he want to do it forever? No. As much as he had admired and respected the neighbor who had employed him—and all those who worked with their hands—Wes didn't think working as a mechanic was his destiny. He still didn't know what he wanted to do as he worked toward rebuilding the life that had been taken from him. But for now he had found a good place, working with honest, hardworking people who cared about treating their customers right.

It paid the bills and was challenging enough not to bore him, but not overwhelming as he tried to ease back into outside life.

"What's going on?"

He could see his boss, Carlos Gutierrez, and his brother Paco watching them through the small front window of the shop.

"You know you don't always have to cut to the chase, right?" Lacey looked exasperated. "We're not having a quick conversation between prison bars anymore. A little small talk would be fine. You could say, *Hi, Lacey. How are you? How's the house? How's the baby?*"

Wes worked to keep his expression neutral. He might have agreed with her, except their marriage hadn't exactly been filled with small talk, even before his arrest.

"How are you feeling?" he asked. He had learned a long time ago it was best to try humoring her whenever possible.

Lacey was a devoted, loving mother to their daughter and he still considered her a dear friend. If circumstances had been different, he would have tried like hell to keep their marriage together.

Still, he couldn't help being more than a little grateful her sometimes volatile moods were another man's problems these days.

"I'm good. Huge. I can't believe I still have ten weeks to go before the baby comes."

They had been divorced for two and a half years. She had remarried her childhood sweetheart a year almost to the day their divorce had been finalized and was now expecting a son with Ron Summers.

Wes was happy for her. When he had little to do but think about his life, it hadn't taken long for Wes to recognize that his marriage to Lacey had been a mistake from start to finish. He had been twenty-one, about to head off overseas with the Army and she had been eighteen and desperate to escape an unhappy home life, with an abusive father and neglectful mother.

They hadn't been a good fit for each other. He could see that now, though both of them had spent years trying to deny the inevitable.

One good thing had come out of it. One amazing thing, actually. His nine-year-old daughter, Brielle. She was his heart, his purpose, his everything.

"That's actually why I'm here. Ron has the chance to take a last-minute trip to Costa Rica for work. He'll be gone ten days and he wants me to go with him, if I can swing it. This is my last chance to travel for a while, at least until the baby is older."

"Sounds like fun," he said, trying to figure out where he came in and why she had accosted him at his workplace to deliver the news.

"The problem is that I can't take Brie. She doesn't have a passport and there's no way to get one for her in time."

Ah. Now things were beginning to make sense.

"Is there any chance she could come stay with you while we're gone?"

A host of complications ran through his head, starting with the building just beyond her. The Gutierrez brothers had been good to him. He couldn't just leave them in the lurch to facilitate his ex-wife's travel plans.

He worked full-time and would have to arrange childcare. Brielle was nine going on eighteen and likely thought she was fully capable of being on her own while he worked all day. Wes definitely didn't agree. But he couldn't bring her down here to the garage with him all day, either.

He would figure that part out later. How could he turn down the chance to spend as much time as possible with his daughter, considering all the years he had missed?

"Sure. Of course. I would love to have her."

Lacey's face lit up with happiness, reminding him with painful clarity that it had been a long time since they had been able to make each other happy.

"Oh, that's amazing. Thank you! Brie will be so excited when I tell her. The alternative was staying with my friend Shandy and she has that five-year-old who can be a real pistol. Brielle will much prefer staying with her dad."

He could only hope he was up to the task. "When do you leave?" Wes asked.

"Next Friday. The last day of school."

It would have been easier if she were leaving during the school year, when he would only need to arrange after-school care until his shift was over, but he would figure things out.

He couldn't say no. He had moved to Cannon Beach, following Lacey and her new family, in order to nurture his relationship with Brielle. He couldn't miss what seemed to be a glorious opportunity to be with her.

"No problem. We'll have a great time."

"You're the best. Seriously. Thanks, Wes."

She stood on tiptoe and kissed his cheek, and as her mouth brushed his cheek, Wes couldn't help wishing that things could have worked out differently between them.

He couldn't honestly say he regretted the end of a marriage that had been troubled from the beginning. He did regret that the decisions made by the adults in Brielle's life complicated things for her, forcing her to now split her time between them.

"You do remember that today is Guest Lunch at the school, right? Brie said you were planning to go. If you're not, I'm sure Ron could swing by on his lunch break."

He really tried not to feel competitive with his daughter's stepfather, who seemed overall like a good guy, if a little on the superficial side.

"I'll be there," he answered, hoping the day wouldn't be inordinately busy at the shop.

The Gutierrez brothers were great to work with, but an employer could only be so understanding.

As he watched his ex-wife drive away, the second time he had been caught in the wake of a woman's taillights that morning, he was reminded of Jenna Haynes and her car trouble.

If he were swinging by the school anyway for lunch, he might as well take a car battery with him and fix Jenna Haynes's car. It was an easy ten-minute job, and that way she wouldn't have to worry about the possibility of it not starting after school.

He told himself the little burst of excitement was only the anticipation of doing a nice, neighborly deed. It had nothing to do with the knowledge that he would inevitably see Jenna again.

Chapter Two

"Stay in line, class. Remember, hands to yourself."

Jenna did her best to steer her class of twenty-three third-grade students—including three with special learning needs and Individualized Education Programs—into the lunchroom with a minimum of distractions.

The day that had started out with such stunning news from Angela had quickly spiraled. Her dead battery had only been the beginning.

As soon as she reached the school, she discovered both of her paraprofessionals, who helped with reading and math, as well as giving extra attention to those who struggled most, had called in for personal leave. One was pregnant and had bad morning sickness and the other one had to travel out of town at the last minute to be with a dying relative.

Jenna completely understood they both had excellent reasons to be gone. Unfortunately, that left her to handle the entire class by herself, and her third-grade students were so jacked up over the approaching summer vacation—or maybe from the sugar in her cupcakes—that none of them seemed able to focus.

One more week, she told herself. One more week and then she would have the entire summer to herself.

The previous summer, she had taken classes all summer to finish her master's degree, as well as working nearly full-time at Rosa's gift shop, By-the-Wind.

She didn't feel as if she had enjoyed any summer vacation at all.

She wasn't going to make that mistake again this year. Though she still had two more classes to go before earning her master's degree, she had decided to hold off until after the summer, and she had told Rosa she couldn't work as many hours at the gift shop.

Addie was growing up and Jenna wanted to spend as much time as possible with her daughter while Addie still seemed to like being with her.

"Don't want spaghetti." The sudden strident shout from one of her students, Cody Andrews, drew looks from several students in the cafeteria. Some of the adult guests having lunch with their students also gave the boy the side-eye.

Jenna felt immediately on the defensive. Cody, who had been diagnosed with autism, was an eager, funny, bright student, but sometimes crowds could set him off and trigger negative behaviors.

He had seemed to have a particularly difficult morning, maybe because Monica, the aide he loved dearly, wasn't there.

"Do you want to get pizza from the à la carte line?" she asked him, her voice low and calming.

"No. I don't like pizza." That was news to her, since his favorite food was usually pizza and he could eat it five days a week without fuss.

"What about chicken tenders?"

He appeared to consider that for a long moment, his blond head tilted and his brow furrowed. Finally he nodded. "Okay. I like tenders."

The lunchroom was crowded with parents and friends of the students who had come for their monthly Lunch with a Guest activity.

She strongly suspected another of the reasons for Cody's outburst might have something to do with that. His parents were recently divorced and his father, who used to come have lunch with him every month, had moved two towns over.

Normally she didn't eat with the students, preferring to grab a quick bite at her desk while they were out at recess, unless she was on playground duty. But because Cody was being so clingy, she had decided to bring her sack lunch to the table. Now he slid in next to her with his tray of nuggets.

She waved to a few of the parents, then pulled out her sandwich just as she felt the presence of someone behind her.

She turned and was astonished to discover her upstairs neighbor standing beside his daughter, Brielle. He was holding a tray that carried both their lunches.

"Hello."

In boots, jeans and the same black T-shirt he had been wearing earlier in the day, he looked big and tough and intimidating. Completely out of place in an elementary school lunchroom.

He should moonlight as a bouncer at a biker bar, since nobody would dare mess with him.

"Hi, Mrs. Haynes. This is my dad." Brielle, his daughter, beamed with pride.

"I know. I've met him. We're neighbors."

"This is his very first time coming to one of the Lunch with a Guest days."

She forced a smile. "Welcome. I hope you enjoy yourself."

"So far so good. It's pizza. What could go wrong with pizza?"

He obviously had not tried the school pizza yet, which could double as a paperweight in a pinch.

Jenna was disconcerted when Wes pointed to an empty spot down the row from her. "Is it all right if we sit here? There doesn't seem to be room with Brielle's class."

It was always a tight squeeze in the small lunchroom when each student brought a guest. Parents ended up finding spots wherever they could. She gestured to the empty spot. "Go ahead."

She was fiercely aware of him as she finished her sandwich.

"I have a dog," Cody suddenly announced. "Her name is Jojo, and she's white and brown with white ears and a brown tail. Do you want to see?"

Jenna realized with some alarm that the boy was talking to Wes in particular, unfazed by his intimidating appearance.

"Um. Sure."

Cody pulled out the small four-by-six photo album he carried with him all the time in the front pocket of his hoodie, a sort of talisman. He opened it and thrust it into Wes's face, far too close for comfort.

"Wow. She's very pretty," Wes answered.

"Does she do any tricks?" Brielle asked, genuine curiosity in her voice as she peered around her father's muscular arm to see the photograph.

"She comes when I call her and she sits and she can roll over."

"I wish we had a dog," Brielle said, a hint of sadness in her voice. "We have a cat, though, and it's the best cat in the whole world."

Jenna thought the interaction would end there, as Cody could be quiet and withdrawn with strangers. She was surprised when the boy turned the page of his well-worn photo album to show other things that were important to him in his life. His bedroom. His bicycle. His father, who had walked out the previous year.

She might have expected Wes to turn his attention back to his daughter. That was the reason he had come to lunch, after all, to spend time with Brielle. Instead, he seemed to go out of his way to include the boy in their conversation.

She couldn't help being touched by and grateful for his efforts, especially because it allowed her a chance to interact with some of the other students who did not have a guest with them for various reasons.

As soon as the children finished lunch, they were each quick to return their trays to the cafeteria and rush outside for recess.

Brielle seemed to take her time over the meal, probably to spend more time with her father. Cody was the last to linger at the table, apparently enjoying his new friends too much to leave.

When he left to go out to recess, watched over by the playground aides, Jenna rose as well.

"I brought over a battery for your car," Wes said abruptly. "I can switch it out for you before I head back to the garage. I thought that might be better so you don't have to worry about needing a jump again after school is out."

This man was full of surprises. "Really? You would do that on your lunch hour?"

He shrugged. "It's no trouble. Will take me less than ten minutes. Brie can help me. She loves to work on cars, don't you?"

His daughter beamed. "Yep."

"I will need your car keys, though."

"They're in my classroom. I'm about to head back there, if you don't mind following me."

"Not a problem."

He and his daughter walked with her, Brielle chattering happily with her father. She didn't seem to mind his monosyllabic responses.

As they made their way through the halls, Jenna couldn't help but be aware of Wes. She was a little surprised to realize she had lost some of her nervousness around him. It was very difficult to remain afraid of a man who could show such kindness to a young boy who could sometimes struggle in social situations.

"Thank you for helping with Cody. He's having a pretty tough time right now. Guest days are sometimes hard on him. You helped distract him."

"I didn't do much. We just talked about his dog."

She wanted to tell him the conversation obviously meant much more to the boy, who was deeply missing his father, but she didn't want to get into Cody's personal problems with him, especially not with Brielle there.

"The distraction was exactly what he needed. Thank you."

Wes didn't quite smile, but she thought his usual stern expression seemed to soften a little. "Glad I could help. About those keys…"

"Yes. I'll get them."

She opened her classroom and headed for the closet where she kept her personal effects. After digging through her purse, she pulled out her key chain with her car fob.

"Here you go," she said.

He held his hand out and she dropped the keys into it, grateful she didn't have to touch him for the handover.

"Thanks. I'll bring them back when I'm done."

"Do you need my help out there?"

"No. We got it."

"Thank you."

The words seemed inadequate but she did not know what else to say. As soon as Wes and Brielle walked out the side door closest to the faculty parking lot, her friend Kim Baker rushed out of her classroom across the hall, where she taught fifth grade.

"Who is that?" Kim asked, eyes wide. "I must know immediately."

"My neighbor."

"*That's* the serial killer?"

Jenna winced, feeling guilty that she had confided in her dear friend after she found out Wes had recently been released from prison.

"He's not a serial killer. I never said he was. He was in prison for property crimes. Fraud, extortion, theft. But Anna and Rosa assure me he was exonerated."

"There you go, then. You should be fine."

"Especially since I have nothing to steal."

"You and me both, honey. We're teachers." Kim looked in the direction Wes had gone. "I have to say, I wouldn't mind having that man on top of me."

"Kim!" she exclaimed.

"Living upstairs," her friend said with a wink. "What did you think I meant?"

She rolled her eyes. "You're a happily married woman. Not to mention soon to be a grandmother."

Kim was only in her midforties but had married and started a family young. Her daughter was following in her footsteps, married and pregnant by twenty-two.

"I am all those things, but I'm not dead. And he is way hotter than you let on, you sly thing."

Jenna could feel her face flush. She hadn't told Kim much about Wes.

"I am curious about why your sexy new neighbor is stopping by in the middle of the day to talk to you. Is there something you're not telling me?"

"No!" she exclaimed quickly. "Nothing like what you're thinking. He jumped me this morning."

"Go on," Kim said, eyes wide with exaggerated lasciviousness.

Jenna let out an exasperated laugh. "My car died, I mean. He jumped my battery. He offered to fix it tonight, but since he was coming by the school today to see his daughter for lunch, he offered to fix it now."

To her vast relief, this information was enough for Kim to drop the double entendres. "That is really nice of him."

"Yes. It is."

"And you're sure that's all?"

"Yes," she said, more forcefully this time. "He's been very kind. That's all."

Kim made a face and reached for Jenna's hand, her features suddenly serious.

"I'm only saying this as your friend, but I can't think of anyone else who deserves to have their battery jumped by a sexy guy. And if he's kind and thoughtful, all the better."

The genuine concern in her voice touched Jenna, even if she didn't agree with the sentiment. She was deeply grateful for the many friendships she had made since coming to Cannon Beach. The people of this community had truly embraced her and welcomed her and Addison into their midst.

She still could not quite believe she was now free to stay here as long as she wanted.

"I appreciate the sweet sentiment, Kim, but I'm fine. Completely fine. I have everything I need. A great apartment, a job I love, Addie. It's more than enough. I don't need a man in my life."

And especially one who intimidated her as much as Wes Calhoun.

Kim did not look convinced, but before her friend could argue, Wes returned to Jenna's classroom, on his own this time instead of with his daughter.

He set Jenna's keys on the edge of her desk. "Here you go. She's running great now. Started right up. Looks like you're due for an oil change, though. You're going to want to get on that."

"I will. Thanks. What do I owe you for the battery?"

He looked reluctant to give a number but finally did, something that seemed far less than she was expecting.

"What about labor?"

"Nothing. There was really no labor involved."

She wanted to argue but couldn't figure out how in a gracious way. "Thank you, then," she finally said. "I'm very grateful."

She would have said more, but the bell rang in that moment and children began to swarm back into the classroom from the playground.

"Glad I could help," he answered. "I'll let you get back to your students."

"I'll settle up with you this evening, if that's okay."

Again she had the impression he wanted to tell her not to worry about it, but he finally nodded. "Sounds good. See you later."

Two students approached her desk to ask a question about the field trip they were taking on Monday to the aquarium in Lincoln City. By the time she answered them, Wes had slipped away.

Chapter Three

"I love, love, *love* pizza night!"

Wes smiled at Brielle, her face covered in flour and a little drip of tomato sauce on her nose. She wore an apron that matched the black one he wore on the rare occasions he cooked. Those occasions mostly consisted of Friday nights, when Brielle came over for her weekend visitation. Their tradition had become centered around pizza night, where they would spend an hour or so making their own pizzas and then would watch a show of her choosing.

The few days he had the chance to spend with Brielle were the highlight of his week. Even when they didn't do anything more exciting than hanging out at his apartment and playing board games, Wes found himself happier than he believed possible three months earlier.

This moment—in his warm kitchen with rain pattering down outside and his daughter giggling at the kitchen table as she made a face on her pizza with pepperoni—seemed worlds away from his life the past three years.

Rich and sweet and filled with joy.

He had been given a second chance and didn't want to waste a minute of it.

"Only one more week of school. Can you believe it?"

Brielle shook her head. "No. And I also can't believe I'm

going to be in fifth grade next year. I hope I get Mrs. Baker. She's super funny."

He had met the woman the day before when he had returned Jenna's key to her classroom, he remembered.

While he was thinking about things that seemed far away from prison life, Jenna Haynes was the epitome.

She was lovely as a spring morning, her life worlds away from the darkness and ugliness he had been forced to wallow through in prison.

As lovely as he found her, he would be wise to remember they likely had nothing in common. He was darkness to her light, hard and jaded and cynical in contrast to her sweet innocence.

And she was terrified of him. He couldn't forget that part.

"Looks like we made too much dough. What are we going to do with it?"

"We can make another pizza!" Brielle said with a grin.

"We can do that, but that means we're going to have a lot of leftovers to eat the rest of the weekend."

"We could invite someone over," she suggested. "What about Mrs. Haynes and Addison? I can't believe they lived downstairs all this time and I never knew until today."

He hadn't exactly been holding out on Brielle. He simply hadn't thought to tell her before now about his neighbors.

He had only been in Brambleberry House for two weeks, after spending his first several weeks in the area paying a ridiculous amount for a tiny studio with a short-term lease, until he had found this place available. This was only his daughter's second weekend staying here with him. She had been delighted when he mentioned the other building tenants.

"Mrs. Haynes is super nice. I don't have her but my friend Reina does, and she really likes her," Brie had said when he told her.

"What about her daughter? Do you know her?"

"She's only in third grade, but we have the same recess so we play soccer sometimes. She's super fast. And she's funny!"

A good sense of humor seemed to be the barometer by which Brielle judged everyone. He couldn't disagree.

"So can we take them our extra pizza?" she asked now.

He was trying to come up with a good excuse to refuse when his doorbell rang.

Wes frowned, instantly on alert. Prison had given him a strong dislike of surprises. He wasn't expecting anybody, but maybe Lacey had forgotten to send something with Brielle for her overnight stay. Vitamins or extra socks or something.

"I'll get it," Brie sang out, rushing toward the door.

Wes hated that his life experience made him constantly brace for trouble.

He followed Brie, ready to yank her back to safety if necessary as she opened the door.

It wasn't trouble. At least not the sort he had become used to. His neighbor and her daughter stood on the landing to his apartment.

"Hi, Mrs. Haynes. Hi, Addie," Brielle said.

"Hi, Brielle." Addie beamed at his daughter.

The two girls looked very different. Addie had blue eyes and blond curls while Brie had long straight dark hair, which she usually wore in a ponytail or braid.

"It smells delicious in here," Addie exclaimed, giving a dramatic, exaggerated sniff. "What are you making?"

"Pizza." Brie grinned. "We make the dough and everything. My dad is the best pizza maker. He learned from my grandpa, who died when my dad was a kid. Isn't that sad?"

"My dad died when I was a kid, too. I was only four."

"I'm sorry." Brielle hugged the other girl, which seemed to touch Jenna.

So Addison's father had died. He had wondered if the man was still in the picture somewhere.

He gave Jenna a look of sympathy, which she met with a strained smile.

"Pizza is a great skill," she said. "We brought you dessert, then. Sugar cookies."

Brielle's features lit up. "Wow. Thanks! I love cookies."

"Here you go," Addie said, handing over a plate covered in pastel-frosted flower cutout cookies that looked like spring.

"You didn't have to do that," Wes said.

She had already paid him for the battery, a check in an envelope she had left tucked in the door frame of his apartment. He was more than a little embarrassed that he had noticed the envelope smelled of strawberries and cream, like Jenna.

"It's the least I can do to thank you for all your help with my car yesterday. I know cookies are poor recompense for giving up part of your lunch hour, but I didn't know what else you might enjoy."

"Home-baked cookies are always a treat. I don't get them very often."

"Well, I hope you enjoy them."

"How is the car running?"

"Great. Everything has been perfect."

"I'm glad."

They stood awkwardly for a moment as he fought the urge to brush the pad of his thumb over that slight tinge of pink rising on her cheekbone.

Brielle saved him from doing something so foolish. "Hey, Dad. Can Addie and her mom stay for dinner? You said we had too much pizza to eat ourselves."

The awkward level had now ratcheted up to a ten.

"I'm sure they have other dinner plans," he said quickly.

"We don't," Addie said. "Pizza would be great!"

"We were going to heat up some soup from the freezer, remember?" Jenna said, not meeting Wes's gaze. "We were just saying how soup is just the thing for a stormy night."

As if on cue, lightning arced through the sky, followed by a sharp crack of thunder that made both girls shriek in surprise, then giggle at each other for their shared reaction.

"I like soup, Mom, but I would rather have pizza," Addie said. "It smells soooo good, doesn't it?"

"We really do have more than enough dough and toppings," Wes said. "We were just trying to figure out what we were going to do with it when you knocked on the door. It was perfect timing."

Another bolt of lightning flashed outside and rain began to pelt the window.

It was beyond comforting to be here inside this warm apartment in the big, rambling house by the sea.

"It does smell good," she admitted.

"And tastes even better," he said, not bothering with false modesty. He had very few skills in the kitchen and was justifiably proud of his pizza dough, a recipe his father had perfected over the years before he died.

"All right," she finally said. "If you're sure we won't be imposing on your time with your daughter."

"Not at all," he assured her. "We were just about to put the toppings on, if you want to come and choose what you want."

She followed him to the kitchen of his apartment, which Wes had considered a decent size. He wasn't sure exactly how it seemed to shrink with the addition of another child and a small woman.

"How can I help?" Jenna asked.

How long had it been since he had shared a meal with a woman besides his daughter? He honestly couldn't remember.

"You could throw together the salad, if you don't mind. I've already rinsed the lettuce and it just needs to be tossed."

"I can do that."

She crossed to the sink and washed her hands then went to work ripping leaves from the romaine and green lettuce heads he had purchased earlier that day before picking up Brielle from her mother's.

"What do you like on your pizza?"

"I'm not picky. What do you usually have?"

"Brie is a big fan of plain cheese and pepperoni. I typically go for margherita, with crushed San Marzano tomatoes, fresh mozzarella, basil and a splash of olive oil."

Her eyes had widened during his geek-out about pizza and she gave a surprised laugh. "That sounds really delicious. Addie will probably be happy with the pepperoni as well."

"Perfect. So two margherita and two pepperoni. I can only cook two at a time on my pizza steel so let's do the girls' first. They don't take long."

"Okay."

While he formed another ball of dough into pizza crust for Addie, then enlisted the girls' help to add the sauce, mozzarella and pepperoni, Jenna began slicing cucumbers and tomatoes to add to the salad.

This was nice, he thought as the girls went to work setting the table. He had bought a kitchen-in-a-box set of plates and silverware and serving utensils that supposedly contained everything a person needed to set up a basic kitchen. Now he wished he had sprung for something nicer.

Once the girls' pizzas were in the oven, he went to work with the other two balls of dough, expertly shaping them and adding the toppings. Jenna watched him work, her expression interested.

"You really do know what you're doing."

He gave a rueful smile. "I'm kind of a pizza geek. My dad spent a year working in Italy at a pizza place during a gap year of college and he taught me a few secrets."

"Brie said you were only a child when he died."

He didn't like remembering the pain of that time. "Ten. He moved from making pizza to opening his own restaurant in the little town outside Denver where he grew up. One night after closing, a couple of drifters broke in, thinking the place was empty. They shot my dad and took off with what was left in the cash register after he'd already made the deposit for the night. Thirty bucks in change."

"Oh. I'm so sorry."

The soft sympathy in her voice, in her expression, seemed to seep through him and he wanted to bask in it.

Embarrassed, he quickly changed the subject as he ripped a couple of basil leaves off the plant he bought at the supermarket.

"I can't get enough of smelling fresh basil," he said as he sprinkled the herb atop the two margherita pizzas. "Sometimes I want to just bury my face in it. Amazing, the things you never realize you missed."

Oh wow. He was just full of brilliant conversation. First he dropped his father's long-ago murder into the conversation, then he started gushing about herbs. He wouldn't be surprised if she scooped up her daughter and went rushing back downstairs, away from the weirdo with a basil fetish.

Instead, she was looking at him again with that same soft compassion. "How long were you…in prison?"

"Three years, two months and five days."

He didn't look at her as he turned on the oven light to check the girls' pizzas.

It didn't matter that he had been cleared of any wrongdoing. The damage was done. He would never get that time back and his reputation would never fully recover.

Guilty or not, he had spent more than a thousand days in prison. Had seen things he couldn't unsee. Cruelty between inmates, intimidation and abuse by guards, people treated more like cattle than human beings until they gradually began to lose their humanity altogether.

He was a different person than he'd been the day he had been arrested.

"I'm not sure what should be the appropriate response to that," she admitted after a moment. "*I'm sorry* doesn't feel at all adequate."

He shrugged. "It happened. It's done. I'm still trying to figure out what comes next."

He wasn't sorry to change the subject again. "Looks like these are ready to come out."

He pulled out the two pizzas, happy to see the crust bubbly with air pockets, then slid the other two into the oven.

"These other pizzas will only take a few minutes. Since the girls' pizzas have to cool down first before they can eat them without burning their tongues, why don't we start with the salad and vegetables?"

He had already prepared a relish plate as it was the only way he could persuade his daughter to eat a few vegetables.

The next few moments were busy finding beverages for everyone and taking the girls' pizzas to the table.

Soon, his timer went off to remove the other pizzas from the oven. He was delighted by the surprise and pleasure on Jenna's expression.

"That looks absolutely delicious."

"I hope it tastes even better."

The girls chattered away about school around mouthfuls of pizza, while he and Jenna worked on their salads. Finally, she picked up her first piece of pizza. He felt silly, but couldn't help holding his breath until she took a bite. The sound of delight she made was gratifying.

"Wow," she exclaimed. "That is really delicious. The flavors come together so perfectly. I'm afraid I might never be happy with pizza delivery again."

"That's the problem with making your own pizza. If you do it right, it kind of ruins you for anything else."

He couldn't help staring at her mouth as it lifted into a slight smile. What would it be like to have her give him a full-fledged smile? Even better, a laugh?

He shouldn't be wondering about that, Wes chided himself. He and Jenna Haynes were simply neighbors, though he wanted to think maybe after the past few days, she would no longer watch him out of those nervous eyes, like he was a mountain lion crouched to pounce on her at any moment.

Her life felt so surreal sometimes, the reality often more bizarre than anything her imagination could conjure up.

A few weeks ago, Jenna would never have believed she would find herself having dinner with her intimidating new neighbor and his daughter.

Or that she would enjoy it so much.

The pizza was delicious, probably the best she'd ever had. And though Wes Calhoun seemed to be going out of his way to be friendly, she still sensed a wary reserve in him.

He seemed to measure each word as carefully as he probably did the flour in his father's pizza dough recipe.

Did he ever completely let down his guard? She doubted it.

She was fine with that. She had to be, since she had her own protective barriers firmly in place.

"Thank you," she finally said, after she had eaten every single bite of her personal-sized pizza. "That was truly delicious."

"It was super good," Addison agreed. "Mom, you should take lessons from Brie's dad on how to make pizza."

She raised an eyebrow. "Should I?"

"You make good pizza," her daughter quickly said. "But Mr. Calhoun makes *really* good pizza."

"He truly does."

"I'm happy to teach you all I know. Which should take maybe five minutes. It's all about not skimping on the quality of your ingredients and putting a little advance thought into it."

"I'll keep that in mind. Thank you again for sharing your pizza night with us."

"You're welcome to come back again the next time we make it," Wes said. "Every Friday night is pizza night. We might even have to do it more than once a week. Brielle is going to be with me full-time for the first few weeks after school gets out, and I don't have that many other specialties. I expect we will have the chance to enjoy a lot of pizza."

"My mom is going to Costa Rica," Brie said. "I think she should take me, but she says she can't because I don't have a passport."

"You'll get another chance to go on a trip with your mom and stepdad," Wes assured his daughter. "Meantime, you get to hang out with me and do all kinds of fun things."

"We can definitely plan some times for you two to hang out while you're staying at Brambleberry House with your dad. It will be great for Addie to have someone her age here."

"My friend Logan used to live downstairs on the first floor, but he moved away with his dad *forever* ago."

"I know Logan. He's nice."

"He is," Addie agreed. Suddenly her eyes widened with excitement. "And guess what? As soon as school is out, we're getting a dog! I've been begging and begging for one, and Mom finally said we can go to the shelter next week to find a rescue."

"Lucky!" Brielle exclaimed. "I always wanted a dog. We just have a cat. What kind are you getting?"

Addie shrugged. "I don't know. We haven't picked it yet. Whichever one needs a home most, I guess."

Jenna did her best to ignore the misgivings she still felt about taking on a pet. She knew full well how much responsibility it would be, adding a dog to their family. But now that she knew for certain they wouldn't have to pack up and disappear again, as she had feared for so long that they would have to do when Aaron Barker was released from prison, she could no longer think of any more excuses.

Addie had been through so much in her short life. Losing her dad. Having to uproot her life and escape here to Cannon Beach. Living for more than two years with a jumpy, scared-of-her-own-shadow mother.

Agreeing to her daughter's relentless pleas to add a dog into their lives felt like the least Jenna could do for her.

"You're so lucky!" Brielle exclaimed. "Can I play with him or her?"

"Anytime you want," Addie said. "You could even help me take him for a walk, if you want. Dogs need a lot of exercise. That's what my mom says."

"Your mom is right," Wes said. "The happiest, healthiest dogs get exercise at least a few times a day."

He sounded like an expert. She really hoped so, since she had no idea what she was doing. Maybe he could give her advice.

While the girls chattered more about what kind of dog was best, Jenna turned again to Wes.

"Thank you again for the pizza, though I just realized that I owe you even more now."

"How's that?"

"First you kindly go out of your way to change my car battery, then you make us the best pizza ever. All I've done in return is bake you a batch of cookies."

"They were delicious cookies, though. I'm sure between Brie and me, they will be gone by morning."

"Cookies hardly compare. You make it tough for a woman to clear her debt to you."

He gazed down at her, something in his expression suddenly that made her cheeks feel hot.

He blinked it away and returned to a polite smile. "You don't owe me anything in return. Cookies are more than enough."

She did not necessarily agree, but couldn't immediately

think of anything she could do to repay him for his kindness. She would have to give it some thought.

"Come on, Addie. It's almost bedtime."

Her daughter predictably groaned but headed for the stairs. "See you later," she called to Brielle.

"Good night." Jenna gave one last smile as she followed her daughter down the stairs.

On the positive side, she suddenly realized, the evening together had gone a long way toward reducing her fear of Wes. It was tough to be nervous around a man who obviously adored his daughter and who found such simple pleasure in the smell of fresh basil.

Chapter Four

"This is the one, Mom. He's perfect. We have to get him."

Jenna looked at the floppy tan puppy in her daughter's lap, all paws and ears and big, soulful eyes. She was watching firsthand the process of two creatures falling in love. The dog couldn't seem to keep his eyes off Addie and her daughter was clearly already long gone.

"He's the cutest dog ever. The very best dog. Please, Mom!"

She had envisioned them leaving the shelter with a small older dog. A Chihuahua or a little Yorkie, some kind of petite, well-trained lapdog who didn't bark or chew or make messes all over the floor.

"He was one of a litter of six mini goldendoodles that were found abandoned down near Manzanita."

The shelter volunteer helping them, a woman in her forties with a name tag that read Pam, gave the dog an affectionate pat. "We've adopted out all but him. You could call Theo here the last man standing, I guess."

"Hi, buddy. Hi."

The clever dog licked Addison's cheek, completely sealing the deal, as if he knew exactly which of them really held the power in this situation.

Jenna was suddenly quite certain there was no possible way on earth she would be able to get out of here now without taking along this dog, who literally met none of the qualities on her own personal wish list.

Her daughter clearly loved him. That was the most important thing, she reminded herself. Jenna would simply just have to figure out how to readjust her own expectations.

"How old is he?" she asked Pam.

"We can't say for sure," the shelter worker said. "The vet thinks maybe three to four months? They were weaned puppies when they were found and he's been here a month. That's just an estimate, though."

"Why would anybody abandon a litter of puppies?" Addie looked horrified, her arms tightening around the dog as if to protect him.

Because people can be selfish and cruel sometimes.

She didn't want her daughter to learn that lesson yet, so Jenna only shook her head sadly. "Who knows?"

"I wish I understood it," Pam said. "I can't comprehend how anyone could think a litter of puppies would be better off there, in the middle of a forest, than here at our shelter. It makes no sense to me."

"Me neither." Addie hugged Theo, her cheek pressed against the dog's fur. "Nobody's going to leave you anywhere now, Theo. I promise. You're coming home with us. You'll love our house. We even have a ghost!"

Pam looked startled. "A ghost?"

Jenna gave a rueful smile. "We live in an old beach house. Brambleberry House? You might know it."

"Oh yes. That wonderful place on the edge of town."

She nodded. "Some of the previous residents are convinced we have a benevolent spirit who watches over all those who live in the apartments."

She still wasn't convinced and found it amusing that her friends Rosa and Melissa spoke about Abigail as if she were an old friend, though she had died more than a decade before either woman had lived in the house.

"A ghost!" Pam looked enthralled. "Oh, that's lovely. How about that, Theo? Want to live in a house with a ghost?"

The dog's tongue lolled out and he actually looked enthusiastic, but that could have been more evidence of his growing adoration for the girl holding him.

"Is he trained at all?" Jenna hated to ask but needed to know what challenges she might be facing.

"He's getting there. He's not a hundred percent but he is very smart, and it shouldn't take him long to learn how to follow some basic commands, as soon as he adjusts to the routine of your house."

"I can't wait!" Addie's eyes glowed. "I'm going to teach him to sit, to roll over, to shake hands and to catch a ball in the air like my friend Logan's dog can do."

"Those all sound great but first things first," Jenna said. "We need to start with teaching him not to go to the bathroom inside the house. After that, we can work on the other commands."

"We can provide you with some great websites and other resources that give good training advice," Pam said. "We can also connect you with a few places locally that offer puppy training classes."

"That would be very helpful," Jenna said, again trying to push down her misgivings. She could handle this. She certainly had done harder things in her life than train a puppy.

"So have you decided for sure?" Pam asked.

Jenna gestured to her daughter and the dog. "I think these two have decided for me."

"Oh great. And since you've already been approved for adoption, you can take him home with you today, if you'd like. We do have a few forms for you to fill out. Addison, would you bring Theo with you to my office?"

"Yes!" she exclaimed. Pam provided a leash from a hook on the wall and Addie attached it to the dog's collar, then proudly walked with him down the hall to a small office decorated with pictures of dogs and cats and their happy new humans.

A half hour and several signatures later, they walked out of the shelter with their new family member padding happily beside them.

All her misgivings came flooding back as she loaded Addie and Theo into the car. What had she done? She went through days when she felt as if she could barely take care of herself and her child. Adding another living creature to her responsibilities suddenly felt overwhelming.

"Can I go show Mr. and Mrs. Anderson downstairs? Theo also has to meet Sophie. Do you think they'll be friends?"

The retired couple who lived in the first-floor apartment of Brambleberry House had a very cute—and very spoiled—toy poodle.

"I'm sure they will be great friends." She hoped, anyway. "The Andersons left this week for their trip, remember? They left Sophie with their friend in Portland."

"Oh right."

"We're going to have to pick up some supplies before we can take Theo home. Toys and food and a crate."

She probably should have purchased all that in advance before taking home the dog, but she had been so busy wrapping up end-of-year school details, she hadn't thought that far ahead.

"Can we take him into the store?" Addie asked. "I don't want to leave him alone in the car."

"No," she agreed. "We shouldn't do that. I know they let dogs into the pet store. We'll go there."

They parked at the pet store and headed inside, after stopping long enough for Theo to raise his leg on a fire hydrant conveniently placed near the door.

It didn't take long to fill a shopping cart for the puppy. At this rate Theo would be as spoiled as Sophie, she thought.

They had nearly finished finding everything on the quick list they had made before coming inside when Addie suddenly exclaimed with delight. "Mr. Calhoun! Hi, Mr. Calhoun!"

Jenna whirled around and found her upstairs neighbor walking through the pet store with a bag of cat food.

"Oh. Hi."

She hadn't seen Wes since pizza night, nearly a week earlier, except for a few brief waves of greeting in passing. She had somehow forgotten how big and tough and intimidating he looked.

And gorgeous.

She hadn't forgotten that part.

She could feel her face heat and hoped he didn't notice.

"Wow." He looked down at the gangly dog. "Looks like you've got a new friend."

"This is Theo. He's the best dog ever. And he's our very own dog now! He gets to come home with us."

"That's very cool. Hi, Theo. Nice to meet you." Wes crouched to the same level of the dog and reached out a hand, which Theo investigated with a sniff followed by vigorous tail wagging.

"I think he likes you," Addie said, beaming.

"Hey, bud." He scratched the dog's ears and under his chin, which seemed to earn him Theo's instant adoration.

"I didn't know you had a cat," Jenna said, gesturing to the food bag.

"I don't." He straightened. "But we've got a couple of strays that hang out at the shop. They're good mousers but I still like to leave a little food for them. Plus I guess I'll be cat-sitting for a couple weeks as Brie is bringing along Murphy when she comes to stay with me."

"That's nice of you."

He shrugged. "If I have to take a bad-tempered elderly cat

as part of the package in order to hang out with my daughter, it's worth the sacrifice."

He looked back at the dog. "You say his name is Leo?"

"Theo," Addison corrected. "The nice lady at the shelter said his real name is Theodore because he looks like a teddy bear but they didn't want to call him Teddy so they call him Theo."

"Nice name."

"I hope he doesn't bother everyone at Brambleberry House," Jenna said. "The shelter said he's not one to bark a lot."

"He'll be great, I'm sure. I'm not worried. I hardly ever hear the neighbors' little poodle."

She decided not to point out that Sophie lived two floors below him and had been gone for a week, where Theo would be just downstairs one flight all the time.

"Fingers crossed," she said.

He glanced into their cart. "Looks like you have everything you need to take the dog home."

"And then some, right? I'm afraid we've gone overboard."

"You can never have too many tennis balls when it comes to dogs. I can help you load your supplies into your car after you check out."

She was a tough, independent woman who had been forced by circumstance to learn how to stand on her own two feet. Still, it was nice to have the option to lean on someone once in a while.

"That would be really helpful. Thank you."

As he only had one item, he checked out first, then waited while she did the same. The final tally made her gulp. Having a pet was not a cheap undertaking.

When her items were bagged and she had paid for them, all three of them walked outside.

"When is Brielle coming to stay with you?"

"Tomorrow night."

"How exciting. I bet it's going to be wonderful to have her there."

"Sure. It should be great."

She thought she picked up a note of hesitation in his voice, but she didn't have a chance to ask him about it before they reached her SUV.

She popped the cargo gate and he helped her load all their supplies into the back, including the heavy bag of puppy food.

"Thank you. I really appreciate your help."

"My pleasure."

He gave a smile, or as close to one as he seemed to offer. It wasn't really much of a smile, mostly just a small lifting of his mouth, but it still made her toes tingle.

"I guess we will see you."

"Yes. Leave the dog food by your car and I can carry it upstairs for you."

She could manage, but it seemed ungracious to refuse. "Thank you. I appreciate that."

"See you later, Addison. Bye, Theo."

Addie waved and Theo wagged his tail with delight.

After she made sure Addie had her seat belt on, Jenna drove away, wondering how on earth she had shifted from fear to this wary fascination in such a short time.

Wes had never smoked but some nights, he really longed for a cigarette.

He knew there were guys in prison who had picked up smoking there as a way to relax and beat the boredom. He had preferred other methods. Working out, reading. Studying.

He had taken Spanish lessons in prison as well as a couple of community college history and rudimentary law classes. He also volunteered for a couple of service programs.

Anything he could do not to sit in his cell and feel sorry for himself and angry at the world.

Now he had the freedom to do whatever he wanted, whenever he wanted. Maybe that was why he felt so…restless. He still didn't quite know what to do with that freedom.

He thought the hour run he had taken earlier might ease this edgy discontent. It hadn't, nor had the long, pulsing, delicious shower after.

He ached for something but wasn't sure what.

After changing channels a dozen times, picking up his book, then putting it back down, scrolling on his phone through news stories he didn't really care about, he decided to take a ride on his bike down the coast. Maybe a little sea air on his face would calm him.

He walked down the two floors of Brambleberry House, sensing, as he sometimes did, the faint, barely perceptible smell of flowers on the stairs.

Rosa Galvez Townsend, who had rented him the apartment, had told him there were rumors that a benevolent spirit walked the halls of the house, the ghost of a longtime owner of the house, Abigail Dandridge.

She had died with no direct heirs and had left the house to two friends and tenants of hers.

She apparently had loved the house so much she had not wanted to leave.

He remembered staring in disbelief at the woman, who had given him an embarrassed sort of laugh. "You do not have to believe it. Most people don't. But I felt like it was only fair to warn you about the rumors before you move in."

A hint of flowers on the stairs was not exactly a convincing argument. Even if there had been a real ghost, how could he pass up a beautiful apartment in a rambling old house on the seashore? He had no problem putting up with the random scent of flowers and the occasional waft of cold air that seemed to come out of nowhere.

As he walked outside, the night smelled of lilacs and lavender, with a salty tang from the Pacific fifty yards away.

And he was not alone in the Brambleberry House gardens, he realized. Jenna stood in the grass, holding the leash of her gangly new puppy.

She spotted him coming onto the porch and waved.

"Hello. Don't mind us. This is about our tenth trip outside this evening. We're working on potty training. I'm not quite sure Theo understands the concept completely yet, so I imagine we'll be coming out frequently to reinforce. So much for my relaxing summer vacation, right?"

She smiled, a white flash in the moonlight, and his entire body seemed to tighten.

"He'll figure it out," he said. "Consistency is the key to training puppies."

She moved closer, and he could smell the scent of her, an intoxicating mix of strawberries and vanilla and sunshine.

"You sound like you have some experience in that area. Have you trained many dogs?"

For a brief moment, he debated how much to tell her and finally decided there was no good reason to withhold the information.

"I was part of a canine training initiative in prison. We did the initial basic training with puppies that might eventually become service dogs. I was lucky enough to have three great puppies during my time. All of them eventually graduated and are working as trained service animals now."

"That sounds like a wonderful program."

The dogs had truly been lifesavers to him, bringing peace and comfort and purpose during those dark years.

"It was a good fit. You have a bunch of people with nothing but time on their hands. That's what dogs need most, especially in the beginning."

He missed those puppies. He had given his heart to each

of the three dogs he had worked with in prison and had been gutted when it was time to pass them on for the next phase of their training.

Now that he was on the outside, Wes had been thinking about getting a dog of his own, though he wasn't sure he was ready to start over with another pet.

He supposed some part of him still worried things might change in a heartbeat, that something could happen to throw his life back into chaos. He didn't know what that might be, but didn't want to take any chances that he might not be ready for that kind of complication and commitment.

That was the main reason he was working as a mechanic at the Gutierrez brothers' shop. He was good at it, for one thing, but he also needed something fairly straightforward to do right now while he tried to figure out the rest of his life.

Before his arrest, he had been running a highly successful security company in Chicago with thirty employees and multimillion-dollar contracts.

All of that had disappeared in a blink. The company. His life savings. And most of his trust in humanity, Wes had to admit.

He wasn't sure he had the bandwidth right now to start over and rebuild everything from scratch.

He knew he had to start somewhere, but he had no idea where the hell that somewhere might be.

He wasn't about to spill his angst all over Jenna Haynes. If she knew the tangled morass of his brain, she would probably be more afraid of him than she had been when he first moved in.

She didn't seem as afraid of him now.

He found that awareness both exhilarating and vaguely terrifying.

Some part of him wanted to warn her she had every right to be afraid. Around her, he felt like the proverbial Big Bad Wolf.

He wanted to swallow up a sweet thing like Jenna Haynes in one delicious bite.

"I could use any pointers you have with Theo here," she said before he could tell her any of those things. "This is my first time training a dog. My first time being responsible for any pet, actually."

He raised an eyebrow. "You didn't have a dog growing up?"

"No. Believe me, I wanted a dog desperately but it never quite worked out."

"Why not?"

"I grew up with a single mom, with no dad in the picture," she said after a slight hesitation. "I don't even have a name, since he took off before I was born and my mom didn't like to talk about it. Mom always worked two jobs to support us, and she didn't think it would be fair to have a pet when we weren't home very often to take care of him. Also, money was invariably tight so she could never quite justify the cost of pet food or vet bills when she was working so hard just to take care of us."

"Is that one of the reasons you gave in to Addie's pleas, even though you're nervous about taking on a dog? Because, like most parents, you want to give her what you always wanted but never had?"

Her gaze sharpened at his insight. "Yes. That's exactly why. Good guess, Dr. Calhoun. I must say, I feel a little called out right now."

He gave a short laugh. "I'm not all that brilliant. I only understand it because I'm the same way. I told you my dad died when I was ten. I missed him fiercely when I was a teenager, so I'm determined to be as present as possible in Brie's life. To the point of being obnoxious about it."

Wes paused, then added, "What about after you married? Why didn't you get a dog then?"

"Multiple reasons, I suppose. We wanted one but our first apartment didn't allow pets. We moved into our first home after we had been married two years, but I was pregnant at the time and we decided to wait a bit until adding a pet into the mix, on top of first-time home ownership and new parenthood."

"Sounds sensible."

"Sometimes I wish we hadn't been so sensible. I only had six years with Ryan. We should have done all the crazy things we dreamed about. Flown to Paris. Quit our jobs and lived on the beach in Mexico for a time. Gotten a puppy. Or a half dozen puppies."

Life's cruelties never ceased to infuriate him. A sweet woman like Jenna deserved to have a long and happy life with the man she loved. "How did your husband die?"

"Cancer. Melanoma. He was only thirty."

"That's tough."

"Yes. Addie was barely three when he was diagnosed. He died a year later. It was a very painful time."

"I'm sorry," he said, the words feeling painfully inadequate.

"Thank you. But I've learned since Ryan died that everybody has something, you know? I don't have the monopoly on pain."

He knew so many people who could take a lesson from her, who considered themselves permanent victims of whatever hardship that came their way and refused to accept that someone else might be struggling, too.

"What about you?" she asked, obviously eager to change the subject. "Did you have dogs when you were growing up?"

He nodded. "When I was young, we lived on the small hobby farm where my dad grew up and there were always dogs around. We didn't really have house pets but we always had horses and dogs and chickens."

"Oh, that sounds lovely."

"It was a pretty good childhood, for the most part. Then my dad died and my mom couldn't keep up with things. She sold the restaurant and the farm and we moved to the Chicago area to be closer to her family."

How differently might his life have turned out if his father had not died? Wes probably would have stayed in the Denver area. He might even still be there.

Instead, they had moved to Chicago, where he had struggled in school and became friends with people who hadn't always had his best interests at heart.

Wes had been involved in a few scrapes during his teen years and had even served a brief stint in youth corrections.

He might have continued on that path, except he had one teacher who had given him the straight truth about the dead-end direction he was headed. For some reason, Wes had listened.

He had determined to change his life. He had enlisted in the Army, where he had worked first as a mechanic and then as a military police officer. He had met and married Lacey while he was still in the service and taken her first to Germany and then to Japan.

Even before he got out, he and a buddy had decided to start a security business. Hard work and determination had turned their fledgling enterprise into a success beyond his wildest dreams.

And then everything had changed.

"Were you going somewhere?" Jenna asked.

It took him a moment to realize she was referring to his leathers and helmet. He suddenly didn't feel like taking a ride anymore. He wanted to stay here with her in this moonlit garden and enjoy the sound of the waves and the scent of a lovely woman beside him.

That was a dangerous road. He would be much better off climbing on his bike and riding off into the night.

"I was going to take a ride. Nowhere special. I do that

sometimes. It's cliché, I know, but I like to feel the wind on my face."

"I've seen you leave at odd hours and wondered where you go."

He wasn't sure how he felt to know she had watched him from her window as he sped off into the night, trying to outrace demons that always seemed to be racing right behind him.

"How long ago did you lose your husband?"

"It's been four years now. I can hardly believe it's been that long. It feels like only yesterday. Addie has spent half her life without her father. She hardly remembers him, which I find so sad. Ryan was a wonderful father and adored her from the moment she was born."

"She won't completely forget. Ryan is part of her, just as she is part of him."

"You're right. I see him sometimes in the way she loves to read every sign we pass on the road or tilts her head when she's studying something she doesn't quite understand."

"He lives on in her."

"Yes."

She was pensive for a moment, then smiled. "I'm sorry I kept you from your ride. Thanks for the encouragement with Theo. Don't be surprised if I become annoying and bring you all my many questions."

"You shouldn't expect veterinarian-level answers," he warned. "I spent a year training puppies. That's the extent of my knowledge."

"That gives you a year more experience than I have."

Her smile flashed in the moonlight, and he had to curl his hands around his helmet to keep from crossing the space between them and reaching for her.

"I'm happy to help with whatever I can do."

"Thank you. Good night. Enjoy your ride. And I apologize

in advance if Theo and I make too much noise going in and out at all hours."

"Don't worry about that. I can't hear anything up on the third floor except the wind."

"Are you sure you're not hearing Abigail? If you smell freesia, that's supposed to be her."

He raised an eyebrow. "Do you really buy into all the ghost stuff?"

She shrugged with a rueful smile. "Originally I was skeptical when we moved into Brambleberry House. Since then, I don't know. I'm less skeptical, I guess. I hope that doesn't make me sound too out-there. I don't usually believe in that sort of thing, but for some reason living in Brambleberry House leaves you open to all kinds of ideas you might once have thought were unlikely, bordering on ridiculous."

"I'm surprised there wasn't a ghost clause in my rental agreement."

"Did you read all the fine print? There might have been. I don't know. It's been more than two years since I signed my agreement, and to be honest with you, when I moved in, I didn't care if there were a *dozen* ghosts living here. Addie and I just needed a safe place, which we certainly found here in Cannon Beach."

He frowned. A safe place? Why? What had threatened them? Her words did certainly explain her general air of unease, especially around him.

Was she still running? Somehow, he didn't think so.

Even in the short time he had known her, she seemed calmer than she had in the beginning, when he first moved into the apartment. Maybe that was only because she had come to know him a little.

He wanted to press her, but she certainly looked as if she regretted saying anything at all.

"I hadn't realized how late it is," she said quickly, confirming his suspicion. "I should go back in with Addie. Thank you again."

"You're welcome. Good night."

He gave the dog one last pat. "Good night, Theo. Be good."

"Considering he's already chewed up one of my flip-flops and a pair of Addie's socks, I think we're past that."

"He'll outgrow the chewing. Get him a couple of nonrawhide bones he can chomp on. Or you can freeze some wet puppy food in one of those sturdy chew toys you bought at the pet store and give him that. When he's outside, of course, where he can keep the mess in the grass."

"I'll keep that in mind. Thanks. Come on, Theo."

With that, she hurried back inside the house, leaving the scent of her, strawberries and cream, floating on the breeze. Along with lilacs and...was that the smell of freesia? He wasn't sure he even knew what that was and didn't know how to find out. Maybe he would have to make a trip to the garden center to see if they had any of the flowers so he could do a scent test.

The concept made him roll his eyes at himself. Was he really buying the idea that the house might be haunted?

It didn't matter. He was staying put, no matter how many ghosts the house might hold.

Jenna hurried up the steps to her apartment and closed the door behind her. Theo plopped down immediately, as if their trek out to the garden had completely sapped him of all energy.

She could only hope.

"You had better sleep all night now," she said sternly. "I don't feel like going out there at 2:00 a.m."

The puppy yawned, stretched and closed his eyes, right at her feet.

"Nope." She scooped him up. "You need to sleep in your crate."

She set him in the large crate the shelter had suggested. Theo seemed completely comfortable in the space. He immediately curled up on the soft blankets she had folded into the corner.

She could only hope she would sleep as well, but something told her she might be up for a while, remembering that conversation with Wes.

Had she really blurted out that she believed in ghosts?

The encounter played back through her mind, and she suddenly realized something that had been haunting the edges of her subconscious since he moved in.

Wes Calhoun was lonely.

She did not know why she had that impression, but she was suddenly convinced of it. He had come out of the house with a glower she wasn't even sure he was aware of. Nor did she think he realized how that glower had lifted when he spotted her and Theo.

Poor man. He had moved to Cannon Beach to be closer to his daughter and likely knew few people except those he worked with and his ex-wife and her new husband.

She understood where he was coming from. She had certainly felt alone when she first moved to town, though she had had Rosa, her dear friend from college.

Rosa had convinced her to come here in an effort to escape the numbing terror she had lived with for months because of Aaron Barker.

She thought she had fled far enough away so that she and Addie would be safe here in Cannon Beach. Aaron had no idea one of her dearest friends lived here. She knew she hadn't mentioned Rosa during any of their three dates, before she broke things off when his obsessive control began to manifest itself.

She had been wrong about being safe here in Oregon.

By a cruel twist of fate, an accident, really, he had discovered where she had fled and had followed her here, with horrifying consequences.

She pushed the darkness away. She could not let him intrude further in her life. She had already given him far more than he deserved. He was gone now. She was safe, at least physically.

She had attended counseling after Aaron had ultimately been arrested. She had worked through much of her trauma from the long months of relentless anxiety. She had come far, especially if she could chat with a big, dangerous man in a moonlit garden beside the sea.

She hadn't been completely comfortable, but she suspected that might have to do with her growing awareness of him as more than simply her neighbor.

The man seemed in dire need of a friend, someone he could turn to when the nights seemed long and empty.

She wasn't sure she could be that person, nor could she completely understand why she suddenly wanted to try.

Chapter Five

Why, oh why, did she always end up having to carry her groceries into the apartment during a fierce downpour?

Was she a victim of poor planning or merely fickle weather?

When she had set off for the grocery store that Saturday morning after dropping Addie off at a birthday party, the sun had been shining and the birds had been singing. Yes, she knew a storm lurked on the horizon. She couldn't miss those dark clouds gathering offshore. But she hadn't expected it to hit so quickly or with such ferocious fury.

Now she sat in her car in the driveway of Brambleberry House, waiting for the weather to cooperate and the rain to slow at least enough that she could carry a few bags inside without becoming completely drenched.

She also had to let out Theo, whom she had left in his crate inside her apartment.

She had just about decided to run for it anyway when a sudden knock on her window startled her. She gasped at the unexpected sound and momentary fear pulsed through her as she saw the large, hulking shape of a man standing outside the door.

He shouted something she couldn't quite hear over the noise of the storm. Lightning flashed nearby, followed almost immediately by thunder. So close!

The instant she recognized Wes standing outside her car with a large umbrella, her instinctive panic eased.

She opened her door just a crack. Even in the small space, rain poured in.

"Do you need help? I saw you pull in from upstairs. When you didn't go into the house, I was worried something might be wrong."

"Yes, something's wrong. We're in the middle of a hurricane, in case you didn't notice."

He chuckled, a deep, pleasing sound that drifted to her even over the tumult of the storm.

"This is not a storm. I've been in actual hurricanes when I was in the Army stationed in Florida. This is only a little squall."

"It's still enough to soak my groceries. I don't feel like eating soggy bread for a week. I was waiting for it to let up a little."

"Makes sense. You could do that, if you want to. Or I brought you out an extra umbrella. You can run up to the porch with it and I'll grab your groceries."

"Thank you. I usually keep a few in my car, but Addie and I both used one last time we had a big rain and I think I left them inside the apartment."

"Open the back of your car and head inside. I'll grab as many groceries as I can."

"I can grab a few bags, too."

Why had she picked today to do the big grocery shopping, her monthly trip when she stocked up on the necessities they used most?

Oh yes. She remembered. Because as much as she adored her daughter, shopping with Addie usually took twice as long. Her daughter liked to look at every book on the racks, every possible cookie at the bakery and each little item in the tempting little toy section.

She scooped as many bags as she could carry in one hand while juggling the umbrella in the other and hurried up to the porch, where she quickly entered the security code on the front door.

Wes was close behind her. He didn't bother with the umbrella, she noted. He simply sprinted inside so the reusable shopping bags filled with groceries didn't have much time at all to become drenched.

"Is that everything? I can go back out."

He held up both hands, where she saw he had at least three shopping bags in each. "This is everything. One question. Are you planning for the apocalypse?"

She shook her head. "I'm on a teacher's salary and only get paid once a month. When I grocery shop, I try to buy in bulk and freeze food to make it last."

She supposed she hadn't ever really lost the fear that she would never have enough to provide for her daughter, which she knew was a lingering worry from her insecure childhood.

"Thank you for bringing it in and helping me keep everything dry. I can take it up the stairs from here."

He gave her a look that showed he clearly took offense at her suggestion. "I've got it. I haven't had a chance to go on my run today, since I had to take Brielle shopping for a friend's birthday present, so I'll count this as my workout for the day."

He hefted the bags high, which made her smile. The gloomy day suddenly felt much brighter. "Brielle must be at Carly Lewis's birthday party, too."

"Apparently it's the social event of the weekend."

"Of the whole month, according to Addie. She was thrilled to be invited to an older girl's party."

"I can imagine." He made it up the stairs without a sign that carrying the heavy bags was any exertion at all.

"So Brielle's mom has left the country?" she asked as she opened her apartment door for him.

"Yep. I'm flying solo. It's a little daunting to know I'm alone right now in the parent department. Lacey is now two thousand miles away. If I had a problem, I know I could always reach out to her, but it's more than a little intimidating to realize I'm on my own."

"You'll be fine."

"I hope so. The prospect of two weeks of being on my own with Brie gives me even more respect for single parents like you, who do this alone all the time."

She smiled as she started putting groceries away. "I'm lucky. Addie is easy."

"So far. The girls haven't hit their teens yet."

She groaned, not wanting to think about how fast her child seemed to be growing up.

From his crate, Theo whined to be let out. She winced. She was a terrible dog mom. She should have done that first thing. "Oh shoot. I'd better take him outside. He's been in his crate for an hour while I went shopping."

"Why don't I take care of that and you can keep putting away your vast quantities of vegetables?"

"That would be great, actually."

"I'll take him out to the fenced area of the garden. That way we won't need the leash, especially since I don't expect he'll be that crazy about hanging out in the rain, either."

"We call that the dog yard, since that's where the Andersons put their little Sophie."

The entire Brambleberry House property had a wrought-iron fence surrounding it, but it was open in front for the driveway. The completely fenced area adjacent to the house was the perfect size for Theo.

She had just finished finding room in her refrigerator for the rotisserie chicken she planned to shred and use in multiple recipes when she heard a sharp rap on her apartment door.

She hurried to open it for Wes and Theo, both of them drenched.

"Oh my! What happened to the umbrella?"

"It broke in the wind ten seconds after I walked outside."

"You're soaked. Let me find you a towel."

She grabbed two—one for Wes and one for Theo.

"Thanks," he said as Jenna picked up her dripping dog and began rubbing him briskly with the towel, trying not to notice how Wes's blue T-shirt clung to every hard muscle of his chest.

He dried off his hair, not seeming to care that the towel left the ends tousled and sticking up in random directions.

He looked as if he had just climbed out of the shower.

Her shower.

She swallowed and turned her attention back to the dog. She did *not* want to go there, even in her imagination.

"You seem to know what you're doing in the kitchen."

"You mean because I bought a little of everything at the grocery store?"

"Yes. Plus I think you have some things there I've never even heard of."

"I like to cook. I don't have a lot of time during the school year so summer gives me a good chance to experiment and try some new recipes."

"I should do that. I'm sure Brielle will quickly get tired of eating pizza or going down to the taco truck on the beach."

"Who could ever get tired of that? We love pizza and tacos."

His mouth lifted into a slight smile that made her suddenly aware that they were alone here in her apartment, without either of their girls.

And she was suddenly aware that he was an extremely attractive man.

"We should grab tacos together sometime while I have Brielle with me full-time."

She swallowed, her mind racing. Was he asking her out? Panic raced through her. She wasn't ready. Not to date again, to allow herself to be vulnerable again. She wasn't sure she would ever be ready.

Just before she would have made some excuse, common sense reasserted itself. He was not asking her out on a date. He was suggesting that, as two single parents, they share a meal together with their children.

She swallowed. "That would be good."

"How about midweek? That's when I get really tired of coming up with something to cook."

"We could probably make that work."

"Great. I'll be in touch."

She remembered suddenly the loneliness she had sensed in the garden, when they had talked in the moonlight.

Wes had been incredibly helpful to her on several occasions. The least she could do was repay the favor, even if it meant stepping outside her comfort zone.

She hesitated, then plunged forward. "I could also show you how I make a few of my basic recipes. I'm far from an expert but I do have a few specialties and I'm always happy to share. It would be the least I can do, after everything you've done to help me the past few weeks."

"You don't owe me anything. But I'm sure Brielle and I would both appreciate a few new recipes to add to the mix."

"We're having lasagna tonight," she said, then went on before she could change her mind. "I have a good recipe for an easy roll-up lasagna that's delicious and Addie never even notices the spinach I slip in. You and Brielle are welcome to join us, if you don't have plans. Consider it my way of paying you back for pizza the other night and also for sacrificing your comfort for my groceries. We could say around seven."

If he was surprised at her invitation, he hid it well. "That would be great. Thank you. I was trying to figure out what to fix for dinner."

"That's one of the hardest things about being a parent. I hate the idea of having to make that decision every single day for the rest of my life until Addie goes to college."

"I hear that."

"On the other hand, I try to remember to be grateful that I'm not like my mother and I've never had to worry that my child will go hungry."

"That's a good way of looking at things."

He gazed down at her, that half smile playing around his mouth. She shivered at the intense light in his eyes and had to hope he didn't notice.

The moment seemed to stretch out between them, soft and seductive.

What would she do if he kissed her right now? Would she be afraid and pull away? Or would she sink into his arms, surrender to the heat simmering between them?

She didn't have the chance to find out. He didn't kiss her. Instead, he broke the connection between them, a small muscle flaring in his jaw.

"I should go change into dry clothes so I can pick up Brielle."

She glanced at the clock on the mantel, an odd combination of relief and disappointment coursing through her.

"Oh, you're right. I can't believe it's that late. There's no reason for both of us to go. I can pick up the girls, if you want."

He nodded, a little tersely. "Okay. That works. I guess we'll see you at seven, then."

She wasn't quite sure what happened next. She only intended to walk him to the door. One moment they were moving together in that direction and then suddenly Jen thought she caught the vague scent of freesias swirling in the air. At the same time the puppy moved across her path. She caught herself just in time from tripping over him but the awkward movement left her unbalanced.

She was going to trip anyway, she realized in a split second. She reached out instinctively, blindly, to brace herself, and her hand encountered damp cotton covering warm, solid muscle.

"Whoa," he exclaimed. "Careful."

His arms came around her and held her upright. She stared up at him, this man whose intimidating looks concealed emotions she suspected ran deep.

All of him was hard, dangerous, except his mouth. That was soft, mobile. Enticing.

She stared at his mouth, just inches from her own.

She wasn't afraid of him kissing her. She *wanted* him to.

The realization left her more off-balance than stumbling over a puppy.

She wanted to wrap her arms around him and taste and explore that mouth that often looked so stern.

She held her breath, waiting, aching. For a long moment, they gazed at each other, the only sound in her apartment their combined breathing.

Before she could do something foolish like reach up and instigate the kiss, take what she suddenly wanted, Jenna came to her senses.

No. She couldn't do that. She was not in the market for a relationship, and she was certainly not in the market for a relationship with a hard, dangerous man like Wes Calhoun.

She quickly stepped away, pulling her hands together so that he did not see them trembling. "Thank you. I'm not quite sure what happened there. Maybe there is something slippery on the floor."

If she didn't know better, she would almost think Theo had tried to trip her on purpose. She could not say that, of course. It sounded ridiculous. Anyway, why would her sweet puppy do such a thing?

That muscle flexed in his jaw again. "I'm glad you didn't fall," he said.

"So am I. Thanks for catching me. I really don't need any broken bones to start out the summer."

"Watch out for wandering puppies."

"I'll do that. I'll let Carly's mom know I'm taking Brielle home, but she might want to text you to make sure it's okay."

"Sounds good. Thanks. I guess I'll see you tonight, then."

Anticipation curled through her, sharply sweet. "Yes. See you then."

By then, she would try to have a much better hold on this burgeoning attraction to a man she knew she shouldn't want.

He had to stop doing this.

Wes hurried up the steps toward his apartment, for the first time feeling the chill of his damp clothing.

He was a glutton for punishment. Jenna Haynes was not the woman for him. He knew that. She was sweet, warm, nurturing. Innocent.

They couldn't have been more different. He possessed exactly none of those qualities.

That didn't stop him from wanting her anyway.

Some part of him had responded instinctively when she stumbled. He had reached for her and had wanted to pull her tightly against him and keep her safe from any harm.

He had almost kissed her. The urge had almost overwhelmed him.

Fortunately, he came to his senses in time, seconds before he would have pressed his mouth to hers.

Kissing her, unleashing his hunger, would have changed everything.

They were forging a fragile friendship, one he was beginning to cherish. He liked talking with her. She was smart, funny, kind.

While he might yearn for much more than a friendship, he knew it was impossible between them. He had to get over it.

She seemed to have lost her outright fear of him, but that didn't make her less wary. She jumped if he accidentally touched her and she still watched him as if not sure how he would react to any given situation.

Why was she so nervous? Okay, yes, he looked tough. He could see himself in the mirror every morning when he shaved. He knew he appeared intimidating and fierce. He had put on muscle in prison, not really as protection or defense but mainly as a distraction.

He might have hoped Jenna would know him enough by now to understand he would not hurt her—or any woman, for that matter.

Maybe her unease didn't have anything to do with him.

If she had not spoken of her husband in such affectionate terms, he might have thought she had been a victim of domestic abuse. That could still be the case, though somehow he doubted it.

Her secrets were her own, he reminded himself. Everyone had them and if Jenna was not interested in sharing hers, he could not fault her for that.

She seemed willing to be friends. She had invited him and Brielle to dinner, after all, and had agreed to take their girls out for tacos some other time during the week.

Could Wes put away his growing attraction for her and be content with only a friendship?

What choice did he have?

He liked being with her. Maybe in time she would trust him enough and would begin to relax a little more in his presence.

He had very few friends here in Cannon Beach. He didn't want to lose this one, even if that meant shoving down his growing attraction for her.

Chapter Six

Later that evening, Wes sat at Jenna's dining table, feeling distinctly uncomfortable.

The food was delicious, pasta in a creamy spinach and tomato sauce with a tossed salad and fluffy breadsticks.

The conversation was fine, too, with the girls chattering away and carrying most of it.

Still, he was aware of a vague feeling of unease.

This felt entirely too domestic, the kind of warm, enjoyable scene that he had dreamed about through all the long months he spent on the inside.

His own marriage had never been this cozy. He and Lacey had been a bad combination from the start. She had been so young, not at all ready for marriage but eager to escape her difficult family.

He had liked her more than most of the women he'd dated. When she had become pregnant about four months after they started dating, despite their use of protection, they both decided marriage was the best course of action.

She had lost the baby a week after their wedding at the county clerk's office in North Carolina, where he had been stationed at the time.

He had once cared about her. Or told himself he had, anyway. Having Brielle two years later had been a joy for both of them, going a long way toward erasing much of the pain of that first miscarriage. But somewhere along the way they had both realized they weren't a good fit and had been talking about ending the marriage before he had ever been arrested.

He knew he had been a lousy husband and blamed himself for the breakdown of their marriage.

He had been a workaholic, completely focused on building up his business. At the time, he told himself he was doing everything for Lacey and Brielle. Lacey had begged him to slow down, to spend more time with them, to help her out more around the house and with their child.

He had made empty promises, again and again, but he hadn't changed.

In prison, he had finally acknowledged to himself that he had always held part of himself back from the marriage. He had never let himself be vulnerable with Lacey, had never truly opened his heart to her.

He had seen how devastated his mother had been after his father's murder, and maybe some part of him had internalized that and prevented him from completely letting down his guard.

Even if he had, he wasn't sure they ever could have healed all that had been withered because of neglect.

By then, Lacey had already reconnected with her childhood sweetheart. She was now very happily remarried, expecting another child with her new husband.

She had found in Ron Summers all that Wes hadn't been able to give her.

When he saw how happy they were together, Wes had decided he had been the problem all along, as he suspected. He sucked at marriage, apparently. Maybe he should just stick with being the best possible father to Brielle to make up for lost time and leave domestic bliss to others more suited to it.

This, though. This felt so comfortable here in Jenna's apartment, easy and natural and soothing. Rain clicked against the windows and the puppy snored at the girls' feet. As she listened to the girls' steady conversation, Jenna smiled with a warmth that made something in him ache with cravings he thought he had buried long ago.

"That lasagna was delicious, Mrs. Haynes," Brielle said.

"We did a good job on it, didn't we? Thanks for helping me. All of you. We have so much left over—you can take some home and put it in the freezer for another day."

"Good idea."

Dinner prep with her had been a delight as she showed the girls with calm patience how to make the sauce and then layer the ricotta and spinach sauce on the noodles before rolling it up into pinwheels on the pan.

"You did most of the work with dinner," he said now to her. "We can clean up."

"We left the kitchen a mess, though."

"We don't mind the work, do we, girls?"

The girls looked as if they minded very much but they didn't argue, simply went to work clearing away the table and carrying the dishes to the sink.

The cleanup did not take as long as Jenna seemed to think it would. After they had finished, Brielle and Addie asked if they could play a new board game Jenna had recently purchased.

He couldn't come up with an excuse, since he had nothing else planned for the evening with his daughter and it was too early for bedtime.

The game was fun and challenging and much giggling ensued as they tried to figure out the rules.

"Looks like Theo needs to go out," Jenna said after the second round. "You three keep playing. I'll take him out."

"It's still raining, though," Addie pointed out.

"Yes. We live in Oregon. It tends to do that. But unfortunately for us, dogs still need to go outside occasionally, especially when they're being trained."

"I can take him," Wes offered.

"You're the one who told me how important consistency is in puppy training, remember? I need to reinforce the training. I don't mind."

He rose from the table, undeterred. "Can I come with you anyway? After all those carbs, I could use a stretch."

He wasn't lying. For reasons he wasn't ready to explore, his muscles felt tightly coiled. She hesitated briefly then nodded. "Will you girls be okay in here? We'll just be outside for a few moments."

Addison rolled her eyes. "I'm eight and Brie is nine. We're fine. Can we play *Mario Kart*?"

"Fine with me. We won't be long."

The girls were already moving to the sofa and pulling out the game controllers as Jenna reached for her raincoat. Wes took the coat from her and held it out, manners drilled into him by his mother coming to the fore.

"You don't have a raincoat?" she asked as they headed for the door.

He shrugged. "I have one but it's upstairs. I'll be fine. I'll stay on the back porch."

He would actually welcome a little rain right now to cool his skin and his overheated imagination, though he didn't share that information with her.

She picked up a small towel he assumed was for wiping down the wet dog and handed Wes an umbrella from a container by the door. When she opened the door, Theo trotted happily down the stairs to lead the way.

The rain had slowed to a drizzle, he saw when they walked outside to the rear of the house and the dog yard. The moon even peeked out from behind the clouds to cast a pale light onto the shrubs and flowers.

She inhaled deeply as she walked down the steps with the

gangly puppy still leading the way. "Oh, I love that smell. Don't you?"

He drew in night air scented with rain and flowers and the sea.

"It's nice," he had to agree.

"When I was a kid, we lived in one apartment building that had a very small playground with a patch of grass no bigger than one of the flower gardens here. I still loved to go out every time it started to rain and stand on that little patch of grass to sniff the air. My friends all thought I was weird."

"I don't think you're weird."

Funny, warm, appealing. Definitely not weird.

"Since I've moved to Cannon Beach, I've decided everything smells even more delicious here, when you add in the ocean and all the pine and cedar trees around, plus the Brambleberry House flowers. It's magical, isn't it?"

She was magical. Wes found her sweet and refreshing and unforgettable. How was any man supposed to resist her, especially a man who had known far too little sweetness recently?

He could not disagree about the air. It was intoxicating. Something told him he would never be able to smell this particular combination of scents, rain and flowers and the ocean, without thinking of this night and this woman.

"The first night after my release, we had a rainstorm. I stood outside my motel for at least an hour and just relished the rain on my face."

It was an admission Wes suspected he could not tell anyone else on earth. Somehow he knew Jenna would understand.

She said nothing for a long moment, attention fixed on the dog, who was currently sniffing the base of a Japanese maple. Finally she turned to face him, eyes solemn and her features sad.

"Why were you in prison, Wes?"

The question seemed to come out of nowhere, like a sudden unprovoked attack from his six that left him momentarily breathless.

He owed her an answer.

He wanted to tell her all of it. At the same time, he wanted to pretend it had never happened.

"I trusted the wrong person," he finally said. The words sounded naive and unbelievable, even to him. Was it any wonder a jury of his peers had not believed them either?

He wished he didn't have to talk about this. He wanted to stand in this delicious-smelling garden and enjoy the simple pleasure of talking to a lovely woman. But the past was part of him now, an inescapable imprint on his personal story, and he suddenly wanted her to know.

"I told you I served two tours in the Army as an MP. Military policeman. When I got out, I got a job providing private corporate security. After a year or two of that, I ended up starting a company doing the same thing with a good friend, another MP I served with. Anthony Morris."

Even mentioning Tony's name left a bitter taste in his mouth, pushing away the remaining sweetness of the boysenberry pie they'd had for dessert.

"Tony was my best friend in the service. I thought I knew him. I trusted him. But unfortunately, the man I thought I knew didn't exist. He said all the right words about honor and integrity but lived a completely different reality. Somehow he managed to conceal it from me and our clients, smiling to our faces while filling his pockets with anything he could find."

"He was dirty?"

"To the core. The whole reason he wanted to start Mor-Cal Security was to use our clients, people who trusted us, as his personal booty chest. He didn't steal just a few things, either. The extent of it was staggering. He stole something from every single client. Large or small. Trade secrets. Account information. Personnel records. Even loose change. Whatever he could pocket or sell to the highest bidder. He was an equal opportunity thief."

That helpless rage swept over him again. "And I was stupid enough to hand him the keys. Literally and physically. I never imagined he would betray our clients like that. Betray *me* like that. I didn't believe him capable."

Maybe he deserved to go to prison for being so unbelievably stupid. But if everyone who trusted the wrong person ended up in prison, there would be no room for the actual criminals.

"People can be capable of all sorts of things we never imagine."

Her tone was tight, resigned, making him wonder who could possibly betray someone like Jenna.

"You are right, unfortunately. If I had given it any thought at all, I would have figured a guy whose life you saved in the middle of a firefight is not going to screw you over a few years later."

Her features softened with compassion. "Oh, Wes. I'm sorry."

Her compassion seeped into all the cold places, taking away a little of the chill from the memories. "I should have suspected something was up, but he handled all the finances. He was the brains, I was the muscle. I was just glad I could help my mom and my sister out a little and buy a nice house for Lacey and Brie, after they put up with years of base housing."

"When did you start to suspect?"

He sighed, remembering the bitter shock. "When I was arrested for grand theft. I denied everything, of course. I thought the feds had made the whole thing up. Tony would explain everything, I told them. Then I discovered Tony had fled to South America, leaving me swinging in the wind. Everything traced back to me. He had cleverly covered his tracks and created a false trail that led straight to my door. From the outside, it looked as if I had planned and orchestrated everything and that he had escaped only to protect himself from me when he uncovered the truth."

"Oh no."

"Right. Tony had completely set me up and I was too naive to see what was happening."

"You must have been in shock when you figured out what was really happening."

"You could say that. He was the closest thing I had to a brother, you know?"

She placed a comforting hand on his arm and he gazed down at her fingers, small and pale in the moonlight. Did she feel this pull between them, the same magnetic force of the moon directing the tides?

"Is he still on the run?"

He shook his head with a grim satisfaction. "A couple of my Army buddies went down and found him about a year ago. They dragged him back to face the consequences. He eventually ended up coming clean and admitted I wasn't involved. The prosecutors didn't buy it, but my attorneys fought like hell to find the evidence to exonerate me. Which is how I can be standing here today enjoying a rainy evening with you."

"So in the end Tony did the right thing?"

"Only because he was backed into a corner and had no choice. Don't paint a rosy picture of him, Jenna. He was a bastard who only admitted the truth after he was caught, in hopes that it might mean a lighter sentence for himself. He was only too happy to let me rot in prison for something I didn't do."

The bitterness in his voice made Jenna want to wrap her arms around him and hold him close to ease some of the vast pain of betrayal.

"I'm so sorry that happened," she murmured. "But at least you learned you had good friends you could count on."

He somehow managed a rusty laugh. "Are you always such an optimist, Mrs. Haynes?"

"Oh, no," she assured him. "Far from it. I've just learned the value of good friends over the years. I would have been lost without them."

He gave her a searching look, and she wondered how much truth she had revealed with her words. She wanted to tell him what had happened with Aaron but now wasn't the time, after he had unburdened himself about something much darker from his own history.

She couldn't think of anything else to say and realized they had been standing for a long moment, gazing at each other silently.

He was an extraordinarily good-looking man. Once a woman could see beyond his intimidating size and fierce features, she began to notice other things. The softness of his mouth. The firm line of his jaw. Those intense blue eyes fringed with long dark eyelashes.

She felt hot, suddenly, as if she had stood too long in front of the little electric fireplace in her bedroom.

"The rain has stopped."

He blinked and looked around. "Yes."

"When I'm going through hard times, I try to remind myself that, just like a rainstorm, nothing lasts forever. Pain and betrayal eventually begin to fade."

"Has your grief for your husband faded?"

He seemed genuinely interested, so she didn't answer with the trite response she might have otherwise. "I don't know if it will ever fade completely. But it has…mellowed over the years. I no longer feel devastated every time I think of Ryan. I now can remember the good times as well as the bad. We had several wonderful years together and I will always treasure them. And he gave me the greatest gift of all, Addie."

"He was a lucky man."

Something in his voice, some odd, yearning note, drew her gaze. He was looking down at her with an expression that made her catch her breath.

He wanted to kiss her.

She recognized the hunger deep in her soul because she shared it. It seemed so odd—so wrong—to be talking about her husband to a man who was completely unlike him but who made her ache with awareness.

"I should…" She pointed vaguely to the house, to the door. The girls were waiting upstairs, she reminded herself.

"Yes," he answered.

He didn't look away, though, merely continued watching her. She drew in a ragged breath, intending to call to the dog, but the words died in her throat.

When she tried to analyze it later, she wasn't sure which of them moved first. One moment, they were staring at each other in the garden, the next, they were reaching for each other.

His mouth was cool and tasted of berries but the rest of him was warm. Deliciously warm.

He kissed her with a raw hunger that took her breath away. His mouth moved over hers as if he wanted to memorize every dip, every curve.

Her arms rested against his chest and it took her a moment to realize he was shaking slightly. Not from cold. From hunger.

Jenna found something incredibly powerful and also deeply terrifying to know this man could tremble with desire because of *her*.

The rain started up again, just a cool mist that landed in her hair. She didn't care. She wanted to stand here forever and go on pretending the rest of the world didn't exist.

He was the first to pull away. She wasn't sure what brought him back to his senses. One moment, his mouth was tangled with hers, the next, he had eased away and gazed down, his breathing ragged and his expression dazed.

"I'm sorry, Jenna. I didn't mean to do that. I've been telling myself all evening that kissing you would be a mistake."

All evening? He had been thinking about kissing her *all evening*? She didn't know what to think, what to say.

"Yes. You're right. It was a mistake."

As soon as she said the word, she thought she saw a flicker of something in his gaze reflecting from the landscaping lights, something that looked almost like…hurt.

He had been the one to say the words first and she could not disagree. They were completely wrong for each other. She was finding herself increasingly drawn to the man. But she knew nothing could ever come of it.

"Let's just blame the moonlight. It's lovely out here, especially after the rain. It's hard not to be…carried away by the moment."

She couldn't look at him as she spoke, hoping he didn't see remnants of her desire on her features.

"We should go in. The…the girls."

Without another word, she scooped up Theo, grabbed the towel off the porch swing and let herself into a house that suddenly, oddly, felt colder than the garden had, almost disapproving.

Jenna hurried up the flight of stairs to her apartment, drying the confused dog as she went.

With each step, she wondered what she had been thinking to kiss him with so much…passion.

That wasn't her.

Or maybe it was.

It was a disconcerting thought.

Maybe there were parts of herself she had never had occasion to explore before, needs and desires that had always seemed warm and comfortable and…*muted* during her marriage to Ryan.

Maybe she was like that ocean out there. On a calm afternoon at low tide, only tiny waves licked at the sand. When conditions aligned, though, and storms blew in, the ocean could be mighty and powerful. Terrifying.

She sensed this thing between her and Wes would be like that—wild, passionate, fierce.

And that she would quickly find herself in over her head.

The rain began in earnest again as Wes watched Jenna hurry into the rambling old Victorian house. Drops slid down his collar, soaking him quickly. But he ignored it, too busy cursing himself for letting his base instincts take over.

After he had kissed her, she had almost looked *afraid*. Did she think he would hurt her?

He had completely screwed up everything.

Why had he kissed her?

He should have simply tamped down his attraction to her, as he had been doing for a long time now.

Maybe he had wondered on some level if kissing her could prove to her he was absolutely no threat to her.

How ridiculous. If he had given her a mild, restrained sort of kiss, that might have been the case, but he had kissed her as if she were his last meal.

Why was she so afraid? She had said something earlier that evening that might have been a clue. He closed his eyes as more rain slithered down his collar.

Who had hurt her? And where was the bastard now, so Wes could make him sorry?

He let out a breath. Her reasons for being jittery around him didn't matter. Nor did it matter if she was actually afraid of *him* or simply of any man.

He had done nothing to ease that fear. By kissing her, giving in to the heat and the hunger, he had only provided her with more reason to be nervous in his company.

How could he help himself? He was finding Jenna increasingly difficult to resist.

It wasn't simply a physical attraction to her, a hunger that kept him up at night and left him aching and empty.

He was quickly developing a thing for her.

Wes curled his hands into fists.

Could he be any more pathetic? He was falling for a woman he couldn't have.

Jenna Haynes was soft and gentle and kind, all the things that no longer fit into his world.

Wes let out a breath, chilled and damp, though he had moved to the porch, out of the drizzle.

As difficult as he knew he would find it, he had to go back up the stairs to Jenna's apartment, for Brielle if nothing else.

He had to forget about that kiss, about his aching hunger for her and about his growing feelings he knew were doomed to remain unreciprocated.

As he made his way up the stairs, he had the strange feeling that the house responded to his turmoil somehow.

He shook his head at his own foolishness. It was a *house*, for heaven's sake. Four walls, a foundation, a roof. It didn't have feelings and certainly couldn't offer sympathy.

When he reached her apartment, his knock was answered almost immediately by Brielle.

"There you are. Did you get lost out in the rain?" his daughter teased.

Yeah. Something like that.

"It's a pretty night. I was just enjoying it."

Jenna sat in an easy chair, watching the girls playing *Mario Kart*. She had Theo on her lap, almost like a shield.

When her gaze met his, the uneasy apprehension in her expression hit him like a blow coming out of nowhere in the exercise yard.

What did she think? That he was going to rush into the room and kiss her again?

"We're almost done with this race, Dad. Do you want to play?"

"We should head off, kiddo. It's getting late and we have to get ready for camp on Monday."

Jenna's daughter lit up. "Hey, I'm going to camp Monday, too. Are you going to science camp?"

Brielle nodded. "My mom signed me up before she even knew she was going to be out of town. I hope it's not lame."

Addison gave her a look of astonishment. "Science camp is not lame at all! It's way fun. I went last year and we always did cool things. Experiments and kayaking and bird-watching and stuff."

"I really do think you'll have a wonderful time," Jenna assured his daughter with that warm smile she seemed to give to everyone but him. "Addie loved it last year. She couldn't stop talking about it. She's been looking forward to it all year."

"I hope so. I'm happy you'll be there. At least I'll have one friend," Brielle said.

"You'll have lots of friends," Addie said breezily. "A lot of the kids from school went last year and I'm sure they'll go again. But we can totally be camp buddies!"

"Definitely!" Brielle said with a grin. Wes thought again how grateful he was that his daughter seemed happy and well-adjusted, despite the divorce and his incarceration.

She was a curious child who was kind to others and made friends easily.

"If you want, I'm happy to take Brielle to camp Monday and I can pick her up again as well. And she's more than welcome to hang out here after camp, until you're done with work."

"That's a lot to ask of you for two weeks."

"Not at all. I know how hard it is to be a single parent, trying to coordinate schedules. I don't mind at all."

He had been trying to figure out how he was going to manage things. He had already talked to the Gutierrez brothers, who were willing to be flexible with his schedule, but Wes hated to take advantage after they already had been so good to him.

At the same time, he needed to stay away from Jenna so he could work on getting rid of these inconvenient feelings he was developing for her. Arranging his life so he was guaranteed to see her at least twice a day probably wasn't the solution.

What choice did he have, though? All his efforts to find someone to stay with Brielle for the hour between camp and the end of his shift had come to naught.

"That would actually be really helpful, unless I can find someone else tomorrow. I was trying to figure out how to squeeze in everything. I was planning to go in late and come home early to work around her schedule."

"You don't have to try. I'm more than happy to help."

"Thank you."

She still hadn't met his gaze directly, he realized, except for that first brief moment.

"Thank you also for dinner," he said. "I definitely need the lasagna recipe to add to my rotation."

"No problem. I can share it with you, if you want to give me your email."

She handed him a notebook and he quickly wrote down the email address he rarely used.

"I'll send it later tonight."

"Thanks. I'll watch for it. Let's go, Brie. Looks like the race is over."

His daughter sighed, clearly reluctant to leave her new best friend.

"Bye, Addie. Maybe I'll see you tomorrow."

"For sure on Monday."

The girls hugged as if they were each heading off on different long sea voyages, and Wes had to hide a smile. He caught Jenna's gaze, finally, and saw that she was smiling, too.

She quickly shifted her gaze back to the dog in her lap, leaving Wes feeling slightly bereft.

Bad enough that he had kissed her, when he had every intention of keeping his attraction to her bottled up.

He really hoped he hadn't completely ruined a friendship he was beginning to cherish.

Chapter Seven

"What time will Brielle be here?" Addy asked for what seemed like the hundredth time that morning.

Jenna sipped her tea, frustrated with herself for the butterflies jumping around in her stomach. She had awakened filled with a mix of anticipation and nervousness about seeing Wes that morning when he brought his daughter down the stairs.

She could not stop thinking about the kiss the other night.

The memory of it seemed seared into her subconscious. Every time she closed her eyes, she recalled the heat of his body next to hers, the strength of his muscles beneath her fingers.

She had wanted more than a kiss.

At some point in the early hours of the morning, she had finally admitted that to herself. For the first time since Ryan's death, she had ached for a man's touch.

For Wes's touch.

Despite two tortured nights of wondering what it might be like, she knew anything more than a heated kiss between them was impossible.

She was the problem.

It was easy enough to tell herself she wasn't ready yet. But Ryan had been gone for four years. While some part of her would always grieve for the future they had dreamed about, she had determined years ago that she couldn't spend the rest of her life aching for something she could never recapture.

She had decided to move on three years ago, when she had first accepted a date with Aaron Barker.

That decision had turned out to be a disastrous one, upending her entire life.

She was only now beginning to put the pieces back together.

She might be fiercely drawn to Wes Calhoun and felt great sympathy for what he had endured, spending three years in prison, wrongly convicted for another man's crimes, but Jenna couldn't picture a future with him.

Wes was rough, hard, dangerous. He rode a motorcycle, ran for miles on the beach, was built like a professional athlete.

What did she have to offer a man like that? Her hobbies included knitting and reading the occasional cozy mystery, not riding on the back of a Harley.

She sighed, more depressed than she had any right to be.

Wes was a very nice man and someday he would find the perfect woman for him. Jenna was more sorry than she would have expected that she couldn't be that perfect woman.

The doorbell suddenly chimed through their unit, distracting her from her thoughts.

Her pulse fluttered like the butterflies in her stomach.

"They're here!" Addie exclaimed, rushing to the door. She flung it open before Jenna could tell her daughter to give her a moment to compose herself.

And there he was.

Everything inside her seemed to sigh as he reached down to greet Theo, who rushed to be the first one to say hello.

Yes, Wes Calhoun was big and hard and dangerous. But his eyes were warm, and the genuine smile he gave both her puppy and her daughter touched something deep inside.

"Good morning, Addison."

"Hi, Mr. Calhoun. Hi, Brielle."

Addie reached a hand to the other girl and tugged her into

the apartment, already chattering about what might be in store for them that day.

Jenna had to say something to him, she told herself. She couldn't stand here all day simply gazing at the man.

"Good morning," she said, forcing a smile to hide her sudden shyness.

"Morning. Sorry we're a little late. We misplaced a tennis shoe."

"I think the Brambleberry House ghost hid it from us," Brielle said from the sofa, where she and Addie were now sitting, heads together, petting Theo. "I swear, I looked in that closet four times before we finally found it, right in front of us."

"But our ghost usually doesn't tease," Addie said, her voice perfectly serious. "I don't know why she would hide your shoe."

Brielle shrugged. "Who knows? Maybe she doesn't want me to go to day camp."

"Or maybe," her father said mildly, "you didn't look hard enough in the closet and your shoe was there all along."

"I did look, though," his daughter insisted.

"Well, you found it and you're here now," Jenna said with a smile. "Did you pack a lunch? If not, I made an extra PB&J."

Wes handed over an insulated lunch bag. "This one is turkey and cheese, along with some carrots and grapes and a small bag of chips."

"Sounds delicious."

"I'm still figuring out the sack lunch thing," he admitted.

"You seem to be doing great."

"I guess I should find my own tennis shoes," Addie said.

"Yes. You should," Jenna said. She had only been reminding her daughter to finish getting ready for the past half hour.

"Maybe the ghost hid my shoes, too," Addie said, looking thrilled at the possibility. "Maybe the ghost doesn't want either one of us to go to science camp. Maybe she doesn't like science."

"Before you start spreading any unfounded conspiracy theories about our poor Abigail, go look in your closet," Jenna said.

"You can come help me find them," Addie said to Brielle. "Four eyes are better than two. That's what my mom always says, anyway."

"Okay," the other girl said cheerfully. The two of them hurried, Theo close on their heels, toward Addie's bedroom door, decorated with drawings of unicorns and flower gardens, along with the occasional bloodthirsty, jagged-toothed dinosaur.

Their departure left her alone with Wes, she suddenly realized.

There was no reason for things to be awkward between them, she told herself. Yes, they had shared a kiss, but they had dealt with it after it happened. Surely they could go back to being friends now, right?

"She's a great kid," Jenna said.

"Yeah. I really lucked out in the kid department. Even with the divorce and all the mess of the past three years, Brielle is great. I thank heaven for it every day."

"Children can be fairly resilient. After my husband died, I was so worried about how it would impact Addie, but she seems to be doing okay, so far."

She couldn't resist knocking on the intricate woodwork of the door frame, which earned her a smile from him.

She did not tell him that while she certainly had worried about Addie losing her father at a young age, she had also stressed about how her daughter internalized their summer two years earlier when they had fled to Cannon Beach. They had been forced to use assumed names, to change their hair color, to be cautious about everyone who came into their tight circle.

She didn't want to share that with Wes, though. That was in the past and she refused to let Aaron Barker take up any more space in her present or her future.

"It's a nice day so we'll probably walk the three blocks to the community center where the camp is based. Is that okay with you? I'm multitasking and walking Theo in hopes of wearing him out so I can get some things done around here today."

"Sounds like a plan. Thanks again."

"The forecast calls for more rain this afternoon, so I'll probably drive to the center to pick them up after day camp."

"I'll be here soon as I can after work."

"No rush. The girls are getting along great and I don't mind having Brielle here at all."

"Thanks. I really appreciate it. I'm definitely going to owe you dinner."

She shook her head. "You don't. This is what friends do for each other, Wes."

His gaze met hers in a searching look that left her slightly breathless.

"I was worried you might not want anything to do with me and Brielle after that kiss the other night."

She studied him, surprised by the note of uncertainty in his voice. Was it possible that he had been left as disconcerted as she was by their kiss?

"Don't be silly. It was only a kiss." She knew that was a vast understatement. It had been much more than that for her. The words *stunning* and *earthshaking* seemed more appropriate. "It shouldn't have happened and we both agree it won't happen again. But it's no big deal."

He didn't answer immediately. "I'll try to keep my hands to myself but I'm very attracted to you and…it's been a long time for me."

His hands had shaken when he touched her, she suddenly remembered. The memory made her toes curl.

"Same here," she admitted. "I guess it's a good thing neither of us is in the market for a quick fling."

"I don't know. I could probably be persuaded."

Her gaze flew to his. Though his tone was sober, there was a sparkle in his gaze, a little devilish glint that made her give a startled laugh.

"So could I, truth be told," she admitted. "But it's not a good idea, right? We're neighbors. Our daughters are friends. I would hate for things to become messy and awkward between us."

After a long moment, he sighed. "I know you're right. But I don't have to like it. It was a really amazing kiss."

She could not disagree.

The girls came out of the room before she could answer.

"Guess what?" Brielle exclaimed. "We found Addie's shoes right away. I guess it was only my shoe that Abigail hid."

"Whew. Good thing." He smiled again at his daughter with so much warmth and affection, Jenna's toes curled again.

"I've got to go. I'll see you all later."

Brielle gave her father a brilliant smile. "Bye, Dad. I'll see you tonight."

"Have fun at camp. Learn all you can about science so you can teach me stuff."

"Okay. But you already know lots of stuff."

"I'm always willing to learn more."

Before he left the apartment, Wes sent Jenna a look that had her wondering exactly what kind of things he knew…and regretting that she would never have the chance to find out.

After she walked the girls to the community center and checked them both into their day camp, Jenna decided that morning was too beautiful to go straight home.

On impulse, she decided to head down to the beach with Theo and walk home along the seashore.

She and Addie had already discovered the dog loved the water. After his initial hesitation, Theo had become a big fan, dancing through the little waves and sniffing every sand mound and seaweed tendril along the beach.

The morning was cool and lovely as they walked along the hard-packed sand close to the water's edge. They certainly weren't alone on Cannon Beach, but it was far from crowded, like it could be on a July afternoon.

A couple of teenagers flew colorful trick kites on the sand and a few hardy souls played in the water, though she considered it still too cold for comfort.

Sometimes Jenna still had to pinch herself to make sure she really was lucky enough to live here, beside the Pacific.

She loved the ocean and found it both invigorating and, conversely, calming.

She wasn't sure if she could ever return to her home state of Utah. While she loved the mountains there, Oregon had mountains, too, whenever she might need a fix.

Utah held plenty of sad memories. She had lost her husband there, had worked to rebuild her life, then had fled, abandoning everything because of one selfish man who didn't know the meaning of the word *no.*

Here in Cannon Beach, she had found peace. Had it been perfect? No. But she had found friends and a community here. Everyone here had been kind to her from the moment she moved into Brambleberry House.

They had nearly reached the beach below Brambleberry House when she spotted a familiar figure moving toward them from the opposite direction with a beautiful Irish setter pacing protectively beside her.

"Rosa!" she called as they approached. "Hello! How are you, darling? And how are you, Fiona?"

"Jenna, my friend. Hello."

Rosa's serene features lit up with happiness. Her friend was round and lovely, her pregnancy giving her a graceful beauty that Jenna loved to see.

"Who is this little sweetheart?" Rosa asked with a smile.

"This is Theo. He's a rescue dog we picked up last week

at the shelter. I've been promising Addie we would get a dog forever. I finally ran out of excuses."

"He is beautiful. I am so happy for you and Addie. She must be thrilled."

"They adore each other," Jenna said. "It's been really sweet to see. How are you feeling? Do you need to sit down? There's a bench over there. Let's stop for a minute and visit. We haven't had the chance to talk in forever."

After a moment's consideration, Rosa nodded and made her way to the bench, where she lowered herself down, still graceful despite her advanced stage of pregnancy.

"I am trying to stay active like my doctor says I must do, but it is not easy at this stage. Every day, moving becomes a little harder."

"I remember too well. I was in my first year of teaching when I was pregnant with Addie. Before she was born, I was so miserable. I wasn't sure I would be able to survive it."

"I am the same. I am ready to turn over the store to Carol."

Their mutual friend Carol Hardesty worked full-time at Rosa's gift shop as the assistant manager. She was competent and efficient but didn't have Rosa's business sense or her creative approach to retail management.

"I'm happy to take a few extra hours during the summer if you need me to," Jenna said. "I can go to three days a week during the busy summer season, if that would help."

Rosa made a face. "It is not necessary. We talked about this. You need to slow down, now that you are done with your school classes. You should take time to enjoy your summer a little bit instead of always working, working, working."

This was the first year of her life that she had decided to take an actual summer break. She still worked twelve to sixteen hours a week at the gift shop, but compared to previous summers, when she had worked full-time and taken extra classes so she could accelerate her advanced degree, that seemed like a breeze.

She knew she would love having time to catch up on projects as well as plan ahead for the next school year.

"I don't mind working, working, working if it will help you out," she said to her friend, to whom she owed so much.

"We will be fine. Do not worry. I have other workers who need the extra hours. You enjoy being with your daughter."

She looked around. "Where is our Addie?"

"Science camp. I am just heading home after walking her and Brielle Calhoun there."

"Brielle. This is Wes's daughter."

"That's right."

"How are you getting along with my new tenant?" Rosa asked.

Jenna remembered the heat of his mouth on hers, the scent of flowers and pine surrounding them as they kissed. She did not meet Rosa's gaze. They had been friends since being paired together as college roommates and Rosa knew her too well. Would she be able to tell the situation had become… complicated?

"He was nice enough to change my car battery a few weeks ago when I had trouble. His daughter is staying with him full-time for the next few weeks while her mother is out of town, so I'm helping out with some gap babysitting."

"That is very neighborly of you. I am sure Wes appreciates your help."

"He seems grateful."

"He is very handsome, do you not think?"

Jenna gave a casual shrug she suspected did not fool Rosa for a moment. "I don't know. I hadn't really noticed. He's just the neighbor who lives upstairs."

Rosa made a disbelieving sound. "I do not believe you. How can any woman not notice a man like that? I am very happily married to my Wyatt and so huge I cannot see my toes right now. And still I would notice someone like Wes Calhoun."

Jenna could feel herself flush. For a moment, she was tempted to confide in her old friend about that kiss two nights earlier and the heated dreams that had left her aching and alone in her bed.

In the old days, they used to wake each other up in their dorm room after dates to talk long into the night. She had told Rosa everything, though she suspected her friend had not ever been entirely truthful with her.

But they were not college students now. She was a grown woman, a respected educator, with an eight-year-old daughter. It seemed undignified, somehow, to dish with her landlady about the gorgeous guy who lived upstairs—even if that landlady was her dearest friend.

On the other hand, she could really use some advice.

She gazed at the dogs, now digging in the sand, probably on the hunt for a crab or some other poor creature.

"Okay," she admitted. "I noticed."

"Ha. I knew it!" Rosa looked inordinately pleased with herself. "I told Wyatt I thought maybe it would be good for you to have such a handsome man living upstairs from you. You spend too much time alone."

Jenna frowned. "Seriously? You were trying to matchmake when you rented the apartment to Wes?"

Her friend tried, and failed, to look innocent. "I would not say matchmake. Maybe just give you a little, what is the word, *nudge*."

Jenna gave Rosa an exasperated look. "I don't need a nudge. And I certainly don't need someone to matchmake for me, especially not with a man like Wes Calhoun."

Now it was Rosa's turn to frown. "How do you mean, a man like Wes Calhoun? What is wrong with him?"

She sighed. "Nothing is wrong with him. As I said, he

seems very nice. He's a good father and clearly loves his child. He has been very kind. He has even given me a few training tips for Theo, who adores him."

Rosa laughed. "See? There you go. Dogs are very wise. They see into the heart of a person. If you find Theo does not like a man, that is when you should be nervous about him."

She wasn't sure she was ready to let a dog vet the men in her life. On the other hand, she also wasn't sure she could trust her own instincts about men, considering what happened with Aaron Barker.

"I don't believe that's scientifically proven, Rosa."

Her friend made a dismissive gesture. "Maybe not science. But I have seen it myself. I would never have considered dating anyone if Fiona did not approve. The men she did not like always proved to be someone I did not like, either."

"But do I really have to base my dating decisions on the opinion of a puppy whose favorite thing in the world seems to be sniffing the behind of any other dog who comes along?"

Rosa laughed. "Fine. You may have a point. What does our Abigail think of him?"

Jenna rolled her eyes at Rosa's mention of the woman believed to haunt Brambleberry House. "I don't know. I'll have to ask her. So far, she hasn't seemed inclined to discuss the matter with me."

"She will let you know if she approves." Rosa smiled, then suddenly winced and rubbed at her protruding abdomen.

Jenna didn't miss the gesture. "Everything okay?"

"Yes. Fine. I am having a few twinges, that is all. For the most part, this has been an easy pregnancy, though Wyatt is nervous enough for both of us."

Jenna adored Rosa's husband, Wyatt, who had temporarily lived downstairs from them when Rosa lived on the third floor. Wyatt was a police detective and she considered him one of the good guys, especially after he had worked so hard to make sure Aaron Barker received a lengthy prison sentence.

They sat for a moment on the beach overlooking the sea. Finally Rosa sighed. “This is so lovely but I should probably go. I have an appointment in a short time.”

Jenna hugged her friend. “Take it easy on yourself. And remember that I’m more than willing to help out if you need me to take additional hours at the store.”

“I will remember. Thank you, my dear.”

Rosa whistled to Fiona, who returned to her side, then the two continued on their walk while Jenna did the same with Theo, heading up the beach toward home.

Chapter Eight

She had come to enjoy this last trip outside before bedtime each night for her and Theo.

With her daughter asleep in her room, Jenna would take the dog down the staircase and out the back door to the fenced dog yard.

In the moonlight, with the murmuring sound of the ocean not far off and the random peeps and calls of the various night creatures who lived nearby, she found it peaceful. Almost meditative.

Once, she had been afraid of the night. Those were the hours when she felt most vulnerable, at risk from a boogeyman whose name she knew all too well.

Since Aaron Barker had been arrested, Jenna worked hard to overcome her fear of nighttime. She wouldn't let him take that from her forever.

Okay, she still walked outside with pepper spray in her pocket. She could be brave and cautious at the same time, couldn't she?

On impulse, tonight she had brought along Theo's leash as well as her phone, where she had a security camera linked up in the living area of the apartment so she could hear if Addie woke for a glass of water. She decided to walk the dog down the beach a short way, only to the water's edge directly west of the house.

As she watched the moonlight dance on the waves, she released a breath, all the pent-up frustrations and concerns of the day floating away on the tide.

She had worked that day at Rosa's gift shop, and her shift had been unusually stressful from start to finish.

The day had started with her catching a shoplifter, her least favorite thing. Worse, the person who had slipped into her purse a handcrafted necklace valued at several hundred dollars turned out to be someone she knew, the aunt of one of her students.

It hadn't been the woman's first offense and not even her first shoplifting incident at By-the-Wind, so Rosa had no choice but to call the police, who had arrested the woman, angry and protesting all the way.

The event had put a pall over her whole day. After her shift and before she had to go pick up the girls from their fourth day at science camp, Jenna had gone to the grocery store to purchase a few things she had forgotten in Saturday's epic shopping trip and had ended up dropping and breaking an entire bottle of pasta sauce.

She had insisted on helping the store employee clean up the mess. As a result, she had been late picking up the girls and had rushed up to the community center to find them waiting on the curb for her.

She hadn't even had the chance to talk to Wes that afternoon when he came to pick up his daughter, as Brielle had rushed away with a hurried thank-you as soon as she saw her father's motorcycle pull into the driveway, eager to tell him about all the things she had learned that day.

Jenna told herself it was for the best. She was thinking about the man entirely too much anyway. It didn't help that for the past four days she had seen him in the morning when he dropped off Brielle and then again in the afternoon when he picked her up.

Each time she saw him, Jenna's awareness of the man only seemed to intensify.

What was she going to do about it?

She sighed. Exactly nothing. She planned to remain friendly with him and keep a safe distance.

"Are you ready to head back?" she asked Theo after a few more moments.

The dog turned its head, tail wagging. At odd moments, she almost felt as if he understood exactly what she was saying. As far as dogs went, Theo seemed unusually intuitive.

Sure. And maybe during those odd moments when he seemed to be staring at nothing in the corner, he was really communing with the Brambleberry House ghost.

She shook her head at herself. He was a great dog but he wasn't some kind of canine medium to the other side.

"Come on, Theo. Good boy."

The dog trotted beside her, already well-behaved on the leash. So far, he was fitting into their little family as if he had been there forever.

She keyed in the password to the locked beach gate and made her way through the garden, pausing occasionally to sniff the lavender and the climbing roses over one of the trellises.

She again felt so fortunate to be living amidst such beauty. Not only were the gardens of the house spectacular, but the view was beyond compare. On stormy nights, she loved watching the clouds roll over the water and seeing the waves churn.

Tonight was calm, though, only a light breeze, lush with the smell of flowers and pine and sea, to send the leaves shivering.

She was nearly to the house when the dark shape of a man stepped down from the porch.

She let out an instinctive shriek and reached for her pepper spray.

"Easy, Jenna," a low voice said. "Easy. It's me. Wes. I didn't mean to alarm you. I had no idea you were out here or I would have given you some kind of warning."

Her chest felt tight and shaky and it took her a moment to catch her breath again. With her heart pounding, she slipped the pepper spray back into her pocket.

"Hello. You startled me."

"I can tell. I'm sorry. Are you okay?"

Heat soaked her face and her skin felt tight and itchy with embarrassment. "Yes. Fine. I was surprised, that's all."

"Are you sure that's all?" He stepped down from the porch and moved closer to her. Jenna fought the urge to back away.

"What do you mean?"

"When I first moved in, I thought something about me was causing you to be so jittery."

She sighed, embarrassed all over again. "It's not you," she whispered. Or at least not *completely* him.

He peered down at her in the moonlight. "I think I'm beginning to figure that out."

He reached out and laid a hand on her arm. She didn't feel threat from him. She felt…comfort.

"Why are you so nervous, Jen? Did someone hurt you?"

His voice was gentle, like a cottonwood fluff floating on the breeze. He sounded concerned, not nosy or intrusive, as if he genuinely wanted to know so that he could figure out a way to help her.

"It's a very long story," she said.

He sat down on the bench there in the garden surrounded by rhododendron, iris, rosebushes. He gestured to the spot beside him, not demanding, only inviting her to share if she wanted to, offering a listening ear.

She wanted to tell him, suddenly.

She did not like to talk about what had happened to her two years earlier, especially nights like tonight when the fear and emotional distress seemed so raw and close.

Yet somehow, she wanted to tell Wes.

After a moment, she lowered herself to the bench beside him, strangely aware of the hard slats of the bench beneath her, the sweetly scented night breeze, the soft knit fabric of her sweater.

"I told you a little about my husband and how he died."

"Yes. I'm sorry again for that."

"I loved Ryan dearly. Together we created the family that neither of us had before. He was a kind man. Not perfect, but perfect for me, if that makes sense."

She glanced at Wes in time to see a muscle twitch in his jaw. "He sounds great," he said.

"He was. I was devastated by his death. So was Addie. I didn't expect to ever date again. But a year after he died, friends pushed me to try online dating. I didn't think I was ready for anything serious, but they persuaded me that I didn't have to marry a man just because I went out on a date with him. It would be good practice, they told me, and would help me figure out what I might be looking for if I ever wanted to let someone else into my heart."

She picked at the cuff of her sweater, unable to meet his gaze. "I didn't want to date anyone. At the same time, I was beginning to feel terribly lonely. I taught all day and then was alone with Addie all evening. I missed adult conversation, especially because Ryan had been sick for so long and hadn't really been a partner for that last year. I thought maybe dating again would distract me from how much I still missed my husband."

"I'm going to assume something went south," he said, his voice low.

She sighed. "You could say that."

She leaned back on the bench, finding an odd sort of strength from Wes's company. How strange, that this dangerous man could make her feel so very safe.

"I met a few guys who seemed nice enough. We went out for coffee or a meal, but things never progressed beyond that. I figured that was enough, then I made one more match on my profile. A man from a nearby town. Aaron Barker."

She couldn't seem to say the name without her whole body tensing. Did Wes notice?

"Aaron seemed very nice on the surface. He was charming and kind. We went for coffee and had a lovely conversation. For the first time, I was tempted to go on a second date with someone. We went to lunch one afternoon. It was pleasant. Enjoyable, even. We talked on the phone a few times and met a few nights later, for dinner this time. After dinner, he walked me to my car and…kissed me."

At this rate, she was going to unravel her sweater, so she forced her fretting fingers to relax.

"It was too soon for me. I got into my car and drove away. Before I could make it home, I had to pull over and be sick."

"Not a good reaction for a first kiss."

She remembered, suddenly, how she had reacted after Wes had kissed her. She had certainly not been sick. She had been achy and hungry and wanted more.

"He called me that night to check that I made it home safely and I…tried to break things off. I explained that I wasn't ready to date yet, that it had been a mistake for me to create a profile on the dating website and that I should not have let my friends push me into it. I tried to be as kind as possible and assure Aaron that he had done nothing wrong. I told him I liked him but that it wouldn't be fair to date him when my own emotions were still so tangled up with my late husband."

"I'm guessing he didn't take it well."

She shook her head. "He refused to listen to anything I said. It was almost as if he didn't hear me. He kept talking about how we clicked and he knew for sure that I felt it as well. I tried to let him down as gently as possible, but he would not listen. Not that night and not the next night when he called me again. He started to became…forceful."

He grew rigid beside her. "Oh, Jenna."

"Not that. He didn't…sexually assault me or anything. He just refused to accept that I didn't want a relationship with him. He would write me love notes, send flowers to me at work, text me endlessly at any time of the day or night. I finally blocked his number, but he would get another number and start all over again. I changed my phone number and my email, but he always seemed to figure out how to connect with me."

"Did you talk to the police?"

"He was the police," she said simply. "He was a patrol officer for a small department in a nearby Utah town. His uncle was the police chief and he wouldn't listen to any of my complaints. Not only that, but Aaron specialized in cybercrime, which made him a tech whiz. He could infiltrate all my social media, my contact info, even my private school email address. I couldn't escape him. This went on for weeks, until I was completely terrified."

"I can imagine."

"And then he went after Addie."

"How?"

The single clipped word contained both shock and hard fury. It should have frightened her, coming from such a fierce man, but somehow only made her want to lean against him and let this man protect her from the world.

"She was in kindergarten and he picked her up from school early one day. I hadn't said anything to my coworkers about what was going on with me. I guess I was too embarrassed. So when he showed his badge to the kindergarten teacher—who was elderly and should have retired years earlier—and told her we were old friends and that he wanted to take Addie to visit her father's grave and pick up a birthday present for me, she didn't blink an eye."

"I hope she was fired," he said, without a note of sympathy in his voice.

"She was retiring that year anyway, so it was all swept under the carpet. Anyway, he returned her to me about an hour after school was out. He kept her just long enough to terrify me and make it clear that he could get to either of us anytime he wanted. I knew I had to leave. He wasn't going to let up. If anything, he was escalating."

"Sounds like it."

"That very day, I happened to get a phone call from my dear friend Rosa."

"Rosa? As in Rosa our landlady?"

"One and the same. We were college roommates. Somehow in the middle of our conversation, I ended up spilling the entire ugly story to her. For so long, I had carried the burden by myself. It felt so good to tell someone else."

"Rosa was a good choice."

"Yes. Her father was in law enforcement so she wasn't naive. She knew what could happen if I didn't take action. She insisted I come to stay with her. She set me up in my apartment, got me a job at her gift shop and basically helped me begin the process of putting my life back together."

"Good for you."

"I can't explain how wonderful it felt to finally start believing I was safe. I really thought Addie and I could make a new start here. I was even thinking about trying to get an Oregon teaching certificate."

Her voice trailed off and she once more gripped her hands together in her lap.

"I take it that didn't happen as seamlessly as you had hoped."

His gentle tone soothed her somehow. The memories were still hard, but they seemed slightly less hard through sharing them.

"Addie and I had a few good months here. We were finally starting to feel safe. And then Aaron found me."

"How?"

"A fluke, really. Apparently someone from his little Utah town came to the coast on vacation and spotted me working at the gift shop. I should have expected it. Many people from other western states come here to enjoy the Oregon Coast. It was my bad luck that one of his friends who had seen a picture of me decided to come to Cannon Beach."

"Did Barker try to come after you?"

She nodded with a shiver she couldn't restrain. The events of that afternoon, here in this very garden, suddenly felt closer than they had since she testified at his sentencing hearing.

"Aaron couldn't understand why I had fled. But he magnanimously told me he was ready to forgive everything as long as I came back with him. When I tried to flee, he… attacked me and especially Rosa, when she tried to protect me. She was so brave. Though she and her dog were both hurt, they still managed to distract him long enough for me and Addie to escape into the house and call 911. I'll never be able to repay her for her courage. She showed far more grit than I did. I was petrified."

"Understandable, after everything you had been through. What happened to Barker? Was he caught?"

"Yes. Rosa hit him with a rock and stunned him. He was still coming to when Wyatt and the other police officers arrived. He was arrested and charged with multiple assault and attempted kidnapping charges. He pleaded not guilty, of course. He would never admit he did anything wrong, but he was convicted and sentenced to serve five years in the state prison system."

"Five years. Hardly seems like enough for what he put you through."

"He was sentenced to five years but was scheduled for a parole hearing in December."

His gaze narrowed. "Was?"

Wes, she had previously noticed, didn't miss much. "Yes. He…he died unexpectedly in prison a few weeks ago. Natural causes. An aneurysm, according to the autopsy."

"Wow. No kidding?"

She nodded. "I finally feel like I can breathe again, you know? For the first time in two years, I can think about the future. In many ways, I feel as if I've been living in suspended animation. Trapped by events beyond my control. I was ready to go into hiding again as soon as he left prison. Now I don't have to. I can stay here in Cannon Beach. We can make this area our forever home. It's liberating."

He looked down at Theo, sleeping at their feet. "Is that what led you to adding a dog to your family?"

She nodded. "I've been in survival mode for so long. It really feels as if Addie and I have been in a constant state of turmoil since Ryan died. We're finally in a good place now. Addie has wanted a dog forever and this seemed like a small thing to do for her, after everything she has endured."

"He seems like a good dog."

"We got lucky. He's really well-behaved and eager to learn."

He petted the dog, and she couldn't seem to stop watching those big, calloused hands.

"So now you know the entire grim story. I don't…trust easily. For obvious reasons."

"Understandable."

"It's easy to fall into the victim mentality. But I don't want to live the rest of my life that way. That is giving Aaron entirely too much power over me. I would rather not have to think about him another moment."

"I'm sorry I dredged up all the bad memories by asking what happened."

She shook her head. "I wanted to tell you. I consider you a friend, and friends share things about their lives with each other, right?"

"I suppose that's true."

"You were honest with me about what happened to you. I should have been honest in return. I suppose I'm a little ashamed that it has affected me so much, when there are others who have been through much worse things. Like you, for instance, convicted for something you didn't do."

"My mom used to tell me not to compare my troubles to anyone else's. I wouldn't want theirs and they wouldn't want mine."

She smiled. "Well, thank you for the sympathetic ear. I'm glad I told you."

"So am I. It only reinforced to me how amazing you are."

She blinked, disconcerted by his words. "Me? I'm not amazing. I told you how terrified I was when Aaron found me. I couldn't think straight. Two years later, I'm still scared of far too many things. I even scream at shadows, as you saw clearly tonight."

"And yet you are inherently kind to your students, to your customers at the gift shop and to random strange men who live upstairs."

He took her hand in his and smiled down at her. Something sparked in his gaze, something warm and glittery, and his throat moved as he swallowed hard.

"Wes."

That was all she said. All she could manage. His gaze met hers and she was unbearably moved when he lifted her hand to his mouth and gently kissed her fingers.

She wanted to kiss him.

An aching hunger bloomed to life, like the rosebushes bursting with color on a June morning.

She looked at his mouth, breathless as she waited for him.

He lowered his mouth and she leaned toward him, heart pounding. At the last moment, he froze, his expression suddenly tormented.

He wouldn't kiss her, she realized. Not only because of what she had told him but because she had been clear that she didn't want more than a friendship with him.

If she were wise, she would count her blessings, gather her dog and rush inside.

She didn't feel very wise right now. Before she could think through the ramifications, she leaned forward, bridging the last few inches between them, and kissed him.

It was as if she had unleashed the storm. He kissed her back with a fierce intensity that pushed every coherent thought out of her head.

Still, she sensed he was holding back. She could feel it in his leashed strength, in the tight control he was keeping over himself.

She wanted that wildness, suddenly. Would this man ever let himself lose control?

She tightened her arms around his neck and tangled her mouth with his, wanting the delicious kiss to go on and on.

Chapter Nine

He was in so much trouble.

As flames of desire licked through him, Wes tried his best to hold on to whatever semblance of control he could manage to dredge up out of the depths of his subconscious.

Jenna tasted so damn good. Like chocolate and cherries and this perfect summer night.

She made a soft, breathy sound deep in her throat and her arms seemed to tighten around him.

He could feel his control slip away, inch by painful inch. All he wanted to do was kiss her, taste her, make love to her.

He traced a hand beneath her sweater, to the warm, luscious skin there. She shivered and arched against his hand, pressing her curves into his chest.

He was aching with need, his brain empty of everything but how much he wanted this woman in his arms, in his bed.

His hand slid from her back to one hip. He wanted to touch those curves she pressed against him.

He was inches from his goal when she made that soft, sexy sound again.

The sound seemed to yank him back to his senses. What the hell was he doing? He had told himself he couldn't do this again. He wanted her too much, though his kissing her again only showed him how very much he was beginning to care for her.

Beyond that, she had just shared with him her harrowing

ordeal. She had been tormented, stalked, terrified by a man who couldn't take no for an answer.

Even though she had made it clear she wasn't interested in anything with him, here he was mauling her in the garden of Brambleberry House, like he was some sort of high school kid making out with a girl behind the bleachers of the football stadium.

He jerked away, disgusted with himself.

She looked small and delicate, lovely as tiny violets springing across the grass in May.

He had spent three years feeling dehumanized, marginalized, discarded.

But he never felt as barbaric as he did right now, taking in the sight of Jenna Haynes staring up at him with huge eyes.

"I'm so sorry. I don't know what came over me."

She blinked a few times and drew in a deep breath. "Why are you apologizing?"

"Because I had no right to kiss you like a starving man who had just been snatched off the streets and plunked down at a table in the middle of a feast."

She made a small, strangled kind of sound. "It was only a kiss, Wes. You didn't attack me or anything. In fact, as I recall, I started things."

He closed his eyes, remembering that heart-stopping moment when she had spanned the distance between them and pressed her mouth to his.

Something told him he would be reliving that moment for a long, long time.

"Maybe," he finally said. "But I took things too far. I shouldn't have, especially after everything you told me about what you've been through. I promise, it won't happen again."

She gazed at him, and he watched as she seemed to regain her composure with every passing second.

She nodded and pressed her lips together, those delicious lips he could have explored all night long.

"Okay," she said. She rose and let out a long breath. "Good night, then. Thanks again for...for listening to me."

She grabbed Theo's leash and the two of them walked into the house, leaving him alone to curse and ache and want.

Jenna walked back up the stairs to her apartment on knees that felt weak, somehow.

She still couldn't quite wrap her head around the realization that she had instigated another kiss with Wes Calhoun.

Hadn't she learned her lesson the first time?

She wanted to blame it on the moonlight or the peaceful garden or the simple release of sharing her story with him finally.

She suspected the real reason for her behavior had nothing to do with that. It had more to do with the man himself.

When Wes first moved into Brambleberry House, she had considered him the very last man in Cannon Beach she might come to trust, someone with whom she had nothing in common.

What an illuminating example of how very wrong first impressions could be. These past few weeks of coming to know him better—of seeing his gentleness with Theo, with his own daughter and with hers—had given her a picture of a kind man beneath the gruff, intimidating exterior.

She respected and admired him more than any other man she had met in a very long time.

What was she going to do about it?

As she reached her apartment, she let herself and Theo inside, where she took off the puppy's leash and harness. The dog rushed to his water bowl, and Jenna closed the door behind her, listening to the small, comforting noises of the apartment settling around her.

Nothing.

That was exactly what she planned to do about this attraction to Wes. They had kissed again and it had been amazing, but now she had to go back to her regular life and try to forget those few stirring moments in the garden had ever happened.

The idea depressed her, even though she knew she had no other option.

They were attracted to each other. She couldn't deny that. The heat they generated could have ignited a dozen beach fires.

Why not give in to it? They were both unattached adults. What would be the harm in finding a secluded spot in the garden, maybe the pergola or one of the padded benches in a dark corner, and surrendering to the attraction between them?

Because she would end up with a broken heart.

She was not a woman who could handle a casual fling. She had seen her mother's heart broken too many times by men who would move in and out of their lives.

She was a forever kind of woman. She knew that about herself and suspected it wouldn't take much for her to fall in love with Wes.

Then what?

Try as she might, she couldn't picture a future with Wes. She again couldn't imagine she could provide anything that a man like him might be looking for in a woman.

Someone adventurous. Audacious. Brave.

She wasn't any of those things. Eventually Wes would figure that out and grow tired of her.

She couldn't go through the pain of loving someone again and inevitably losing him.

Better to stop things now, before either of their hearts were involved. Before she could make a fool of herself over him and destroy a friendship she was coming to cherish.

Theo went to stand by the door of his crate, ready for bed. She opened it for him and watched him curl up on the soft blankets, then headed for her solitary bed.

Chapter Ten

Somehow, she and Wes managed to maintain a cordial relationship over the next week while she helped fill in the gaps of Brielle's care, between his work schedule and the girls' science camp schedule.

He was friendly enough when he would drop his daughter at Jenna's apartment in the morning, a half hour before she had to take the girls to camp.

He would chat with Jenna about her upcoming day and would ask questions of Addie about camp and what other activities she was doing that summer.

A few mornings when he had extra time, he even offered to take Theo outside to the garden so that Jenna could focus on finishing up breakfast and getting ready for her shift at the gift shop, on the days she worked.

In the evenings, the routine was reversed. He would come to pick up his daughter about an hour after camp finished for the day. He never lingered long but took time to chat a little about the day and their respective plans for the evening.

Despite her lingering tumult over the kisses they had shared—and the secret part of her that undeniably wanted more—she quite enjoyed the routine they had fallen into. She sensed he did as well.

Everything changed on the morning of the girls' last day of science camp.

The morning started like all the others. She and Addie both got up early to walk the dog on the beach as the morning mist hung heavy on the shore and the gulls swooped to scavenge for juicy treasure along the detritus left from high tide.

She wasn't quite sure what happened. One moment, they were enjoying the morning, the next, the dog stopped to sniff directly in front of Jenna and she got tangled in his leash.

She could feel herself topple and reached a hand out to brace herself. Under normal circumstances, she would have been fine, simply annoyed at her own clumsiness. She landed on soft sand, after all.

Something in the sand wasn't soft, though. She felt a slicing pain as her palm caught on something jagged buried in the sand. A piece of shell or driftwood, perhaps, or maybe even a shard of glass left by some unknown beach visitor.

She gasped at the pain and immediately rolled to her side, clutching her hand.

Addie looked down at her, wide-eyed. "What happened? Are you okay?"

"I'm fine," she lied.

She pulled her hand away and saw she had a nasty cut about four inches running right through her life line, between her right thumb and forefinger. "I'm afraid I'm bleeding, though," she admitted to her daughter.

She could only be glad she had been the one to fall and not Addie.

"Oh no! How did you cut yourself?"

"I'm not sure. Something sharp in the sand. I should find whatever it was so it doesn't hurt someone else."

"I can look."

"I'll do it," she said quickly, with visions of Addie being cut as well. "I don't want you to hurt yourself, too. Why don't you keep walking Theo down the beach a little more, and I'll dig around and see if I can figure out what it was."

Addie looked undecided but after a moment, her daughter obeyed. She and the dog headed away from Jenna a short distance.

Her hand was now bleeding copiously, which was one of the reasons she had sent Addie away. She didn't have anything with her to stop the bleeding so she grabbed a corner of her T-shirt and ripped, feeling a pang as she did.

This had been one of Ryan's T-shirts that she had packed away after he died. She wore them as sleep shirts and to work out.

She still had several of his shirts left, including three that she had sewn into pillows for Addie's room. Still, losing this one stung worse than her cut, like slicing one more thread between her and her past.

She quickly wrapped the strip of cloth around her hand, hoping to stop the worst of the bleeding, then dug through the deep sand there until she found the culprit, a shell from what looked like a Dungeness crab, with a broken, jagged edge.

She tossed it into one of the garbage cans set at intervals along the beach, then caught up with Addie.

"Mom, you need a real bandage," her daughter said, taking in the makeshift bandage that was also now covered in blood.

Jenna strongly suspected she needed stitches, but she didn't want to worry Addie. A trip to the doctor or urgent care clinic could wait until after she dropped off the girls at day camp. Meantime, she would do some rudimentary first aid back at their apartment to staunch the bleeding.

They reached the second floor landing to their apartment just as Wes came down the stairs from the third floor, chatting with Brielle.

He stopped on the stairs halfway to the landing and stared at her.

"Good Lord. What happened to you?"

He looked gorgeous, she couldn't help but notice, in worn

jeans, work boots and a T-shirt that stretched over his hard muscles.

She, on the other hand, looked like she had gone a few rounds with an angry badger. She had tried to hold her arm above her heart to slow the blood flow. As a result, blood had dripped through her makeshift bandage to streak down her arm.

"I'm fine. It's nothing. I stumbled while we were walking. When I reached out to catch myself, I landed on a broken shell with a sharp edge in the sand."

"That looks like it really hurt," Brielle exclaimed.

"It looks worse than it is."

"My mom didn't cry at all. She's tough."

Addie's admiring tone made Jenna feel about a thousand feet tall. She only hoped her daughter still looked up to her after she reached the difficult teenage years, just on the horizon.

"Let me take a look at it," Wes said, holding out a hand.

She didn't want to show him, though she wasn't sure if that was embarrassment at her own clumsiness or hesitation to have him touch her again, given the heat that flared between them at any given moment.

"You don't have time," she protested. "We're late returning from our walk. You'll be late for work. Don't worry about me. I'm fine."

"I have time for this," he said, in a tone that brooked no argument.

When her gaze met his, the implacable hardness there told her she had no choice. He intended to look at her hand. She should be grateful for his concern, not frustrated by his stubbornness.

With a resigned sigh, she unlocked her apartment and opened the door for all of them to follow her inside.

Theo, who had caused the whole disaster, trotted into the

house, planted himself on his haunches and grinned at the four of them, clearly delighted to have his favorite people all together.

"Addie, will you clean up the breakfast dishes and load the dishwasher?"

"Okay." Her daughter headed for the kitchen, Brielle right behind her.

"I'll help," her friend said.

Meanwhile, Wes pointed toward Addie's bathroom, the closest to the living room. "Let's start by rinsing it to get the sand and blood off so we can see what we're up against."

She followed him to the bathroom, wondering why she had never noticed how small the room was.

"I don't want to get blood all over you."

"By the end of the day, I usually have oil and brake fluid and any manner of other things all over me. This is nothing."

He turned on the water while he unwound the scrap of T-shirt from her palm. She winced as the fabric caught in her jagged wound.

"Sorry."

"It's not your fault I'm so clumsy. I still don't know quite how I tripped. I think I got tangled in the leash and caught myself before I could fall on Theo."

"Bad luck that you would land right on a broken shell."

"Yes. Out of the entire beach filled with soft, forgiving sand where I could have fallen, I had to choose that very spot."

She shook her head, trying at the same time to catch her breath as he gently held her hand this way and that under the stream of warm water.

He smelled so good. He was obviously just out of the shower and smelled like a combination of laundry soap and some outdoorsy kind of male shampoo.

He was warm, too. After their chilly walk along the beach,

she couldn't help wishing she could snuggle up against him to draw some of his heat back inside her.

"How bad is it, Dr. Calhoun?"

"I'm afraid you're going to need stitches. It's not long, but it's pretty deep. You said you landed on a broken shell? When was your last tetanus shot?"

She thought back to her most recent medical history and remembered getting one around the time that Ryan had died, when she had scraped herself on a nail trying to plant some flowers in the small fenced yard of their apartment.

"I should be good in that regard."

"Do you want me to take the girls to day camp and then run you to the urgent care clinic? I can call my bosses and let them know an emergency has come up."

She was very tempted to lean on him, to let him take over. It was very hard to ignore the allure of that broad chest, those strong shoulders.

She was tough, she reminded herself. She could handle this, even though her hand throbbed with pain, which was also giving her a headache.

"I should be all right. If you could just help me wrap it better, that would be really great. It's my right hand and I'm right-handed, so I don't think I will be able to do a very good job with my left hand."

"You got it."

Using her first-aid kit after she showed it to him, he applied antibacterial ointment with a gentleness that made her shiver.

She could only hope he didn't notice as he rooted through the kit to find the largest bandage she had.

"This should hold you for a little while, until you can have someone take a look. You should definitely take care of it sooner rather than later."

"Thank you."

Bending low over her hand, he applied the bandage to her

palm, pressing carefully around the edges to ensure the wound was protected as much as possible.

"I wish I could do more."

"You've done enough. I'll be fine. I'll call my primary care doctor right now and see if I can get in this morning to have Dr. Sanderson take a look."

"You see Eli Sanderson?"

"Yes. Do you know him?"

"I knew him in the military, only peripherally. But we have friends in common. He and his wife invited me to dinner when I first moved to town. They were very kind."

"Melissa actually lived here in Brambleberry House before I did. We've become friends through Rosa, who is her good friend."

"She's the one who convinced Rosa to rent me an apartment when I was looking."

"I'm glad she did," Jenna said.

His gaze met hers and the moment seemed to stretch between them, taut and fragile, like the thread of a spider's web, gleaming with morning dew.

Something sparked in his expression as he looked down at her, something hot and glittery that left her a little dizzy.

Maybe she had lost more blood than she thought, she told herself. Or maybe it was simply a result of being in such close proximity to Wes Calhoun.

He was the first to look away.

"That should do it. Are you certain you don't want me to take you to urgent care? I feel wrong leaving you in your hour of need."

"No. Definitely not. I'm fine. Thank you, though. You've been very kind."

"Right. That's what I've been," he said, his voice gruff.

She sensed he wanted to say more, but Addie and Brielle came to check on her and the moment was gone.

* * *

After she had been treated at Eli's office, Jenna returned to the house to let Theo out, then moved him to the fenced dog yard, placing his open crate in the shade under the covered porch, along with plenty of water and food.

When she was certain the puppy was settled and comfortable, she drove to the By-the-Wind gift shop for her noon shift.

The morning fog had blown away, as it usually did during the summer, leaving the day sunny and mild. She parked as close as she could manage. She would have been better off walking, judging by the number of vehicles clogging the downtown area.

The tourist season was in full force. From here, she could see the wide, long Cannon Beach stretching north for miles. It was dotted with umbrellas, bikes, swimmers and the occasional kite.

The crowds of visitors descending every summer could be a nuisance but so much of the Cannon Beach economy depended on them that she couldn't be too upset.

Crowds were a small price to pay for the sheer delight in living in such magnificent surroundings. And if the masses of people became too overwhelming, she could always take a drive down the coast and find an isolated beach somewhere or she could hike into the hills east of town and find a beautiful mountain river wending its way to the ocean.

That was the beauty of the Oregon Coast. It was long, vast and certainly not overpopulated.

She let herself into the employee entrance of the store just as Rosa was coming out.

"What is this?" her friend cried, looking aghast at her bandage. "What have you done to yourself?"

"It's nothing. Just a bit of bad luck. I fell on the beach this morning when I was walking with Theo and Addison and managed to land on a broken shell. I'm fine. Eli gave me only five stitches and some local anesthetic so I can't feel a thing right now."

"Oh, you poor thing. You must go home and rest your hand. I can work for you instead."

Jenna rolled her eyes at this very pregnant woman trying to be protective of her over a little scratch.

"Absolutely not. Please don't worry about me. The bandage is annoying but it should not stop me from doing anything."

"I am sorry this happened to you. Did Addie help you with your bandage?"

She held up her bandaged hand. "Dr. Sanderson and his staff get the credit for this one. But Wes helped me with the initial triage."

Rosa gave her a side glance. "Did he? I told you, he is a good man."

Jenna was beginning to agree. Whenever she remembered the tender way he cared for her injury, she felt warmth seep through her.

She did not tell her friend that Wes was not only a good man. He was definitely a good kisser.

"Do not worry about me," she said again to Rosa. "I'll be just fine. Go and put your feet up."

Rosa sighed. "Wyatt will probably come with his police car and drag me home if I don't rest. If not him, Carrie and Bella will do it."

Carrie was the sister of Rosa's husband and Bella was Carrie's daughter. Both of them adored Rosa and were even more protective of her than Jenna was.

"Good. You should listen to them. I'll see you later."

She hugged Rosa and hurried into the gift shop, grateful again for good friends.

Chapter Eleven

On his lunch hour, Wes decided to eat his brown-bag lunch while he walked three blocks downtown to find a birthday present for his sister, who lived in a little town in Idaho called Pine Gulch, on the west slope of the Tetons.

He had a single destination in mind, the gift shop owned by his landlady, Rosa. It was the logical choice, he told himself. By-the-Wind carried unique local products that represented the best artists and craftspeople in the area. His sister would love something handmade, especially something he had specifically picked for her.

As he walked toward the store, he reminded himself there was little chance he would bump into Jenna, though he knew she worked part-time at By-the-Wind during the summer.

Logic did nothing to stop the little buzz of anticipation as he made his way through town.

The sidewalks were busy, but it wasn't the kind of crowd he had been warned to expect in summer. Mostly families were browsing for beach toys or T-shirts or fudge.

He still could not believe he lived in this busy little beach community on the Oregon Coast, that he was working as a mechanic, of all things, and enjoying all of it.

Life had a funny way of taking a guy on adventures he never could have imagined.

Four years ago, he thought he had his life completely figured out. He had loved the hard work of making the security company a success. While his marriage definitely had its ups and downs, he was trying hard to make that a success as well.

He thought he would continue on that same path and eventually attain everything he wanted.

His life hadn't gone exactly as planned. Three years behind bars had a way of derailing an entire future.

Wes had always been a planner, goal oriented and ambitious. Now he tried to focus on the moment. The smell of ice-cream cones from the parlor he passed, the sound of children laughing as they watched someone making saltwater taffy at another shop, the hum of conversation between shoppers. All of it was underlined by the constant song of the sea, which gave him more comfort than he ever could have guessed.

When he finally reached By-the-Wind, he pushed open the door and immediately felt out of place.

Wes didn't consider himself sexist but this didn't really feel like the kind of store that catered to a guy like him. It was filled with scented candles, wind chimes, floral-patterned shopping bags and rows of handcrafted jewelry.

He was the only man in the store, he couldn't help but notice. A trio of older ladies were looking at carved lighthouse figures while a couple of teenagers spun a rotating rack of silver earrings.

What would his sister like here?

He had no idea. While he and Maggie had always been close as children, separated by only a few years, as adults, their paths had diverged. After his arrest and especially after his conviction, Wes had tried to build in more distance between them. Maggie's husband was a small-town lawyer with state political ambitions. He didn't need to be associated with someone who had been convicted on multiple felony charges.

Maggie had tried to stay in touch but he had discouraged contact. She hadn't given up, no matter how tough he made it on her.

He was scouring through some decorative ceramic vases when he saw Jenna emerge from a back room. She did an almost comical double take when she spotted him. He again felt large and ungainly in this store filled with delicate items.

"Hi." She smiled. "This is a surprise."

"For me, too. I wasn't expecting to see you. I figured even if you were scheduled to work, you would have taken time off because of your injury."

She held up her heavily bandaged hand. "Good news. They didn't have to amputate. I only needed a few stitches. Five, but who is counting?"

"Whew." He managed a smile. "Does it still hurt?"

"The local anesthetic they used to put in the stitches has worn off so it's throbbing a bit, but it's not too bad."

"Good. That's good."

Silence descended between them and he didn't want to do anything but stare at her. That wasn't creepy or anything, right?

Around Jenna, he experienced a strange paradox of emotions, both fierce awareness as well as an odd sort of peace.

"Was there something I could help you find?" she asked after a moment.

"Um. Yes. I'm looking for a birthday present for my sister."

"You have a sister?"

She seemed genuinely surprised, and he realized he hadn't mentioned his family much to her, other than to tell her about his father's death.

"Yes. Maggie is three years younger than I am. An artist and writer. She lives in Idaho with her husband and their two kids."

"Wow. Okay. Um, what are her tastes? Does she collect anything? You said she is an artist?"

"Yes. She paints. But I know she also collects pottery. I was looking at your vases here."

"They are very nice. Do you know what kind of pottery she collects?"

He felt stupid for his ignorance. Again, he wished he had not come, that he had simply picked out something for Maggie online.

Had his subconscious led him here, in the random hope that he might find himself in this very situation, speaking with the woman who fascinated him so much? He did not want to admit it, but the truth was becoming increasingly difficult to ignore.

Jenna Haynes was becoming a vital part of his life. He didn't want to think about how bereft he would feel when his daughter returned to her mother and stepfather's home and he had no more excuse to see Jenna at least twice a day.

He turned his attention back to the problem at hand, finding a gift for his sister. "To be honest, I am not at all sure what to get her. I don't know what she likes. Maggie and I haven't talked much for the past few years. Only a couple of times since I was arrested, actually."

"Why? Did she believe you were guilty?" she asked with a frown. He could almost see her mind working, possibly condemning his sister. He couldn't have that.

"I tried to keep Maggie and her family away from all the ugliness," he said quickly. "She had enough on her plate, with new twins and her husband opening his law practice. She didn't need to be dragged down by worry."

"You don't think she worried about you, whether you were in regular communication or not?"

"Probably," he admitted. In truth, he hadn't wanted the baby sister he adored to see what a mess his life had become.

"We've texted and emailed back and forth a few times since I was released. I was going to swing by and visit on my way to Oregon but it didn't quite work out."

She studied him and he had a feeling she saw right through his excuses and explanations.

"A birthday gift is a lovely way to reconnect," she finally said, her tone gentle. "Though perhaps the best thing you could give Maggie for her birthday would be a video call from her brother and niece so she can catch up on your life."

That was not a bad idea. Because his contact with the outside world had been limited while he had been incarcerated, he had lost the habit of remembering he could pick up the phone at any time now.

"Maybe I can do both. Send her a gift and also catch up over the phone."

She smiled. "That works. I can't help you with the phone call, but let's try to find something wonderful to send her. We have one section of pottery created by local artists. Would you like to take a look?"

"Definitely. I would love to give her something that represents the Oregon Coast."

He looked at the offerings on the shelves she indicated and was immediately drawn to a small, delicate bowl the same iridescent colors found on the inside of an abalone shell. It was even shaped a little like a shell.

"That is beautiful," he said, holding it up to admire the colors.

Her gaze softened. "That is by one of my favorite local artists. She is eighty years old, a real character who lives alone on an isolated stretch near Heceta Head and throws pots every day. You should meet her on one of her visits to town."

"I would like that," he said. He had never been one for art galleries or museums when he was younger but his time in prison had given him a true appreciation for those who could create beauty no matter their situation.

"This one works for me. That was easy. I might even make it back before my lunch hour is over."

"I can wrap it up for you. If you would like to pick out a birthday card while you're here and write a message, we can even ship for you. We have some nice original birthday cards as well as some all-occasion."

While it would certainly take a weight off him not to have to deal with the inconvenience of mailing, he suddenly caught sight of that glaring white bandage on her hand.

"I don't think you should be wrapping up anything right now, with your bum hand. Just slip it in a bag and I can take it home. Brie can help me deal with it tonight."

She made a face. "I appreciate your concern, Wes, but I'm really fine. I've already packaged things for other shoppers today and didn't drop a single thing. If I have trouble, someone else here can handle that part of it."

She was a difficult woman to win an argument against.

"Thank you, I guess. Though I don't feel good about it."

She laughed. "Sorry about that."

He wanted to gaze at her for whatever time was left of his lunch hour but forced himself to head to the cards, where he finally found a lovely hand-painted card he knew Maggie would appreciate as much as the bowl.

Jenna handed him a pen from behind the counter and after a moment's reflection, he wrote a quick message wishing her the happiest of birthdays and expressing his love. It seemed inadequate but he couldn't think of anything else to say.

When he finished the card and slipped it into the envelope, he handed over his credit card and Jenna ran it through.

It sometimes struck him how amazing it was to be able to walk into a store and purchase whatever he wanted. For three years, he had been limited by the prison commissary and what friends on the outside could provide him.

All of his pre-arrest personal assets had been restored to him following the acquittal, along with a healthy settlement for wrongful prosecution. He had plenty of money right now. He couldn't work forever fixing motorcycles. He knew that, but he wasn't in any hurry to change the status quo.

After years of the grind to build his company, then the

stress and helplessness of the past three years, Wes found he enjoyed the work he was doing.

He liked taking something broken and repairing it to be as good as new…and sometimes better.

Maybe he would open his own shop somewhere, though probably not. He didn't feel right about going into competition with Paco and Carlos, after they had been so good to him.

"Thank you," Jenna said, handing him the receipt. "I'll try to get this wrapped up and shipped today. It should go out tomorrow at the latest. That's our guarantee. She should receive it within a week. Will that work?"

"It should. Her birthday isn't for a few more weeks. Thank you for your help."

"My pleasure."

He needed to return to work but he was loath to leave her.

"Why don't you let me take care of dinner for us and the girls tonight?" he said on impulse, gesturing to her hand. "It's the least I can do, after all you've done to help me out with Brie this week."

"It has really been no trouble," she protested.

"You keep saying that, but surely it's been a *little* trouble. You've got a sore hand and don't need to be rushing around tonight trying to fix dinner."

She gave a quick laugh that sounded prettier than any of the wind chimes in this charming little store ever could.

"You seem to have this idea that my hand has been grievously wounded. It's only a few stitches. I am really fine."

"Okay, let's take the hand completely out of it. For two weeks, you have stepped up to bail me out with my daughter. I would love the chance to repay you in some small way. Why don't we celebrate the last day of the girls' camp and my last day with Brielle full-time? We could explore one of the nearby state parks, if you have a favorite."

"Have you visited Oswald West State Park? It's just south

of town. It has lots of tide pools and trails through the forest that look like something out of *Lord of the Rings*. Addie loves it. It also has a picnic area close to the beach."

"I have not been there. That sounds perfect. The girls can show us everything they learned at camp and, bonus, Theo can get some exercise."

"That is actually not a bad idea," she said after a moment's thought. "It sounds really fun."

He felt a ridiculous sense of accomplishment. "Great. I'm done working today at four. I can pick up some picnic supplies. We can take my truck and load the back with whatever we might need."

"That sounds great. I'm off by three, in time to get the girls."

"Let's plan to leave about five. That will give us several hours before dark to enjoy the scenery."

"Perfect. We'll be ready."

He wanted to stay and talk to her more, but he had already taken too long and needed to return to the bike he was working on.

Besides that, the store had begun to fill with more customers, and he realized he had been completely monopolizing Jenna's time for the past fifteen minutes.

"Thanks again for your help. I'll see you this evening," he said.

"Great."

That buzz of anticipation carried him toward the door. Before he reached it, he spotted a few women with familiar features whom he knew he had seen around town before. He nodded to them but didn't miss the way the mouth of one of the women tightened. If she had been wearing long skirts, he had a feeling she would have brushed them out of his way with a dramatic sweep.

He wouldn't let it ruin his mood, he decided. Not when he had a fun evening ahead with Jenna and their respective daughters.

Chapter Twelve

As Wes made his way to the exit, Jenna released the breath she hadn't realized she had been holding and tried not to stare at his narrow hips or his broad shoulders in that snug T-shirt.

Seeing him in this setting, surrounded by lovely, fragile objects, only seemed to reinforce his contrasting masculinity.

She finished packaging up the lovely bowl for his sister, catching only bits and pieces of the conversation around her until she heard the word Brambleberry House.

Two women were looking at a collection of handmade jewelry close to the counter, local women she knew vaguely but who weren't close acquaintances.

Donna Martin was a former teacher with a reputation at the elementary school for having been rigid and cold to her students during her time there. She had retired before Jenna took a job at the school, and Jenna knew there were few students or parents who were sorry when she left.

She had always struck Jenna as being thoroughly unpleasant.

Her companion, Susan Lakewood, was tall, almost gaunt, a woman who volunteered at the library as well as managed a string of rental properties on the other side of town. When she wasn't in Donna's company, she could be quite pleasant.

The two had also apparently noticed how out of place Wes seemed in the store. It took Jenna a moment to realize they were talking about him.

"I don't know what Rosa was thinking, to let his type move into that house. Abigail would be rolling in her grave," Donna muttered.

"He has always been very nice in our few interactions."

"He's a criminal! I heard it on good authority that he hasn't even been out of prison four months. It's outrageous that someone like that is allowed to live in Cannon Beach at all, let alone in such a nice place as Brambleberry House."

"I don't know," Susan said in a timid sort of voice. "He seems polite enough when he comes into the library with his daughter. She likes to read the Magic Tree House books."

Donna made a derisive sound. "Doesn't matter how polite he is. You can't change the facts. He looks like a man who just got out of prison, doesn't he? I would be afraid to have him living anywhere close to me. Who knows what he did?"

Jenna frowned, her palm suddenly throbbing worse than ever with the itch to slap the woman, though she knew she never would.

She did not want to have any sort of confrontation with Donna, who had a reputation for being vindictive to anyone who crossed her. At the same time, she would not stand by and let the woman malign a good man who had done nothing wrong and didn't deserve her disdain.

Under normal circumstances, Jenna would never confront a customer at all, but somehow she sensed Rosa would back her a hundred percent if she were here.

"Can I help you two find something?" she asked loudly.

Susan, at least, had the decency to blush.

"We're just looking," she said quickly.

"Let me know if I can help," she said. Before she could move away to help someone else, she lowered her voice. "For the record, Wes Calhoun was wrongfully convicted and has been exonerated of all charges. He is a loving father and a hardworking employee who is trying to rebuild his life here in Cannon Beach so that he can be closer to his daughter. Don't you find that admirable? There are so many men out there who are only too willing to abandon their children after a divorce. I'm sure as a former educator, Donna, you saw evidence of that as well with your students. What a tough situation that can be on children."

"It's outrageous. Parents don't care about the harm they're doing to their children. All they care about is having what they want."

She let the woman ramble on for a few moments, then finally gave a polite smile.

"Yes. That's why it's so refreshing to see a man like Wes Calhoun, who is trying his best to be a positive influence in his child's life. Don't you agree?"

"Very refreshing," Susan said.

Donna still wore a sour frown. "He still looks like he just held up a bank somewhere."

"It's a good thing most people don't judge others wholly on their appearance but on their behavior, isn't it?"

She walked away before either woman could answer.

She was shaking a little but told herself it was simply a reaction to the pain shot wearing off.

"What was Donna going on about?" Carol Hardesty asked after the two women quickly bustled out of the store.

Jenna sighed, wishing she had handled things a different way. She would have liked to tell Donna she was a sanctimonious cow.

"Donna was bad-mouthing my neighbor. Wes Calhoun. I was gently trying to set her straight."

"Oooh. He's Lacey Summers's ex-husband, right?"

"That's right."

"Who would walk away from a guy like that?" Carol asked, shaking her head in disbelief. "I don't care if he was in prison. He's the sort of guy worth waiting for on the outside, you know?"

Yes. Jenna understood completely.

"He was innocent," she muttered. "He was cleared of all wrongdoing. That's what bugs me. It doesn't seem fair for people like Donna to treat him like some kind of criminal when he didn't do anything wrong."

"I wouldn't listen to anything she has to say. That woman is perpetually unhappy. She finds fault in everyone."

"It just bothers me. Wes is a wonderful father and a really good man."

Carol shrugged. "Here's the thing about Donna. If you don't fit the mold of what she considers acceptable, nothing else matters. You'll never measure up to her expectations. Some of us figured out a long time ago that it's not worth even trying."

Jenna knew Carol was right. What bothered her most about the encounter was that Jenna had been exactly like Donna. She had judged Wes as scary and intimidating when he first moved into Brambleberry House.

She cringed when she remembered that day he had jumped her car, when she had reacted to him out of fear and nerves.

Since then she had learned he was a kind man who made delicious pizza for his daughter, who loved his sister, who savored the smell of basil leaves and the Brambleberry House gardens after a rain.

And who kissed her until she forgot all the reasons why they weren't right for each other.

The girls were chattering with excitement when she picked them up after their last day of camp.

"That was the most fun *ever*," Brielle said as she slid into the back seat, her cheeks a little sunburned and her bucket hat hanging down her back.

"Yeah. It was so fun," Addie agreed. "I'm sad it's over. I wish we could go to science camp all summer long!"

"Wouldn't that be fun?" Jenna said. "But then you would miss soccer camp and art camp."

"I guess."

"How's your hand, Mrs. Haynes?" Brielle asked as Jenna turned her vehicle toward Brambleberry House. "Did you have to get a hundred stitches?"

"Not a hundred, no. Only five."

"Do you have to wear a cast?" Addie asked, peering around the seat to see.

"Only a bandage." She held up her right hand for the girls.

"I've never had stitches," Brielle said. "Does it hurt when the needle goes into your skin? I always thought it would be so weird."

"No. They give you a shot first that numbs your skin. You're right. It is a weird feeling. You can tell when they're tugging the stitches. But it wasn't bad."

"I'm really sorry you were hurt, Mom," Addie said. "Me and Brie can take care of Theo if you want. We can even take him out late tonight so you don't have to do it."

Her daughter's thoughtfulness touched her. "Thank you. I might need your help a little more than usual for the next few days."

"Maybe we can cook dinner tonight," Brielle suggested. "I know how to make nachos."

"Actually, your dad thought you might like to go on a picnic at the beach tonight for dinner, since it was your last day at camp today. Plus you'll be going back home tomorrow."

"Oh, that's right," Addie said, her voice disappointed.

"I totally forgot my mom and Ron were coming home tomorrow." Brielle seemed disappointed at the prospect of leaving Brambleberry House.

"It's not like you won't come back and will never see us again. You stay with your dad like every weekend," Addie reminded her.

Brielle's features brightened. "Oh yeah. We can totally hang out when I come stay with him."

For the remainder of the short drive, the girls chattered about their favorite part of science camp and what they planned to do the next week when they didn't have camp. When they pulled up to the house, the first thing Jenna saw was Wes's motorcycle. His daughter spied it as well.

"Dad's home from work already. Yay! Can we leave now for the picnic?"

"I'm afraid I will need some time to take care of Theo, change out of my work clothes and gather a few things," Jenna said, trying to ignore the little buzz of anticipation she felt at knowing she would be spending the evening with Wes and his daughter. "I'm sure your dad could use a little time as well."

They started for the house when the door opened and Wes walked out, arms loaded with blankets and lawn chairs.

Her little buzz became a full-on tremor.

"Oh. Hi. You're home," he said. His face seemed to light up when he spotted them. For his daughter, she told herself. Certainly not for her.

For a moment, she let her imagination wander, wondering what it might be like to have his hard features glow with welcome like that for her.

"There's my girl."

"Hi, Dad." Brielle launched herself at her father, who managed to set down the lawn chairs and blankets in time to catch her.

Jenna found the affection between the two of them sweetly touching, even as it made her ache a little for her fatherless child, who watched their joy-filled reunion with a little glint of envy in her expression.

How Wes must have missed his daughter during those three years he had been incarcerated. When children were young, even a few months' development could mean fundamental changes in maturity, communication and social skills. Jenna couldn't imagine how much Brielle had changed in the three years they were separated.

He lifted his gaze from his daughter to Jenna and something in his expression warmed her to her toes.

"Hi. I'm sorry I wasn't home half an hour earlier or I could have picked up the girls so you didn't have to."

"It's no problem. I was planning on it."

"How's your hand? Were you okay to drive?"

In truth, her hand was throbbing more now than it had since the initial injury but she didn't want to tell him, for fear he would suggest canceling the outing.

She didn't want to disappoint the girls. At least that's what she tried to tell herself was her motive for ignoring the pain.

"It's fine. I'm a little bit sore but not bad."

"Are you sure you're up for a picnic? If you're not, we can do it another day."

She shook her head. "We're all looking forward to it. Aren't we, girls?"

Brielle and Addie both nodded with enthusiasm.

"Give me a few moments and I'll be ready," she told him. "I have to change and take care of Theo."

"Take as long as you need."

The only trouble was, she had no idea how long it would take her to figure out how to protect her heart so she didn't completely fall for Wes Calhoun.

Chapter Thirteen

Could this really be his life or merely some delicious dream he didn't want to end?

Throughout the afternoon and evening Wes spent with Jenna and their respective daughters at the beautiful state park south of Cannon Beach, he had to stop more than once to soak in the moment.

It was a perfect summer evening, in company with his daughter, whom he loved more than anything else in the world, as well as the lovely Jenna Haynes and her daughter.

Only months earlier, he would have been standing in the chow line waiting for his bologna sandwich and pudding cup. If he was lucky.

Now he was sitting on a blanket a few dozen yards from the Pacific Ocean, watching the sky light up with color as the sun began its slow descent into the horizon.

The air was filled with the sound of the girls' laughter as a cute puppy with gangly legs loped around with enthusiasm, trying to catch the tennis ball they chucked between them.

Across from Wes on the blanket, watching the girls with a soft smile, was the warm, beautiful woman who was becoming increasingly important to him.

He wanted to bottle up this moment, to take it out when life felt hard or when he gave in to his occasional bouts of self-pity at all that had been taken from him by someone he had trusted.

"What a beautiful evening." Jenna gave a contented sort of sigh. "Thank you so much for suggesting this. It was exactly what I needed."

"Tough day? I mean, besides the stitches in your hand?"

She looked back at the girls. "Not really. It was busy, but no worse than usual for a Friday. I did have to deal with some... unpleasant customers, but I handled it the best way I could."

"That's always tough, isn't it? That was the hardest part for me of running a business. I tend to be impatient with people who are rude and demanding. It's hard not to want to respond in kind."

"What do you do?"

"Usually just try to remind myself that everybody has a bad day once in a while and I have no idea what they might be going through outside of this momentary interaction. Don't get me wrong. As you know probably too well, there are some garbage people in the world."

"Like your partner who set you up."

"He heads the list."

He didn't like thinking about Anthony Morris for even a moment longer than necessary.

"I doubt I'll ever be able to forgive him for trying to pin his crimes on me."

"And getting away with it for years," she pointed out.

"Right. But even with Tony, I try to remember that he is now behind bars, where he belongs, paying for what he did. I, on the other hand, am currently sitting on a spectacular beach watching the sunset with a beautiful woman."

He hadn't meant to add that part but had to admit he enjoyed seeing the wash of pink across her cheekbones.

She gazed at him for a long moment, then quickly looked away.

"Not so close to the water," she called to the girls, who

changed direction and returned to the blanket, with Theo leading the way.

The dog plopped onto the blanket, tongue panting.

"Oh. You're a thirsty guy, aren't you? That's what happens when you play so hard," Jenna said to the puppy.

Working around her injured hand, she opened her own water bottle and poured some into the dog's bowl they had brought. Theo lapped at it gratefully, which made the girls giggle.

"I'm thirsty, too," Brie declared. "Can I have another root beer?"

"I'm thirsty, too," Addie said.

"We have plenty of water but only one root beer left," he answered.

He had picked up a four-pack of craft root beer bottled by one of the local breweries. He and the girls each had enjoyed one but Jenna declared she was happy with water.

The girls studied the sole remaining bottle, clearly understanding the dilemma. Only one of them could have it. But which one?

"It's okay," Brielle said after a moment. "You have it."

Addie shook her head. "No. You have it."

"How about this," Jenna suggested. "You can share it. I can pour half the bottle into one of your empty water bottles."

"Good idea," Brie said, clearly thrilled with the solution.

"My water bottle is empty," Addie said, tipping it for the last drop to be sure.

"Why don't you let me do that?" Wes held out a hand to take the root beer bottle. "We don't want you to splash soda all over your bandages."

Jenna made a face but handed over the root beer bottle and Addie's water bottle.

Wes moved a few steps away from the blanket in case of fizzing and opened the bottle of root beer, carefully pouring out half into the water bottle.

As he returned to the blanket and handed the soda bottle to Brie and the pink water bottle to Addie, Wes couldn't help thinking about the time one of the guys in his block, a particularly nasty guy named Victor, had shivved a guy at lunch over a peanut butter cookie.

He remembered the scream and the blood and the shouting guards as if it happened that morning.

Would memories of that dark time always taint his future happiness? He didn't want it to. He wanted to be able to completely put it behind him, but he wasn't sure that would ever be possible.

He could not pretend it had never happened. Those three years were part of him, just like the time he had spent in the Army and the years of his childhood when he had lived on that breathtaking Colorado farm.

He had to hope that eventually moments like these, pure and perfect, would overwhelm the darkness.

"Thank you for everything," Jenna said as the girls sipped at their respective root beers. "This was so fun going tide pooling with you girls and having you show us all the creatures you learned about at camp."

That had been one of Wes's favorite parts of the evening. Jenna had orders from the doctor to keep her hand dry, so Wes had set up a beach chair for her on the sand just above the surf. She watched, the dog at her side, while he and the girls scrambled carefully over the rocks looking at starfish, sea urchins and anemones of every color.

Addie and Brie used Wes's cell phone to snap pictures of what they found for Jenna, so she could enjoy the experience, too.

While he had set up their picnic dinner of fried chicken, pasta salad and kettle chips, Jenna had scrolled through the photos, asking the girls questions about their discoveries.

After dinner, the girls had begged to take a walk on one

of the lush trails around the state park. With the girls racing ahead, he and Jenna had walked together, chatting about places they had visited and bucket list destinations they would like to see.

Finally, they had returned here to watch the sunset.

"We should probably head back soon," Jenna told the girls as they finished their soda.

"I wish we could stay here all night," Addie said, lying back on the blanket and gazing up at the few pale stars beginning to appear.

"I'm afraid there's no camping allowed at this park," Jenna said. "But maybe one weekend this summer we could borrow a tent from Rosa and Wyatt and camp at one of the other places along the coast."

"Can we come?" Brie asked.

Wes gave an inward wince at his daughter's forwardness.

"That would be so fun!" Addie exclaimed. "Can we go camping together, Mom?"

That lovely pink rose on her cheeks as she sent Wes a quick look. "I'm not sure Rosa and Wyatt have a tent that would fit the four of us."

"We could bring our own tent!" Brie said. "You have one, don't you, Dad? If not, Mom and Ron do."

"I do have a tent. But maybe Jenna and Addie wanted to have their own trip together."

"It would be so fun to have you come, wouldn't it, Mom?"

Jenna lifted her gaze to his again. Heat surged between them. "Sure," she finally said. "We can probably make that work. We'll have to see."

He would love nothing more than spending a weekend camping with Jenna and their daughters. He had visions of talking by the fire until the early hours of the morning, gazing up at the stars, kissing her again until they were both shaking with need…

Wes sighed. He would be smarter to come up with excuses to stay away from Jenna, instead of letting his mind run wild, imagining mythical future outings together.

Though he didn't want this particular evening to end, he turned his energy toward loading up his pickup truck with all the things they had brought and making sure they carried away everything from their picnic site.

"Dad, can we stop and have gelato before we go home?" Brielle asked him when they were all finally loaded into the truck and he was about to drive out of the parking area.

His gaze met Jenna's and she shrugged. "Fine with me. I love gelato."

Wes pulled out onto the road back to Cannon Beach, feeling as if he had been handed a reprieve.

Maybe Jenna didn't want the evening to end, either.

After driving back to Cannon Beach, he parked down the street from the small storefront selling gelato in at least two dozen varieties, handmade on the premises.

He and Brielle had discovered the place shortly after he arrived in Cannon Beach, and stopping here occasionally had become something of a ritual for them.

The night was lovely and pleasant, not too warm and not cold enough for a jacket. The streets of downtown were bustling with visitors but the line at the gelato shop moved quickly.

After they ordered and received their gelato—chocolate chip for him and the girls and butter pecan for Jenna—they found an empty picnic table outside the shop and sat down, licking at their cones and people watching.

This was another moment he would store in his memory bank. The girls giggling about something, Theo lapping the ground of any drips from the cones, and Jenna pretty and soft in the lamplight as she tapped her sandal along with the live music coming out of the restaurant next door.

"This has been a perfect evening," she said as she worked to finish off the final few licks of her cone. "Thank you so much for suggesting it."

"Yeah," Addie said. "Thanks. It was really fun."

"Can we do it again the next time I come to stay with you?" Brielle asked him. "Maybe we could go to another beach and try tide pooling there."

"Sure."

He wasn't sure whether Jenna wanted to spend any more time with him, but Wes figured he could always take his daughter on his own.

Same for the camping trip. As much as he would enjoy going with Jenna and Addie, he and Brie could still have a great time, the two of them.

"Looks like somebody is pooped." Jenna gestured to Theo, who had plopped down at her feet and didn't look like he wanted to move.

"He's not the only one. I think I know two girls who are going to drop the moment they get home."

"I'm not tired," Addison insisted.

"Me neither," Brielle said.

"Well, Theo certainly is," Jenna answered.

"Because he's still a baby and babies sleep all the time," Brielle informed her. "That's what my mom says, anyway."

"They do sleep a lot," Jenna said. "All except Addie."

She smiled at her daughter. "You were up and down all night long and didn't sleep through the night until you were eight or nine months old. Your dad used to say you were afraid you were going to miss something. You were an early adopter of FOMO."

"What about me, Dad?"

Through his own choices, Wes had missed so much after Brie had been born, too busy trying to build the company. At least his time in prison had helped him realize that any success he earned professionally could be gone in an instant. This. This was the important thing. Family. Friends.

Love.

He didn't want to go there. Yes, he was developing feelings for Jenna but he certainly wasn't falling in love with her. That would be completely self-destructive of him.

"You are *still* afraid you're going to miss something," he said, focusing back on his daughter. "It's one of the things I love most about you."

She rolled her eyes at him. "I can't help it if all the good stuff happens after I go to bed!"

After they finished their gelato, he helped all three of them back into his pickup and drove the short distance back to Brambleberry House.

"Thank you again," Jenna said when he pulled into the driveway. "That was the most enjoyable evening I have had in a long time."

"Same for me," he admitted, his voice somewhat gruff.

"We can help you carry things back inside."

"I've got it. Don't worry."

"Okay. Well, um, have a good night."

He pushed down a hundred things he wanted to say. Especially *Can I carry you to my bed after the girls are asleep and keep you there all night long?*

"Thanks," he finally managed. "If you need help with Theo after Addie goes to sleep, let me know."

All evening, the girls had been taking turns holding the dog's leash so Jenna didn't have to risk reinjuring her wounded hand.

She nodded. "If I need help, I'll call. But I'm sure we'll be fine."

Before she headed toward the house, she shocked him one last time that day by reaching up and brushing her lips against his cheek.

It was all he could do not to turn his mouth to meet hers and devour her. Desire for her seemed to have become a steady beat through his veins.

"Good night," she murmured, then hurried into the house, leaving him to watch after her and ache.

Chapter Fourteen

She couldn't sleep.

Jenna opened one eye and glared at the clock on the night-stand. It was after 1:00 a.m. and she had been tossing and turning for an hour.

She was so tired but her mind couldn't seem to shut down. While she wasn't scheduled to work at the store the next day, Saturday, she had a packed agenda anyway. She and her friend Kim were cohosting the Brambleberry Book Group, consisting of twenty friends who gathered monthly, taking turns to be in charge.

She thought it would be fun to have dinner in the garden, shaded by the trees and the pergola. Kim was handling the meal, street tacos and taco salad catered by their favorite Mexican food place in town.

While Jenna was only baking a couple dozen cookies, she had plenty of other things to do. Cleaning off the lawn chairs. Setting up tables. Picking up the margarita mix.

She flipped her pillow over to the cool side, punched it with her good hand a few times for more fluff and rolled over.

She needed sleep so she could take on her chores the next day. But sleep still seemed a long way off. Instead, she couldn't seem to stop rehashing the evening spent with Wes and his daughter.

What was wrong with her?

She knew the answer to that, even before she asked it of herself.

She was lonely.

She wanted someone to hold her, to touch her, to cherish her and make her feel wanted.

And not any someone. She wanted Wes Calhoun.

Her mind kept replaying the hot, hungry look in his eyes when she had kissed his cheek several hours earlier.

He shared her attraction, which made it even harder for her to continue resisting him.

What was she going to do about Wes? She was developing feelings for the man, even though she knew anything between them was completely impossible.

Not feelings, she told herself. She couldn't be coming to care for him. They were friends. That was all.

Even as the thought popped into her mind, it rang hollow. Friends didn't make each other yearn. Friends didn't think about each other all the time. Friends didn't kiss each other until they were achy with need.

Wes made it so blasted hard to resist him. That evening with the girls had been magical. Even with her hand aching, she had loved spending time with him and his daughter. He had teased the girls, made them laugh, protected them.

Jenna sighed, turning over again before she finally sat up and pulled off her duvet. She had struggled so much with insomnia during the worst of Aaron's assault on her peace of mind that she was all too familiar with how it worked for her.

She likely had no chance of falling asleep anytime soon, not until she climbed out of bed and tried to do something else to distract herself and calm her mind for an hour or so.

Reading worked best for her, especially if it was something dry and uninteresting. While she focused on something else, all the worries keeping her awake either receded or sorted themselves out.

She had the perfect title in the living room, one of the recommended reading texts left over from her master's program. She had only made it through about a third of the book, despite months of trying.

When she walked out to the kitchen, Theo greeted her with a tail thump inside his crate.

She could also take the dog out for a quick walk through the garden before she settled in to read. The flowers and shrubs laid out in the Brambleberry House landscaping never failed to soothe her, especially in the moonlight.

For a long time, all her instincts had told her to hide behind triple-locked doors and away from any open windows. Going outside by herself after dark would have been out of the question.

Maybe if she still lived in Utah, that might have been the case. As irrational as it might seem, she felt safe here in Cannon Beach.

Yes, bad things happened here. Bad things had happened to *her* here. Aaron had terrorized her and had physically hurt her dear friend and the wonderful Fiona.

Every time she remembered that awful time two summers ago, she felt a little nauseated and had to fight the urge to stay inside where she knew she would be safe.

All the more reason to go outside, she decided. She didn't want to be a person who cowered.

Without taking more time to think about it, she slid into her garden shoes, pulled a hoodie on over her pajama top and went to the dog's crate.

"I know you were all settled for the night, but would you like to go out one more time?"

Theo thumped his tail on the floor, which made her smile. What a joy the dog had been, even in only the short weeks he had been part of their family. She had almost forgotten what their life had been like without him.

Theo jumped from his crate and stretched in a good imitation of a yoga pose, then followed her eagerly out the door as she made her way quietly downstairs.

The house was hushed in these early hours of the morning. She didn't know whether Wes was asleep up on the third floor but the ground floor apartment was empty. The Andersons, the lovely older couple who lived there, were expected home the following week. The retired pair had gone on an extended trip through Europe, including a long cruise, and their weekly email updates filled Jenna with no small degree of envy.

Maybe she should take Addie on a cruise. She could plan it around fall break. They didn't have to go to Europe. Instead, they could stick close to home and take one of the cruises that traveled the Pacific coastline.

The idea was deeply appealing. Four or five days when she didn't have to make all the decisions in life, where someone else would feed them, entertain them, show them beautiful parts of the world.

Still, she couldn't ignore one inescapable truth.

If she was lonely in Cannon Beach, she was going to be every bit as lonely on a cruise, if not more so, surrounded by couples and families having fun together.

How would she ever meet someone new? Jenna wondered as she reached the bottom step. Her job as an elementary teacher didn't bring many unattached men into her life. She didn't socialize much, except with her female friends and other teachers. She would certainly never dare try a dating app again, though she knew several friends who swore by them and had found deep and lasting relationships that way.

Jenna sighed as she pushed open the exterior door to the front of the house.

She didn't want to meet a man, anyway.

Especially a man who wasn't Wes Calhoun.

She pushed away the thought, focusing instead on the fresh,

sweet night air, thick with the scent of roses and lavender. She inhaled deeply, feeling tension in her muscles instantly begin to ease.

This was her home. She didn't need to leave Brambleberry House, unless things grew too uncomfortable between her and Wes.

Yet another reason to try putting things back on a safer footing.

Theo lifted his leg on a tuft of grass, then followed after her as she walked through the garden toward the pergola overlooking the water. Jenna wanted to take one more look to see how many tables would fit in the small structure.

Before they reached it, Theo's tail began to wag and he gave a little yip of greeting, her first signs that she wasn't alone in the garden.

Inside the pergola, Wes wore a headlamp to light his task, which seemed to be tightening a screw on one of the wooden lawn chairs. Three other chairs were upside down, apparently waiting their turn.

He must have heard Theo's doggy greeting because he shifted in their direction, the headlamp aimed up at the sky like a beacon, forever guiding her toward him.

"What are you doing out here?" she asked when they approached.

"I noticed the chairs all felt a little wobbly so I thought it wouldn't hurt to reinforce them before one fell apart."

"In the dark, at one in the morning?"

"Is it that late? I hadn't noticed. What about you? What brings you out? I thought everybody was settled for the night. The house seemed quiet."

"I couldn't sleep so I got up to read for a bit. And as soon as I walked out into the living room, I realized Theo would see me and decide he needed to go out."

"It's a beautiful night, isn't it?"

She lifted her face up to the glitter of stars overhead, endless and lovely.

"It really is."

"Everybody told me to be prepared for gray skies and rain when I moved to Oregon. We've had a few of those, but it seems like we have far more sunny days than not."

"You came at a great time of year. Our winters can be cold and stormy."

"I'm looking forward to watching the storms roll in."

Jenna loved the drama of sitting in front of her bay window as the sea turned dark and frothy. "You might get your wish earlier than later," she told him. "A summer storm is supposed to hit tomorrow night. Tonight, I guess. Around ten or so. I just hope it holds off until later than that as I'm having my book club out here tomorrow evening."

"That sounds fun."

"What's not to love about it? Good friends talking about books, eating food and enjoying adult beverages."

He nodded to the overturned furniture in front of him. "Good thing I had a wild hare to fix the chairs, then. I would hate for one of your book club friends to sit down, only to have the whole thing fall apart."

"Yes. Great timing. Can I help you with anything here?"

"I'm nearly done. You could hold the flashlight for me, if you'd like. I've got the headlamp, but every time I turn my head, I can't see what I'm doing."

She picked up the flashlight he indicated, perched on one of the chairs he had apparently already tightened, and aimed it at the chair in front of him. Theo spent a moment sniffing around the pergola, then found a spot to curl up on atop one of the chair cushions.

A subtle intimacy seemed to curl around them, here in the quiet of the garden. Was this the reason she had been drawn outside? Had some part of her suspected he might be out here, the part of her that couldn't seem to stay away from this man?

She didn't want to think so.

"What time are you expecting Brielle's mom to return?"

"Their plane lands in Portland around noon, so a few hours after that."

"I'm sure Brie has missed her."

"They've talked on the phone nearly every day, but yeah. They're very close. Lacey is a great mom."

"That's good of you to say. I've heard other divorced parents who aren't nearly as complimentary of their exes."

He made a sound that was somewhere between a grunt and a sigh. "We're much better friends now than we ever were when we were married."

"Has it been hard for you, seeing Lacey go on with her life?" He must have loved her once, dreamed of a future with her.

This time the sound he made definitely sounded like a laugh. "Not one tiny bit. She deserves to be happy. Lacey had to carry a lot after I went to prison. She really stepped up. I can never repay her for that."

"How did you meet her?"

She wasn't only making conversation. She genuinely wanted to know, Jenna thought, as he turned that chair over and moved to work on another one. She followed with the flashlight, taking a seat on the chair he had just fixed.

"Friend of a friend. I was stationed in North Carolina and she came down from Michigan to visit a friend in the area, who happened to be dating one of my buddies. We went on a couple of double dates and then just sort of…fell into a relationship."

He was quiet, his muscles flexing as he tightened the screws on the underside of the chair. "She was desperate to escape a tough family life, and I was getting ready to head overseas after a transfer to Germany. We decided to tie the knot before I left so she could come with me. Not an uncommon story in the military."

"How long were you in Germany?"

While he worked, he talked about his military service and some of the experiences he'd had, not only there but during a short stint in the Middle East, protecting the base and being fired on by militants.

As they talked and she came to understand him a little, Jenna was aware of a grim realization.

She was doing a lousy job of resisting him.

In fact, quite the opposite.

She was falling for him.

The truth washed over her, and for an instant, she wobbled the flashlight in her shock. He looked over and she quickly corrected it.

Oh no. What had she done?

This wasn't simply an attraction. She was falling in love with him.

He definitely didn't feel the same way. Yes, he was attracted to her, but that was it. He had given her no indication that his feelings might run deeper.

Oh, what a mess.

They lived in the same house. Yes, they had different apartments, but it was impossible to avoid the other Brambleberry House tenants. How would she be able to live one floor below him? Could she possibly return to merely being friends when she was beginning to realize how very much more she wanted?

She didn't want to move out. She loved this house and so did Addie. But how could she stay here and keep her feelings to herself, when she saw him day after day and when their daughters were becoming such close friends?

"What's wrong?" he asked. She looked up to find him watching her, an expression of concern on his face.

She couldn't tell him any of the thoughts racing through her head. He wouldn't want to hear that his foolish neighbor was getting all kinds of inappropriate ideas about him.

She pasted on a smile, hoping the darkness would conceal her sudden distress. "Nothing. Everything's fine," she lied.

"Are you sure? You were frowning like you just spotted a skunk walking through the lilac bushes."

"Oh, I hope not! Don't you think Theo would alert us to any wandering creatures making their way through the yard?"

"Him?"

He pointed to the dog, curled up on the cushion and snoring softly.

She was grateful to turn the subject. "He's not turning into the greatest watchdog, is he? On the plus side, he's the most mellow dog ever and loves everybody. Not an aggressive bone in his body."

"I'm sure he still has enough protective instincts to watch out for you and Addie if the need arises. Dogs are amazing like that."

They talked about some of the dogs he had worked with in prison and the two great dogs he'd had when he was young, before his father died.

Jenna wasn't at all tired, though she knew she would pay the price the next day. She would be lucky to stay awake until book club.

She knew she should go inside, to figure out what she was going to do next, but she couldn't seem to make herself move.

After she had been outside about a half hour, he set the last chair upright and took off his headlamp, switching it off. "There you go. That's the last one."

She handed him the flashlight. He aimed it downward, though didn't shut it off.

"Thank you for doing that. I'm sure my book club members will appreciate chairs that don't fall apart in the middle of dinner."

"Always a good thing, right?"

She managed a smile, and as he gazed down at her, sparkling awareness seemed to shiver to life between them.

Jenna wanted him to kiss her, even though she knew it would only leave her wanting more. She saw him swallow and had the most inappropriate urge to press her mouth to the strong column of his neck.

"I should..." She pointed to the house.

In the light cast from the flashlight, his expression seemed remote, hard. "Probably a good idea." His voice suddenly seemed abrupt and she wondered what she had done.

"Are you staying out a little longer?"

"Yeah."

"Are you sure? It has to be nearly two."

"I'll get there eventually."

Though she knew she needed to go inside, she was reluctant to leave him out here by himself.

They gazed at each other for a long moment as the night air seemed to sigh around them.

"Do you want to know the real reason I came out here?" he asked, his voice low and his features in shadow.

She shook her head, suddenly unable to find her voice.

"I had to do something physical to keep myself distracted from wanting something I can't have."

Her breath seemed to catch at the intensity of his words, the raw emotion there.

"What's that?" she finally asked, her voice barely above a whisper.

"I think you know, Jenna. You. You are what I want."

Heat rushed from her brain to pool in her belly, her thighs.

She swallowed, not sure how to answer him, finally settling on the truth.

"That's the reason I couldn't sleep, either. I keep remembering…kissing you."

He made a low sound, raw and hungry, and then the flashlight tumbled to the ground, pitching them into darkness as he reached for her.

When he kissed her, everything inside her seemed to sigh a welcome. She had wanted him to kiss her again for days. Forever, it seemed.

The reality was far better than any of her memories, and she was lost in the magic of his touch.

They kissed for a long time, tasting and exploring while the dog snored softly and the night breeze stirred the flowers around them.

She was only vaguely aware of Wes lowering down to one of the pergola chairs and pulling her with him onto his lap, where she seemed to fit perfectly. She felt a fleeting moment of gratitude that he had reinforced the chairs. How mortifying if one clattered apart underneath them.

The thought made her smile a little and he eased his mouth away.

"What's so funny?"

"I hope you knew what you were doing when you tightened the screws or we might be in for an unpleasant surprise."

His mouth lifted with a smile that left her breathless. "I wouldn't care. I would still want to kiss you amid the rubble of a dozen chairs."

She shivered at the intensity of his expression, the heat of him surrounding her.

"You're cold," he murmured.

She shook her head, though reality was beginning to push through the haze of desire.

What were they doing? What was *she* doing? A few more moments out here and she would have completely surrendered.

Though it was painfully hard, she slid off his lap. "I should never have come out here. I'm sorry. We…we can't do this."

He froze for a long second, heat and desire mixing with confusion in his gaze. "Why not?" he asked on a growl.

She released a long breath. "We both know where it would lead. Where would we go? Your apartment? We can't because Brielle is inside. My apartment? Addie."

He gazed at her, his breathing ragged.

"Even if the girls weren't inside, you know it wouldn't be a good idea," she said, hating herself for what she had to do.

"Right now, it feels like a damn good idea."

The fierce hunger in his voice thrummed through her.

He rose as well and in the darkness, she could only make out his profile. "You should know, this isn't just physical for me, though that's certainly a factor. I think about you all the time, Jenna. When I'm not with you, I want to be. When I *am* with you, I want to savor every second of it until I get the chance to spend time with you again."

A torrent of emotions poured through her at his words. Tenderness, joy, heat, need.

She wanted to lean into his words, to grab them and treasure them against her heart.

This seemed so very different from the love she and Ryan had shared. Their relationship had been like hot cocoa on a cold winter night. Warm, comforting, sustaining.

This thing between her and Wes was something else entirely.

More like cocoa with a heavy dash of hot sauce.

As much as she longed to consume every drop, a cold fear seemed to spread from her stomach outward, like frost blooms on the window.

She had fought so hard to be in a good place. Wes threatened to ruin all of that peace and calm.

She already had feelings for him. If she gave in to this heat between them, she would fall irrevocably in love and would end up bruised and broken.

But what if she didn't? a little voice whispered. What if they were able to work through all their differences and find happiness together?

It would be amazing. She had no doubt.

I think about you all the time, Jenna. When I'm not with you, I want to be. When I am *with you, I want to savor every second of it until I get the chance to spend time with you again.*

His words seemed seared into her heart. Was it possible he could be falling in love with her, too?

No. She couldn't believe it. His world was tattoos and motorcycles, while hers was book clubs and parent-teacher conferences. This heat would pass, like the storms that blew through Cannon Beach. After it was gone, what would they possibly have between them?

"I can't," she whispered, despising herself for giving in to the fear but unable to face the alternative.

"Because I've been in prison."

At his flat, emotionless tone, she stared at him, wishing she could see better in the darkness, could grab the flashlight from the ground and aim it at him so she could read his expression.

"No. That has nothing to do with it. Do you want the truth? Okay. I'm afraid, Wes. There it is. Four years ago, my husband died and left me devastated, then just as I was beginning to come back to life, I became tangled up with the wrong man and ended up in another version of hell. I'm finally beginning to figure things out again. I can't… I don't want to mess that up. Not for me and not for Addie."

"Why would this mess everything up?"

She sighed, moving away. "I love living here in Brambleberry House. So does Addie. I don't want to leave. But what if we give in to this heat between us and something goes wrong? How would I possibly be able to stay here?"

He was quiet for a long moment. When he spoke, his voice was low. "But what if everything between us goes *right*?"

His kisses certainly felt right to her. And she loved being with him and could spend all night talking to him out here in the pergola.

For a moment, she was tempted. So very tempted.

But she had ignored her instincts once with Aaron by going on a second date with him. She couldn't take that kind of risk again when she had so much at stake.

She didn't for a moment think Wes would hurt her intentionally. But she was already half in love with the man. If they gave in to this desire between them, how would she possibly protect what was left of her heart?

"I'm sorry," she said again. Despising herself, she grabbed a confused Theo and hurried back to the house.

After Jenna left so abruptly, Wes stayed in the pergola, staring at the night sky peeking through the open slat roof.

If this was love, he didn't want it. This ache in his chest, in his bones. In his heart.

He couldn't blame Jenna for not wanting to further explore the attraction between them and pursue a relationship.

How could he?

Wes wasn't exactly a prize. She had talked about her baggage, but he had so much he needed a damn cargo tanker to carry it all.

He sighed, frustrated all over again at the circumstances of his life that had led him here.

Would he change it if he could?

It was a stunning thought.

If he hadn't been arrested, he probably wouldn't be here in Cannon Beach, living upstairs from her.

He looked at the house, cold and dark now where it was usually so warm and filled with life.

She was right. How would they both be able to remain here, with these raw, unfulfilled emotions between them? He would find it excruciating to live one floor above her, to be so close to her but know she would remain forever out of reach.

Even now he wanted to march up those stairs, break down her door and pull her into his arms.

How could he stay here?

She had said she didn't want to move. He didn't want to leave Brambleberry House, either. The house was warm and comfortable, and the view and proximity to the water would be hard to beat somewhere else within his price range.

He would have an easier time moving, though. He had brought very little with him, and it would be simple enough to pack it up into his truck and find somewhere else to live.

It made the most sense. She had been here for years. This was her daughter's home. If they found the situation completely untenable, he would have to start looking for another place. He didn't know where he would go, only that he had to stay in town. He had been separated from Brie for long enough. He wouldn't do it again.

Would anywhere else along the coast be far enough to help him get over Jenna?

He wasn't sure.

What choice did he have? Whatever her reasons, she had made it clear she didn't want things to move forward.

His only option was to try like hell to put away his feelings, to focus on Brie and the future and rebuilding his life.

Chapter Fifteen

The encounter with Wes in the early hours haunted Jenna the rest of the day as she prepped for the book group meeting.

She had been looking forward to the meeting with her friends all week, but now she wasn't certain she would be able to get through it.

She was exhausted, for one thing, after returning to her house to toss and turn again in her bed until she had finally fallen into a fitful sleep.

She also wasn't in a cheerful mood. She had snapped at Addie when she complained about having to do her chores, then had to apologize. She explained that she was having a cranky morning and shouldn't have snapped…but that Addie still had to do her chores.

The rest of the day was busy as she cleaned her apartment, went to the grocery store and had Addie help her make cookies.

She didn't see Wes all day and tried to tell herself she was relieved, not disappointed.

Finally, an hour before the party, as she was covering the tables with linen cloths, she spotted his pickup truck pulling into its usual parking spot.

He climbed out, paused a moment as if trying to make up his mind, then approached her.

"Hi."

"Hello." She tried a smile, even as she felt a sharp pang of longing. "Did Brielle go back to her mom's?"

He nodded. "Yes. I took her there this afternoon. We went to a matinee this morning of a movie she's been wanting to see. Sort of our last hurrah together."

"It must have been tough to say goodbye."

"I won't say dropping her off with her mother becomes any easier with practice. But I'm slowly beginning to accept that I can see her anytime I want and she'll be here again in a week, not every few months when Lacey could arrange a prison visit."

"You're a good father, Wes."

He made a face as if he disagreed but didn't argue with her. "What time does your party start?"

She glanced at her watch. "Another hour. People should be arriving around seven. I've got a babysitter coming for Addie in about a half hour. Rosa's niece Bella is great with her and Rosa's stepson is coming to play, too."

He glanced out to sea, where she could see a rim of dark clouds on the horizon. "Forecasters are saying the storm should hold off until later. Maybe ten or eleven."

"We should be done by then."

"Good to know. I'll be sure to stay out of your way. I might take my bike for a drive down the coast."

She knew that was one of his outlets when he was particularly restless. Was she the cause of his current tumult? She didn't like thinking it.

"You don't have to stay away. In fact, you're welcome to join us at book group, if you'd like."

"I don't think I would quite fit in with your crowd."

She thought of her group, mostly women but a few men, too. "You might. We're open to everyone willing to read the featured book and offer insight."

He gestured to the tables and chairs. "Can I help you set things up? It can't be comfortable, with your injured hand."

She didn't want to feel beholden to him for even one more

thing, especially with these currents seething between them. But she had to admit she had been struggling all day to work around her stupid bandage.

"Would you mind carrying out some of the folding chairs from the shed? That would be very helpful."

"No problem. How many?"

"All of them. I think there are about a dozen there. That should give us enough, with the furniture you fixed last night."

As soon as she said the words, conjuring up memories that hadn't been far from her mind all day, her face felt hot. He gazed at her for a long moment, and she knew he was remembering their intense embrace as well.

"Sure. No problem."

He headed toward the shed at the bottom of the garden and returned with three chairs in each hand. He set them up, then returned to the shed for the rest, finishing in about two minutes when the job would have taken her at least ten.

He set them up where she indicated, at the folding tables she had already brought out with Addie's help.

"They're pretty dusty. I gather they haven't been used much lately."

She nodded. "When Rosa still lived here, she liked to have gatherings, but I'm afraid I'm not as social as she is. The Andersons do often have friends over to grill, but a few at a time, not enough that would require them to pull out the extra chairs."

"I can clean them off for you."

She started to protest that he didn't need to do that, then swallowed her words. She was running out of time and still needed to bring down a few more items for the party from her apartment. This was also a good test as to whether they could set aside their feelings and be friendly enough to both stay here at the house.

"I've got a few cleaning supplies stored under the serving table there."

He nodded and went to work without another word. For some reason, his simple thoughtfulness made her eyes burn with tears.

Wes was a good man. Any woman smart enough to build a relationship with him should consider herself very lucky.

She wanted to be that woman, suddenly, with a fierce intensity that brought a lump to her throat.

She swallowed it down quickly. "I've got to run upstairs for a few more things. Thank you so much for your help. I'll save you some cookies."

"This is the kind of thing friends do for each other, right?"

Was that a shadow of bitterness in his voice? She couldn't quite tell…and her daughter's excited shriek distracted her from trying to figure it out.

"Hi, Logan! You're here!"

She looked up to see Rosa walking toward them, along with Bella and Rosa's stepson, Logan, who had become fast friends with Addie when he and his father temporarily lived in Brambleberry House after a fire at their own home.

"Hi, Addie." Logan beamed at her. "Where's your dog? I can't wait to meet him! I wanted to bring Hank, but my dad said he should stay home since a book party might not be the best time to see if he and your new puppy get along."

"Theo likes everybody," Addie said. "Don't you, buddy?"

In answer, their new puppy licked at Logan, who giggled.

Rosa gave Wes a curious look as he continued wiping off the chairs. "I do hope you're joining us for book group."

"Not me. Sorry. I don't even know what book you're reading."

She told him and he shook his head. "Haven't read that one, thought I did read the author's last book."

"You should come next month," she said with a warm smile.

"By then, we'll have a new baby." Wyatt's teenage niece Bella beamed at Rosa.

"Are you sure you'll be okay with these three?" Jenna asked, pointing to the children and the dog, who were chasing each other around the part of the yard not currently set up with tables.

"We'll be great," Bella answered. "We'll go for a long walk on the beach and build sandcastles and tire everybody out, then come back and watch a movie. I can't wait to hang with them."

Bella was a sweet girl who looked enough like Rosa to be her sister.

Another car pulled in behind Rosa's. Kim, Jenna saw, with the food.

She hurried over to help carry the catering trays to the tables. By the time she returned to the pergola, Wes had disappeared.

"It was nice of Wes to help you set up for the party," Rosa said sometime later, after the book club gathering was in full swing.

Jenna knew she shouldn't feel this little pang in her heart just at the mention of his name. "Yes. He's been very kind."

"I wish he had stayed for the book group. He could have made more friends."

"Too bad he didn't," Kim said. "Maybe we can talk him into helping us move some tables or something later. All those muscles. *Mmm.*"

Jenna fought down a little spurt of annoyance with her friend, which she knew was completely unreasonable. Kim was extremely happily married and was only teasing about Wes. That didn't stop Jenna from feeling protective of him.

She had no right to feel that way. He wasn't hers. She had made sure of that.

She forced a smile. "I think Wes is making himself scarce on purpose tonight. He said doesn't want to get in the way of our fun."

"Are you talking about Wes Calhoun? I heard from Lacey that her ex was living here."

Jenna looked over at Erin Lawson, a yoga instructor who

always recommended motivational self-improvement books when it was her turn to host book group.

"Yes. He lives in the third-floor apartment," Jenna said, her tone guarded. "Do you know him?"

"Not personally, no." Erin looked at the house. "My friend Jewel is friends with Lacey and she told her about him. I just think you're really brave to live in this big house alone with an ex-con, especially with the Andersons still out of town."

Jenna frowned. "Wes is an excellent neighbor. And he was cleared of all charges."

Erin shrugged. "Innocent or not. Prison changes people. My sister's husband went away for a white-collar thing. He spent a year inside and came out a completely different man. And not in a good way, either. I just don't know if I could do it. I admire you."

Jenna had to bite down a sharp retort. First, she was the least brave woman she knew. Second, she had absolutely no reason to be afraid of Wes.

He would never hurt her. He would rather go back to prison than do that. She suddenly knew that with absolute conviction.

How horrible for him, that some people would always judge him for circumstances completely beyond his control.

She opened her mouth to say as much, but Erin had turned away to talk to someone else and the conversation turned away from Wes, much to her relief.

She tried to focus on the conversation and her friends instead of Wes, though she noted she was not the only woman who watched him when he came out of the house sometime later, started up his bike and rode off into the evening sun.

Chapter Sixteen

"That was a terrific book group," Kim said as she carried the last of the folding chairs back to the shed.

"It was fun, wasn't it?" Jenna said, smothering a yawn.

"And the best part is, we don't have to host it again for a whole year."

She smiled. "At least we made it through the book discussion before the storm hit."

"Barely." Kim gestured out to sea, where dark clouds gathered. Lightning arced over the water and she could hear the distant answering thunder.

"I'd better get home. Thanks for hosting. This was a lovely spot for the party."

Her friend hugged her and hurried to her car as the first few drops of rain hit.

Jenna carried the last few serving dishes into the house, worried about Wes. She had seen him leave the house and ride away on his bike during the first hour of the party and he had yet to return.

She hoped he wasn't caught out in the rain. She had heard raindrops could feel like tiny bullets to a motorcyclist.

Her hand throbbed as she made her way up the stairs to her apartment. She needed some ibuprofen and her bed.

She pushed open the door to her quiet apartment. Bella had left a half hour ago with Logan and Rosa, leaving Addie fast asleep in her bed. Jenna had checked on her fifteen minutes earlier when she had carried a load of items upstairs.

She spotted the empty crate as soon as she walked into the kitchen. Oh shoot. On that earlier trip up to the apartment, she had taken Theo back down with her to let him out for the night one last time and then got so busy talking with Kim and cleaning up the final debris from the party that she completely forgot him in the small fenced dog yard.

She made her way back down the stairs and out the back porch.

"Theo? Come on, bud."

She waited for the puppy to come bounding over to her. When he didn't, she frowned. "Theo? Come."

Still nothing.

The storm was moving closer, she saw. A flash of lightning illuminated the yard, revealing no sign of the dog.

She moved down the steps. Where could he be?

When she reached the back of the dog yard, which accessed the beach gate, everything inside her turned cold. The gate was ajar slightly, with just enough room for a puppy to squeeze through.

A few of her guests who lived close had opted to walk home via the beach. She could only guess that one of them must not have closed the gate completely.

Theo was gone.

A storm was coming, her daughter was alone in the house and their small, defenseless puppy was lost somewhere on the beach.

This was her fault. She should have checked to make sure the beach gate was closed before she ever let Theo out into the yard.

Anything could happen to him out there. She couldn't bear thinking about the hazards to a small puppy.

She had to find him, no matter if she had to search all night.

She turned and raced back into her apartment for her phone and a flashlight, tossing extra batteries in her pocket just in case, then hurried back downstairs.

Her fatigue, the ache in her hand and the ache in her heart were all forgotten for now as she focused on finding Theo.

After a long bike ride down to Pacific City and back, Wes hoped he might be tired enough to sleep.

Instead, his mind still raced, his heart still ached and now he was damp and cold from the rain that had caught him about fifteen miles from home.

The party was apparently over, he saw as he pulled into the driveway. The only other vehicles he could see were his pickup truck and Jenna's small SUV.

He looked up to the second floor, where he saw only a dim light on.

Just as he was climbing off his bike, the front door flung open and Jenna raced down the porch toward him wearing a raincoat and carrying a flashlight.

"Oh, thank heavens you're here," she said, her voice frantic. "I am so glad I heard your bike. I need your help."

"What's wrong?" he asked instantly, forgetting all about his wet clothing or the chill beginning to seep in.

"It's Theo. Somehow he wandered off through the beach gate." Her voice bordered on hysteria. "I'm just about to go look for him. Can you help me?"

"Of course." He didn't hesitate for a second. "I've got a flashlight and my headlamp in my pickup. Let me grab them."

He unlocked the truck and found the lights immediately. On impulse, he also threw in a couple of road flares. They might come in handy.

He shut the truck door as another flash of lightning rippled through the night, still distant but moving closer.

"What about Addie?" he asked suddenly. "You can't leave her for long. Why don't you stay with her and I'll go look."

She shook her head vigorously. "I called my friend Kim and she is on her way back to stay with Addie in case she wakes. She should be here in a few minutes. She knows the code to get in the house and I left my apartment unlocked. It's my fault. I should have been more careful and made sure the gate was shut after some of my guests left that way."

Ah. That explained how Theo had managed his escape.

"How long do you think he's been gone?"

"Maybe fifteen or twenty minutes. I don't think it can be longer than that."

A dog could move quickly in that amount of time.

As they hurried toward the beach, he wondered how they were supposed to spot a little tan-colored dog in the sand in the dark, in the middle of a storm.

He didn't want to be the voice of doom by raising the worry. Maybe the dog hadn't gone far. Maybe he would hear them calling him.

"I think we should split up," Jenna said, once they left Brambleberry House property. "Why don't you go north and I'll go south?"

He wasn't thrilled with the idea of separating from her, though it did make the most sense. They could cover twice the ground that way.

"Here. Take a flare. If you find him, light it so I know to come back. I should see it from far down the beach."

"Okay. And you'll do the same, right?"

In another flash of distant lightning, her features looked pale and frightened. He wanted to pull her against him, to keep her warm and safe from the storm, but he knew this wasn't the time for that.

"We'll find him, Jenna. I promise."

"I hope so. Addie has lost enough. She'll be devastated if something happens to him."

"We don't have long. As soon as that storm hits in earnest, we have to find shelter. Puppy or not. I'm sorry."

"I know."

"It's moving this way. We've maybe only got fifteen minutes before we'll have to head back. There's no safe shelter on the beach."

"Let's pray we find him soon then."

She raced toward the water, scanning the sand with the beam of her flashlight and calling the dog's name.

Still reluctant to leave her alone, he headed off in the opposite direction.

He had been looking for perhaps ten minutes. When he turned around, he could see her light still bobbing across the sand, though it was growing dimmer.

He called the dog but it was hard to hear anything with the waves beginning to crash and the wind blowing hard.

Lightning split the sky again, closer this time. In that instant of light, he thought he saw movement in the waves about ten yards from shore, a tiny dark head.

He thought at first it might be a seal or a sea turtle, then wondered if he had imagined it. He aimed his powerful flashlight in that direction. In a second flash of lightning, he realized it wasn't a sea creature, it was a small dog, swimming furiously for all he was worth toward shore and being tossed back again and again by the waves.

"I see him," he shouted, though he knew even as he did, she wouldn't be able to hear him.

Without another thought, he lit his flare, hoping she could see it, then kicked off his boots, yanked off his leather jacket and waded into the cold waters of the Pacific.

He had hoped he might be able to walk to the puppy, but the waves were too intense. They almost knocked him over twice.

Finally he dived over the next one as lightning illuminated the water and his path to the puppy. The thunder that followed only a few seconds later confirmed the storm was moving closer.

The puppy was tiring. He could tell. The next wave went over its head and it didn't pop up again for a long moment. With a fierce burst of energy, Wes swam the last few yards to the dog and scooped him under one arm, then began the journey back to shore.

When he was a few yards from shore, he stood up and fought his way through the waves to the sand as Jenna came running down the beach.

She gasped, trying to catch her breath. "Was he in the water? I saw your flare and then you jumped in and I was so scared. Did you find him? Is he...?"

He hadn't even had the chance to assess Theo's condition. He held the puppy up and felt vast relief when Theo gave a weak-sounding whine.

Jenna, her breath still coming harshly from her run down the beach, reached for Theo and hugged him tightly. "Oh, you poor thing. I'm so glad you're safe. Don't do that again. You scared me so much!"

The labradoodle licked her cheek and rested his wet head against her chest.

Wes couldn't help thinking he would like to do the same thing, just pull her into his arms and bask in her heat.

They couldn't stay here, though. Not with that storm moving ever closer.

He scooped up his boots and his jacket, not bothering to put them on now.

"We have to get back to the house. The lightning is too close."

"Are you okay? I can't believe you did that!"

"I'm fine," he said as they quickly raced back toward the house. "He wasn't that far out. I wouldn't have seen him if he'd been even a little farther out. I didn't think I would have to swim but the waves were stronger than I was expecting, which might be what happened to him. I can carry him. He's soaked, so he has to weigh twice as much as usual."

"I've got him," she said, racing along beside him.

The rain hit hard as they made it the final hundred yards to the Brambleberry House beach gate.

He opened it and together they ran to the back porch.

"Is he okay?" he asked.

"He seems to be." Jenna set the dog down. He sat on his haunches, looking far more alert in the glow from the porch light, but he didn't seem to want to leave her side.

"Wes, thank you," Jenna said as thunder rumbled just beyond the safety of the porch. "I don't know what I would have done if you hadn't been here. You have come to my rescue more times than I can count."

"I'm glad I made it back from my ride in time to help you."

"So am I. Oh, Wes. Thank you."

She wrapped her arms around him and he held her tightly. She was shaking, he realized.

"Let's get you inside. You're freezing."

She shook her head. "I'm a little cold but I'm not the one who went for a dip in the Pacific. I was so scared when you jumped into the water. Terrified. I have never felt so helpless. I could do nothing while you risked your life for my daughter's dog."

"He's a sweet little guy. I didn't want something to happen to him. Not if I could help."

She made a sound halfway between a laugh and a sob. "I can't believe you risked your life for a puppy. I'm so glad you did, but I feel sick when I think of all the things that could have happened to you. To both of you. An undertow. A rogue wave. Or a shark, for heaven's sake."

"Nothing happened," he said, his voice gruff. "I'm here. Just a little wet, but I was wet anyway from my ride."

"Thank you. I can never thank you enough."

When she placed her warm hands on either side of his face and pressed her mouth to his, she completely shattered him.

He closed his eyes and held himself still as she kissed him with a tenderness that made him yearn for more. Finally, he couldn't bear it another moment and he stepped away.

"You're killing me, Jenna. I can't do this anymore. There isn't enough pavement in Oregon for me to ride away how much I want to have you right here in my arms."

Without looking at her or waiting for an answer, he turned around and hurried into the house, already trying to figure out how soon he could move out so he could start the process of trying to get over her.

Jenna watched him go, her heart beating hard. She had been about to tell him she was falling in love with him. What might have happened if she had spoken sooner?

She hadn't. Once more, she had let her fear control her.

At her feet, the still-bedraggled puppy whimpered and she pushed away her angst to focus on his needs for now.

She carried him into the house, where Kim was waiting.

"You found him. Oh, I'm so glad. Where was he?"

"I didn't find him. Wes did. He somehow had gone into the water and then couldn't swim back out. Wes went in after him."

"Is he okay?"

She grabbed the microfiber towel she used to dry him and rubbed him vigorously. He was warm and alert, his eyes bright as he looked over at Kim. After a moment, the puppy wriggled to be let down, and Jenna set him on the floor again, where he trotted to his water bowl and drank it empty. Poor thing, surrounded by all that salt water he couldn't drink. There was a metaphor in that, she was fairly certain, but she couldn't put her finger on it.

She filled his bowl again, not caring that it meant she would have to take him out to do his business again in an hour.

After taking a few more sips, the puppy ate a little of his chow, then padded to his crate, where he curled up on the blankets and went immediately to sleep.

Kim, watching all of this, smiled. "Looks like he's fine. Exhausted, but fine."

"Thank you for coming back to stay with Addie."

"Glad to do it. I haven't even been here twenty minutes."

"Well, thank you. I had no idea how long it might take to find him."

"And you and Wes would have looked all night, wouldn't you?"

Jenna gave a little laugh. "Yes. Wes was going to make me stop if the lightning got too close, but as soon as the storm passed, we would have gone back out."

She knew she wouldn't have stopped looking and suddenly had no doubt that Wes would have been right there at her side.

He was a man she could count on. A man any woman could rely upon to help her through the storms of life. He would do anything for a woman he loved.

She closed her eyes as the realization filled her with a peaceful assurance. She wanted to be that woman, sharing troubles and joys and life with him.

The last of her fear, any lingering doubts, seemed to shrivel away. She wanted to be with Wes. The differences between them didn't matter. They had many more things in common.

"He's a good guy, isn't he?" Kim said, as if reading Jenna's thoughts.

"The very best," she answered.

"You should probably tell him you're in love with him. A guy deserves to know, don't you think? Especially after he risked his life for your dog."

"Yes. Probably." Jenna could feel her face heat.

"Want me to stay with Addie a little longer while you do? I can even stay all night, ahem, if necessary. I don't mind sleeping on the sofa."

Jenna could only shake her head. "Not necessary. I need to change into some dry clothes, then I'll go talk to him. Thank you again."

"Anytime. Though I hope your little buddy over there learns to stay put after his little adventure."

Kim let herself out while Jenna hurried to change into dry clothes. What did a woman wear when she was about to put her heart on the line? She had no idea, so she settled on a pair of yoga pants and a soft sweater that always gave her comfort.

After checking on her sleeping daughter and puppy, she opened her door, drawing on all her courage to make her way up the stairs to his apartment.

As she went, she thought she smelled flowers on the stairs. Was Abigail there, giving her strength? It was a comforting idea, though she still wasn't sure she was buying the whole ghost thing.

At his door, she lingered for a long moment. What if he was asleep already?

He wasn't. She was suddenly sure of it.

There isn't enough pavement in Oregon for me to ride away how much I want to have you right here in my arms.

She shivered, took a deep breath and knocked softly, then waited what felt like an eternity for him to open the door.

He had changed into dry clothes, too. Had possibly showered. His hair was damp and sticking up and he smelled clean and masculine and wonderful.

"Is something wrong?" he asked, his voice so remote she had to pause, some of her uncertainty fluttering back.

No. She wouldn't give in to it. This man had risked his life to save a puppy from drowning in the Pacific in the middle of a lightning storm.

She could certainly take a chance and tell him how she felt.

"Yes. Something is wrong," she murmured.

"What?"

"I need to tell you something. May I…come in?"

He appeared reluctant but finally opened the door further. She walked into the apartment, so different now than it had been when Rosa lived here. It was comfortable and clean, though fairly utilitarian and sparsely decorated. Rosa had taken all her personal things when she moved out to marry Wyatt.

Now that she was here, she didn't know where to start. Doubt began to creep back in but she firmly pushed it away and faced him.

"When my husband died, I told myself I was done with love. I didn't need or want the vulnerability and pain that went hand in hand with it. Then everything happened with Aaron, which only reinforced that relationships were far too messy."

She let out a breath and realized her hands were shaking. She curled them into fists and hoped he didn't notice.

"I told myself I was happy on my own. I had Addie and my students. A life here in Cannon Beach. I didn't need anything else."

She met his gaze but couldn't read anything in his features that looked as if they had been carved from a block of wood.

"And then you moved in and…everything changed. You kissed me. You made me feel cherished. You reminded me that I'm still a woman. A woman who…who apparently can still fall in love."

He gazed at her, still expressionless except for his eyes, which suddenly blazed with emotion.

"Are you?"

"In love? Yes. I'm afraid so. I didn't want to be, but you rode into my life and changed everything."

The last word barely emerged when he crossed the space

between them in a blink, pulled her tightly into his arms and kissed her with a humbling mix of ferocity and tenderness.

"Oh, Jenna," he said against her mouth a long moment later. "I love you. I think I have from the moment I moved in, when you were terrified of me."

"Not you," she assured him, kissing the corner of his mouth, arms around him as tightly as she could manage. "It was never you. It was the image of who I thought you were."

"An ex-con."

"A big, intimidating man who rode a motorcycle and had tattoos."

"I'm still that guy," he pointed out.

"No. You're so much more." She kissed him again, loving the feel of his arms around her and the knowledge that she was exactly where she wanted to be. Where she needed to be.

Where she belonged.

"You're so much more," she repeated. "You're a loving father. A loyal friend. A man willing to drop everything to come to the rescue of a fourteen-pound puppy."

She paused and kissed him again, her mouth slow and lingering. "And you're the man I love with all my heart."

He gave a low sound, picked her up as if she weighed nothing and carried her to the sofa.

"You are the most amazing woman I've ever known," he said, his voice low and rough. "We both know I don't deserve you, but I don't care. I swear to you, Jenna, that I will spend the rest of my life trying to be the man you need."

His mouth brushed hers with a tenderness and care that made her eyes burn.

"You already are," she whispered.

She loved this man deeply. This was right between them.

No. Better than right. It was perfect.

* * * * *

A MOTHER'S HOPE

Chapter One

"You're late."

The gruff words slammed through his headache like a Brahma bull making kindling of a flimsy fence, and Jace McCandless barely managed to hide a wince.

"I know. Sorry. I, uh, overslept."

Though it was the truth—or most of it, anyway—it was a lame excuse, and he knew it. Worse, he was fairly sure Hank knew it, too. The old man raised one of his bushy gray eyebrows at him.

"This ain't the circuit, son, or one of your fancy Hollywood commercials. You're not a star here, just the hired help."

Jace's laugh was short and pithy. "Hired help? You paying me now? That's the first I've heard."

The other man patted him on the shoulder. "Who needs a paycheck when you're gettin' paid in blessings and goodwill?"

Jace snorted. "Fancy words for what amounts to slave labor."

He wouldn't be here at all if not for Hank's wily skill at emotional blackmail. The man was slicker than cow snot. His grandmother's second husband had called him up the night before, with his unerring gift for finding and capitalizing on a man's weak moments.

Jace had no idea how Hank had known he was scraping emotional bottom, that he was haunted by cries of those he couldn't help.

Next thing he knew, the crusty rodeo promoter had been reminding him of the long ledger of favors Jace owed him from their days on the circuit together—and worse. With that same uncanny skill, Hank had managed to drive the blade into his insides and give it a good, sharp twist.

"You ever think that maybe you survived that hotel fire for a reason?" he'd said, and even through the phone line Jace could hear the bite in his voice. "I have to think sitting at home with a bottle ain't what God had in mind for Jace McCandless."

He wasn't quite sure how it happened, but by the time he hung up fifteen minutes later Jace was fairly sure he had promised the man a whole host of things he hadn't intended, including helping out at the equine therapy center Hank had started after retiring from the rodeo ring, marrying Jace's grandmother and moving her to his spread in this dusty, quiet corner of Utah.

That ought to teach him not to answer the phone when he was drunk off his butt.

"You ready?"

Jace glanced at the bright red steel building behind Hank. His insides tightened, but he couldn't have said whether it was nerves or his lingering hangover.

He hoped to hell it was the latter. During his time on the circuit he developed a reputation as a broncobuster with steel guts and a cool head. He wouldn't like to think he was losing either after only eighteen months away from the business.

"I guess," he mumbled.

Hank grinned, showing off the perfect, blindingly white dentures that were such a contrast to his raw, craggy features. "You are in for a real treat, son."

He highly doubted that, but he still obediently followed the man into the building.

Even with his sunglasses, it took his tired, gritty eyes a good three minutes to adjust from the brilliant spring sunshine outside to the dimmer arena lights.

When he could see again, he immediately wanted to bolt right out the door. What the hell was he doing here?

He even started to turn around, but Hank stood between Jace and the door, almost as if the old man guessed at the thoughts of escape racing through his brain.

"Hey, Mr. Hank! Look at me! I can go fast." One excited youngster waved from the back of a swaybacked nag that looked as though it should have been sold for glue about two decades ago.

Hank—the same crusty old rodeo promoter who had a reputation for chewing up greenhorns and using their bones for toothpicks—grinned right back at the kid.

"You're doing great, Toby. Just great. You won't even need the lead line in another few weeks."

In response, the kid smiled as big as Texas as he was led around the dirt-floor arena.

"So what do you think of the place? Terrific, ain't it?"

Jace didn't quite know how to respond as he gazed around the ring, which was filled with about a half dozen kids in riding helmets atop placid-looking horses. Each rider was accompanied by spotters, one on each side of the horse, and at least one girl rode tandem with an adult who helped support her weight.

These weren't normal riding lessons, Jace knew. And they weren't regular kids. Toby—the one who had waved to Hank—and another girl had the broad, distinctive features of those born with Down syndrome.

Two more had tightly contracted muscles that he thought might indicate cerebral palsy—not that he was some kind of expert—and yet another boy of about twelve rode past wearing opaque sunglasses and receiving visual cues from one of the spotters, so Jace figured he was probably blind.

Jace did *not* belong here.

His head throbbed in time to the plodding hoofbeats of

each horse that passed him, and he fiercely wanted to push past Hank, head back to the ranch he had bought right after he retired and visited exactly twice and climb back into a bottle.

But he thought of the grim mood that followed him wherever he went, the survivor's guilt that somehow seemed darker when he was alone, and decided maybe this wasn't such a bad place after all.

He cleared his throat. "You look like you've got plenty of staff. What am I doing here?"

Hank's rusty laugh echoed through the open space.

"Right now, looks like you're getting them thousand-dollar boots covered in horse crap."

Jace made a face. "What do you want me to do?" he clarified.

"I've got a special job in mind for you. One I think will be perfect. We've got a new client coming in a few minutes. For her first few times around she's probably gonna need somebody strong enough to ride up behind her and support her in the saddle while the physical therapist does an assessment to figure out what would help her most. You up for that?"

Though he wanted—quite fiercely—to give in to the headache and tell Hank no way just before slipping past him out the door, Jace knew he couldn't.

Unpaid debts were a major pain.

Instead he nodded tersely. "Whatever you need."

Hank chuckled. "Until Hope and Christa Sullivan show up, why don't you just watch the action for a few minutes. I've got things to do and can't sit around babysittin' you all day."

He didn't leave him much choice, Jace knew, so he nodded and leaned against the railing that encircled the arena, the smell of leather tack and manure heavy in the air.

Jace sure wouldn't have believed Hank would spend his retirement running an equine therapy center for kids with disabilities if he hadn't heard it from his grandmother, who never lied.

Hank had a reputation as a hard-ass. But when Jace had been a stupid eighteen-year-old with empty pockets at odds with his big dreams and bigger ego, Hank had spied potential in him. Without him, Jace would never have made it as far as he did. Hank had shown him the ropes, hooked him up with the right people who could help him figure out what the hell he was doing and guided him behind the scenes through those rocky early days.

In return, when Jace's career had taken off, he hadn't forgotten. Hell, Jace had introduced Hank to his own grandmother, who had turned out to be the love of the old man's life, apparently. Who would have thought?

He knew he owed him. Without Hank, he would probably have given up after the first few months of mistakes and gone back to trying to make a living out of the dirt and sagebrush of the few acres left of his grandmother's tiny Nevada spread.

Maybe that wouldn't be such a bad thing, since his current situation wasn't anything to write home about.

The door behind him opened, letting in sunlight. He instinctively turned and found a woman fumbling her way through the door, trying to maneuver a wheelchair over a low threshold. He stepped forward, extending a hand to hold the door that opened outward so she could make it through.

"Here. I've got this."

"Thanks." She backed the wheelchair into the arena, and as she passed him, he smelled the light, delectable scent of strawberries.

She was amazingly pretty, with sun-streaked shoulder-length blond hair and the most incredible green eyes he had ever seen, and for a moment he could only stare at her, struck dumb.

"Doorways can still sometimes be tricky business, I'm finding," she said. "They're never wide enough and they usually have that stupid threshold that's a serious pain in the butt when you're trying to get a wheelchair through."

She rose from the chair and turned to face him, and he was struck by two things. One, that the girl in the wheelchair had to be her daughter. They looked alike, except the younger girl's hair was a few shades lighter and much shorter.

The second thing he saw was that the mother was no longer blinking at the contrast in light from outside, and now that her eyes had apparently adjusted, she didn't seem particularly happy to see him, which wasn't a reaction he was used to in women.

"I guess this is where we're supposed to be." The original rueful smile she had given him when she first came in had faded, and he would have to say she had turned downright cool. "Hank told us to come straight to the arena."

"If you're here for equine therapy, this is the right place," he answered.

The girl's head had been tilted to one side as her mother had pushed her in, long, dark lashes flat against her cheeks. He assumed she was asleep or something—what did he know?—but as soon as he spoke, she squinted up at him, then her eyes suddenly widened.

She made an indistinguishable sound, and her muscles tightened so much he was afraid she would fall right out of her wheelchair.

He studied her, awkwardness burning through him. He wasn't at all sure how to act with her and decided his safest bet was to treat her just like any other teenager.

He smiled. "Hi. I'm Jace."

She didn't answer for several seconds, long enough for her silence to stretch painfully. Her mouth moved laboriously, and it seemed to take an extreme exertion of energy before she could answer him.

"I'm Hope," she finally answered, the words slightly slurred.

He grabbed her fisted right hand and shook it. "It's a real pleasure to meet you, Hope. You ready to go for a ride?"

She gave him a brilliant smile that slammed into his gut as if her mother had just shoved the wheelchair right into him.

It was the lingering effects of the hangover, he told himself, but somehow the explanation rang hollow.

"Where's Hank?" the mother asked, her voice as cool as an ice cube trickling down his back. What was the deal with her? he wondered. They had never met—he was positive of it. Surely he would have remembered those stunning green eyes. So why this instinctive dislike?

Before he could ask, though, Hank returned. "I'm here. Sorry, Christa." He gave his too-white smile to both women. He reached out to hug the mother—Christa—then bent down to squeeze Hope's hands.

"You've got your boots on, I see, Miss Hope. Looks like you're all set for some trail ridin'."

"Yep. I'm ready." She looked as if she wanted to climb right out of her chair and onto the back of a horse, but her mother rested a restraining hand on her shoulder.

"Not yet, baby. We need to figure out what's going on first."

She didn't look any more thrilled to be here than he had been, Jace realized. Her skin was slightly pale and her hands seemed to clench and unclench convulsively on the handles of the wheelchair.

One of the riders passed them, waving frantically at them, and while Hope was distracted watching the horse, her mother pulled Hank aside.

"I still don't know about this," she murmured in a voice too low for her daughter to hear. "I really don't. I'm just not sure she's ready."

"Whether *she's* ready or whether *you* are?"

She made a face. "Either of us. Okay, me, probably. Hope

isn't worried about a thing. She's been over the moon ever since my mother suggested it—and that was before she knew *he* was going to be here."

She didn't look at Jace, even when Hank gave that rusty-saw laugh of his and nudged Jace with his shoulder. "Don't blame me for that. You can blame Ellen and Junemarie. They cooked it up between them. Your mom figured Hope might work harder for McCandless here than for a washed-up old rodeo hound like me."

Reality was slow to sink through his aching head. When it did, Jace straightened from the arena railing. The whole time Hank had been laying on the guilt the night before about all the chances Jace had been given and how maybe it was time for a little payback, he'd thought the old man was just looking for general labor. He didn't realize Hank had a specific mission in mind for him—to be the carrot for some poor teenage girl.

He had been played, he realized grimly. And he had been too stupid or too drunk to realize Hank had been setting him up.

He was angry at Hank, for some reason.

Christa had barely met Jace McCandless, but she could sense it in the tight set of his wide shoulders and the sudden steel in his dark blue eyes.

She had no idea why he was here, but she had the sudden impression that he didn't want to be.

Join the club, Mr. McCandless, she thought. Actually, she didn't mind being here. But she didn't want Hope anywhere near those horses. Not yet.

This was a crazy idea, and Christa wanted to push Hope past both men and back into the spring sunshine, away from this arena that smelled of the painfully familiar scents of leather and horses and the sweet tang of hay.

Now she didn't know which was stronger: the nerves skittering through her at the idea of her medically fragile daughter on one of those big horses or embarrassment that Jace McCandless—Jace McCandless, for heaven's sake!—had been dragged into her family's problems.

Drat her mother and the rest of the Busybees. Ellen's quilting circle certainly lived up to its name. Christa hated that she and Hope were the topic of conversation among the ladies at their weekly gossip session.

She never would have dreamed when Ellen told her Jace McCandless's grandmother was a member of the Bees that one day Ellen and Junemarie Stevens would conspire to drag Junemarie's grandson into Hope's limited world.

But then, she had become used to weird, convoluted side trips on the wild journey that had become her life in the five months since Hope's brain injury.

This was only the latest in a long line of unexpected detours.

What was she supposed to do now? Her instincts were urging her to drag Hope out of there, kicking and screaming, if she had to. But her daughter had been so looking forward to coming to the equine therapy center. It was all she had talked about for days. How could Christa withhold such a treat from her?

"Let's go!" Hope suddenly burst out, slamming her curled hands on her armrests. "I want to ride!"

A lot of words for her, Christa thought. Hope's expressive speech was one skill that had been slow to return since the accident. She struggled to find the right words, and those she could manage were often slurred or garbled.

When it came to horses, she apparently didn't have any trouble getting her point across.

"The boss has spoken," Hank said with a grin.

She didn't return his smile as those nerves jangled in her stomach again.

"Just give it a chance, Christa. Even if she only goes a few times around the arena, her muscles will get a good stretch. We'll be careful, I swear."

She could feel herself weakening. Hope had shown more excitement about this than anything else in a long time. She supposed she shouldn't have been surprised. Her daughter had been horse-mad for most of her life and had followed the rodeo circuit faithfully, reading rodeo magazines the way other girls devoured fashion magazines.

Of *course* Hope would be thrilled to see Jace McCandless. Long before they moved back to Utah, to the same town where he had a small ranch near his grandmother's place, Hope had followed his career, claiming some kind of link to the man since their respective grandmothers were friends and quilted together.

Even after he retired from the rodeo world and translated his success and stunning good looks into product endorsements for things such as blue jeans and soft drinks, Hope had followed his career.

Her daughter probably *would* work harder for him than anyone else. But that didn't ease her nerves.

"I don't know. What if she falls? What if she has a seizure? She's still so...breakable."

Hank sighed. "We've been over this, Christa. I swear, she'll be well protected. She'll be wearing a helmet and she'll have a spotter holding her on—Jace, here—and one more on each side of her. Our therapist has picked a horse with a slow, even gait for Hope to start out during the initial assessment. Jace, it's that big roan over there. You mind grabbing her and meeting us at the mounting block?"

The man gave Hank a long, unreadable look, then shrugged and headed toward the horses tied up across the arena.

"Please, Mom." Hope gave her a lopsided smile. "I can ride. I want to. Please."

She studied her daughter, once so fiercely independent, and

the ache that never seemed to quite leave her burned through her chest. Hope had been through so much these last five months.

How could Christa deny her this momentary pleasure?

She squeezed Hope's fisted hands. "All right. Just be careful while you're having so much fun up there. No jumping the gate, okay?"

Hope grinned, looking so much like her old self that Christa was helpless against the tears that burned behind her eyelids.

She wanted her daughter back, prickly teenage moods and all. If this equine therapy would help get them closer to that goal, it was worth a little maternal anxiety.

Chapter Two

From the moment Hope was helped onto the horse in front of Jace McCandless, Christa knew she had lost the battle.

She supposed it really wasn't a battle she should have been fighting at all—but how could she help it after everything her daughter had endured? Up until a few months ago Hope had even been missing a piece of her skull, temporarily removed to allow the swelling around her brain to subside.

Christa had earned the right to be overprotective. What mother wouldn't be? It wasn't easy to see Hope up on that big horse, knowing how just one tumble could set back all the progress they had fought so hard to attain.

It was tough to let go of her fears, but for her daughter's sake she could do her best.

They passed her again, Jace McCandless and her daughter. The lean, sexy cowboy sat behind the saddle supporting Hope's weight atop the raw-boned mare. He sat easy on a horse, as she would have expected from someone who had made a very good living on the rodeo circuit, and with each pass through the arena he seemed more comfortable with his duty.

And Hope, Christa saw, didn't just glow with excitement, she exploded with it. Her eyes were bright and she laughed out loud several times though the horse was only moving at a sedate walk.

She watched them go around again, then Jace slowed the

horse and slid off, keeping one reassuring hand at the small of Hope's back.

"Is that it?" she asked Hank, who had stopped to watch.

"Looks like they're going to let her have a few go-rounds on her own," he answered.

He must have seen her sudden panic, because he gave her a reassuring smile. "Don't worry. McCandless wouldn't leave her alone up there if he didn't think she could handle it."

Despite his attempt to comfort her, she clenched her fists so tightly she could feel her fingernails gouging the skin of her palms. She needn't have worried. Hope seemed to pick up riding again better than she had anything else since the accident.

They would have to come back, Christa realized with some dismay. How would they possibly afford it with all the co-pays and deductibles piling up? Her medical insurance didn't cover equine therapy, so she would have to cover the entire cost out-of-pocket.

She would just have to juggle both her budget and her time to make it happen, she thought as McCandless used the lead line to guide the horse back to the mounting block.

As she hurried to join them, she saw him lift Hope down from the horse and set her gently in her wheelchair.

"How was it?" Christa asked. "You looked great up there! Did you have a good time?"

Hope looked tired but jubilant. "Loved it! Want to barrel-race now!"

Jace gave Christa a wide grin she could swear sizzled through her, clear to her toes. She frowned, upset at the reaction, while Jace squeezed Hope's shoulder.

"Not yet, champ. Maybe next time."

She beamed up at him, as susceptible to that smile as her mother, apparently.

"Nice work, Hope," Hank Stevens said as he joined them. "Nice riding!"

Hope bestowed her delighted smile on him, as well.

"Glad you had fun. We usually make the riders brush down the horses when they're done—works their arms and shoulders, see?—but seein' as it's your first time, we'll let you off the hook."

"I can do it," Hope insisted with the mulish determination that had carried her through eight surgeries in five months.

"I'm sure you can. But next time." He turned to Christa. "Same time next week?"

A hundred doubts still swirled through her mind, but they all paled next to Hope. "Okay. Sure. Thanks, Hank."

She would find a way to make it work. She'd been doing just that since those dark days as a stupid eighteen-year-old girl alone in a strange city with a newborn.

"Can I give you a hand out to your car?" Jace asked, still holding the handles of Hope's wheelchair.

Her first instinct was to refuse his offer of help, to show him she was tough and independent. Hadn't she been from the beginning?

But the bald truth was that Hope weighed as much as Christa, and all the transfers she required in the course of an average day were physically exhausting.

Right after the accident, a wise physical therapist urged Christa to always accept help when it was offered, no matter how it stung her pride not to be as self-sufficient as she would like.

For some reason, accepting help from Jace McCandless seemed particularly galling, but she forced herself to do it anyway.

"Thanks. I appreciate it."

"You handle the doors and I'll be the muscle."

Christa decided she wasn't going to allow her weak mind to dwell on his muscles—or on how edgy and uncomfortable he had looked at first with Hope up on that horse or how he had relaxed until he was teasing and joking with her.

She *especially* wasn't going to think about how delicious he smelled right now as they walked out of the arena and into the spring sunshine—or how long it had been since she'd been close enough to any gorgeous male to fully appreciate his pheromones.

She led the way to her vehicle, a small Jeep Liberty she was immensely grateful she had been able to pay off before she moved back to Sage Flats and cut her salary in half.

When they reached the SUV, she opened the door to the backseat and reached to help Hope transfer in, but Jace beat her to it.

"Just tell me how to get her inside. Do you lift her or does she do the work?"

Christa had to admit, she appreciated a man who didn't mind asking for help. "Usually she can transfer on her own if you just hold her hands for stability and take some of her weight. Yes, that's it. Perfect."

He eased Hope into the backseat while Christa watched, not used to her position as observer in her daughter's care.

She couldn't help comparing the laborious process of settling her into a car now to those days before their world had changed, when Hope used to jump into the backseat after school, her long hair flying behind her. More often than not, she had her cell phone glued to her ear, already talking up a storm to the friends she had just left.

Oh, how Christa missed those days. Even when Hope had been at her angriest, surly about their move to Utah or caught up in the inevitable teenage dramas between her friends, she had been like a bright, vivid beacon, full of energy and life.

Hope had always been the center of every crowd. She had been funny and smart, with a world of possibilities beckoning her.

Oh, she hadn't been thrilled when they moved from the hip and happening college town of Austin to some Utah backwater, leaving all her friends behind. But she had quickly gathered a new circle of friends and seemed to be adjusting to life in Sage Flats, to the freedom to ride her grandfather's high-strung horses, to her new school.

Until the accident. Now that busy social butterfly seemed so frail and solitary. The steady stream of friends who had come to the hospital bearing flowers and cards and get-well posters had trickled over the last five months to a valiant few who continued to visit every week despite Hope's garbled speech, short attention span and flagging energy level.

She had reached the limit of her endurance now, Christa realized. The minute she was settled on the backseat, she leaned her head back against the upholstery and closed her eyes.

"Tired," she mumbled.

"I know. Just rest, sweetheart. We'll be home in a moment."

She closed the door and shook her head.

"She's exhausted, poor thing," she said to Jace, who stood watching. "I'm guessing she'll be asleep before we pull out of the parking lot."

"I hope today wasn't too much for her."

"It probably was. But she would definitely say the ride was worth a little fatigue."

While she spoke, she started breaking down the wheelchair so it would fit into the cargo area of her vehicle, disconnecting the foot plates and the head support, then folding the rest down. He stepped forward to help her lift the heavy body of the chair inside.

"Sure seems like a lot of work. I've got a buddy who had a bull roll over him and broke his back a few years ago. He has a van with a ramp where he just rolls right into it in his wheelchair, without all this hassle. Can't you get one of those?"

She pressed her lips together. Sure, if she had a spare fifty thousand dollars sitting around. Since she didn't, she would make do with her paid-off Jeep Liberty and keep praying Hope wouldn't need the wheelchair much longer.

"Someday, maybe," she answered in a noncommittal tone. She set the brake on the chair so it wouldn't roll around, then closed the hatch.

"Thank you again for helping with her today. I guess you could tell I was more than a little nervous. It helped to have someone experienced like you to lend a hand."

"You're welcome. It was…not what I expected."

"Better or worse?"

He smiled and her insides quivered, until she forced herself to breathe. She sternly reminded herself she wasn't interested in a man—and especially not a man like him.

"Just different," he answered. "The kids are amazing. I wouldn't have expected them all to be so…happy."

She finally couldn't resist asking the question burning through her. "So how did Hank con you into coming today?"

He blinked for half a second, then burst out laughing. "I guess that's one way of putting it. Probably the most accurate. Hank Stevens is amazingly good at finding weakness and exploiting it six ways from Sunday. In my case, he happened to catch me at a low moment when I was…upset about something. He called in about a half dozen favors."

Upset about what? she wondered a bit resentfully. His life seemed so charmed from the outside. He had fame, money, extraordinary good looks. What could possibly put those haunted shadows in his blue eyes?

Not her business. She had enough problems of her own without worrying about someone else's. "Well, I appreciate your being there, whether Hank blackmailed you or not. Hope was a big pro-rodeo fan before her accident."

He was quiet for a moment, his gaze on the backseat of the SUV.

"I don't quite know how to ask this politely, but..." His voice trailed off.

"What happened to her?" she filled in the question she had been expecting, the one she dreaded most.

"Yeah. Do you mind my asking?"

She wished with all her heart she had the nerve to tell him that she *did* mind, that she hated remembering the instant when her daughter's world—and hers—had changed.

She didn't want to answer, she wanted to climb into her vehicle and leave him behind in a cloud of dust and spewing gravel. But she thought of his gentle patience with Hope for the last hour, the care he had taken transferring her into the backseat, and knew his question wasn't asked just to be nosy.

"She was hit by a car while she was walking home from school just before Christmas."

The awful, familiar guilt burned through her.

Her fault, her fault, her fault.

Oh, she hadn't been the driver behind the wheel of the truck that had been speeding far too quickly for conditions and had slid on black ice directly into Hope.

She hadn't caused the accident, but she might as well have. If only she and Hope hadn't fought that morning about the cell-phone bill and all of the excessive text-message overages. If only Hope had come to the store after school as she usually did instead of deciding, in her lingering pique over losing her phone for a week, to walk the mile home.

If only they had stayed in Austin instead of moving home after Christa's father died to help her overwhelmed and grieving mother with the grocery store.

She pushed the futile speculation away. *If onlys* didn't do a damn thing to help with the day-to-day care of her daughter.

"She was thrown about twenty feet and broke both arms and her right femur. Worst of all, she suffered severe head trauma. She was in a coma for three weeks and things were… uncertain for a while. But she's making an amazing recovery."

They had miles to go, but every single step forward was progress, better than where they had come from.

That poor, sweet kid. Jace looked through the window, where Hope was curled up against the seat, then back at Christa. He had a wild, completely inappropriate urge to pull her into his arms to offer whatever small comfort he could.

"I'm so sorry."

It seemed terribly inadequate, but he didn't know what the hell else a guy was supposed to say in these circumstances—especially a guy as selfish and superficial as he was.

She shrugged. "Every day she regains more skills. The progress is slow but steady. Just today she was able to hold a fork on her own and eat three or four bites of her lunch by herself. I can't begin to tell you how hard she's worked to get to that point."

He couldn't even imagine it. Jace thought of his own nightmares, the cold sweats, the phantom screams and cries he heard at the oddest moments.

He was alive and in one piece. He hadn't been through nearly the ordeal that Hope and Christa had endured. So why wasn't he dealing better?

"You must be a strong person to cope with all this. The therapies and doctor appointments and the uncertainty and everything."

How? he wondered.

She gave him a rueful smile that pierced through all his defenses.

"Who says I'm coping?" she murmured.

Again he had to fight the urge to pull her into his arms, intrigued that a woman who seemed so in control could be hiding such vulnerability.

She seemed to think she had lingered long enough, because she moved to the driver's door and opened it, a clear dismissal.

"Thank you again for your help, Mr. McCandless. Both in the arena and out here."

"I'm happy I could do it," he answered, and realized with some shock that he meant the words—and that he was actually looking forward to coming back, especially if it meant seeing her again.

Chapter Three

One hazard of working in a small grocery store in a sleepy town was that she usually had far too much time on her hands.

Christa sat at the untidy desk in her second-floor office at Sully's, gazing out the glass window that overlooked the sales floor at the few customers moving through the aisles.

Business was slow in the typical afternoon lull, though she knew it would heat up again in an hour or so, when people started poring over the contents of their cupboards and refrigerators and recipe boxes to find something to cook for dinner.

She was supposed to be working on the time schedule for the next two weeks. But as they had far too often, her thoughts kept straying in one uncomfortable direction.

All afternoon she couldn't seem to stop thinking about Jace McCandless. It was completely ridiculous.

She was a grown woman—a mother of a fifteen-year-old, for heaven's sake! She was far too old for a silly crush and she had no business obsessing over him like some giddy junior high student. Next thing she knew, she would be writing his initials on the time sheets and surrounding them with cute little curlicue hearts.

She certainly knew better. In the first place—and on a completely superficial level—he was way, way out of her league. His last girlfriend had been the lead singer of a Grammy-winning country music group, and the one before that a Hollywood starlet.

Not that she read the tabloids or anything, but she worked in a grocery store, for heaven's sake. She couldn't exactly miss his sexy features when she was running him across the checkout scanner, usually with some equally beautiful person wrapped around him.

With the whole world to choose from, why would he possibly have any interest in a thirty-four-year-old who lived with her mother, ran her family grocery store and had a U-Haul stuffed full of emotional baggage?

Even more important than what *he* might be looking for in a woman were all the reasons *she* ought to be running as fast as her legs would take her in the opposite direction.

He was a player, a sexy, irresponsible cowboy, and hadn't she had enough of that particular breed of man? The last thing she needed right now in her chaotic, messed-up life was a distraction like Jace McCandless. This afternoon just proved it.

She had a hundred things to do, a thousand pressures bearing down on her, but here she sat mooning over him.

She knew all that, knew she shouldn't be thinking about him at all. But she couldn't deny that something inside her had been irresistibly drawn to him, to the warm light in his eyes and the broad, comforting strength in those shoulders.

She sighed, grateful when the phone on her father's scarred old wooden desk bleated a distraction from her thoughts.

She recognized her mother's phone number on the caller ID and picked up after the second ring. "Hi, Mom. I was going to call you in a moment. How's everything at home?"

She and Ellen alternated days at the store so one of them could be home with Hope at all times.

Ellen was great with the employees and the customers, but she hated anything to do with ordering or inventory or payroll.

Sage Flats was five miles from the nearest town, literally

five miles from any other sign of civilization except far-flung ranches. For three generations now Sully's had served as a combination gas station, grocery store and gathering spot for not only the residents of town but also outlying ranchers who didn't want to drive the half hour to Park City when they only needed a gallon of milk.

Her whole childhood had been tied up in this store—evenings and weekends and holidays spent mopping the floors and stocking the candy aisles and, later, checking out customers. Back then, she had hated the provincial, old-fashioned feel of it and couldn't wait to leave.

Since she had returned after her father's death, she was surprised to find her perspective had undergone a massive paradigm shift. Now she found amazing comfort in the familiar—in the quiet, steady rhythm of life in a small town.

"Been a good day so far. Quiet," Ellen answered in the brisk, no-nonsense voice that had driven Christa crazy when she was a teenager. Then again, *everything* about her mother had rubbed her like metal scraping metal in those days, from her poodle perm to her unshakable faith in the goodness of people to the way she couldn't seem to put on lipstick without leaving a little smudge on her teeth.

Fifteen years ago, when she had been a stubborn, foolish girl, she never would have believed she could come to rely so heavily on her mother, but she would have been completely lost those first days after the accident—really, the entire last five months—without Ellen's quiet strength.

"She seems worn-out from yesterday," her mother went on, "even though she was still talking a mile a minute about horses. The occupational therapist could barely get her to settle down and work this afternoon. She fell asleep on the way home from therapy, but she's up now, watching TV."

"How did school go?"

"Her teacher said she's almost passed off a couple of her

goals. She wondered if you want to schedule another IEP meeting to discuss new ones."

Christa sighed. More decisions she didn't feel at all qualified to make in the new reality they had been thrust into. Hope attended school only half a day, since that was all the stamina she could muster. Even then, she was in a life-skills classroom—what in Christa's generation had been called "special education"—working on regaining basic skills in hopes that she would be close to grade level when school started again in the fall.

"Oh, I almost forgot why I called. Can you bring home some cilantro?" Ellen broke into her thoughts. "I'm making black bean soup for dinner and forgot to pick some up."

She scribbled a message to herself on a sticky note and stuck it on her computer. "Okay. Cilantro. Anything else?"

"That should do it, I think. Thank you, dear. You remember that tomorrow night it's my turn to host the Busybees, right?"

She barely caught herself before groaning. Just what she needed—a house full of chattering quilters who spent more time gossiping than they did working any needles. "I'd forgotten. Hope and I will stay out of the way. Maybe we'll watch a DVD in my bedroom or something."

"You don't have to do that. It's your house, too. I'm sure the girls would love to have you both come out and join us. We're working on the most beautiful Shooting Star pattern. I can't wait for you to see it. The star is pieced with graduated diamonds of rust and orange and peach against a blue background and it looks like the whole thing is exploding in the night sky."

Ellen continued talking about her passion, quilting, but Christa was only half listening now. Through the glass of her office she could see a customer standing at the checkout but no sign of a cashier.

Sully's usually got by with only one cashier during the

afternoon lull, who stocked shelves between ringing up groceries. During busy times—when more than two customers were in the store—Christa would step out of her office to lend a hand as needed.

But she couldn't see Michelle Roundy, the cashier on duty, who had just finished her second year of college and was home for the summer.

She scanned the store and finally found her in a cereal aisle, her back to the checkout counter while she conversed with a tall man in a cowboy hat. Because of the angle, she couldn't see who it was, but even from here she could see Michelle putting out the vibe—tucking her hair behind her ear, tilting her head, touching the man's arm as she smiled.

She sighed, not at all in the mood to play the big, bad boss interrupting a promising flirtation. "Mom, I've got to go," she said. "Looks like the afternoon rush is hitting."

"Okay. Don't forget the cilantro. Oh, and maybe some of those blue corn chips you ordered last week."

Christa hung up and hurried down the office stairs just as the bell on the checkout counter dinged with what sounded like increasing impatience.

She approached the pair in the cereal aisle without sparing a glance at the object of the cashier's attention. "Michelle, would you like me to check for you? It looks like Mrs. Salazar is ready."

Michelle's smile slid away and a flush instantly climbed her cheeks. "Oh! I'm so sorry, Christa. I guess I wasn't paying attention to the bell. I've got it."

She gave one last flustered smile to the object of her flirtation, then hurried away, leaving Christa alone with the man.

He tilted his black Stetson back and her stomach suddenly danced a little jig. No wonder Michelle had been fluttering around him like a pretty little moth. Few women had the strength to resist Jace McCandless's rugged, gorgeous features.

She did, though. She had been immunized a long time ago against charming cowboys.

Right?

She forced a polite smile. "Mr. McCandless. Hello."

"Jace, please," he said with an aw-shucks kind of smile that played exactly right in all the ad campaigns he did. "I'm not sure who you're talking to when you call me mister."

She wondered if that self-deprecating smile fooled anyone. It certainly didn't her. He had to be smart as the proverbial whip to turn a few good years on the rodeo circuit into his kind of fortune.

She gestured to his shopping cart. "Don't you have people to do this sort of thing for you?"

"You'd think, wouldn't you? I'll confess that I do pay a personal chef from Park City to stock my freezer with ready-to-eat meals that even a dope like me can heat up. But, believe it or not, I can't always find what I'm craving."

She raised an eyebrow at the contents of his cart, which included three boxes of cereal high on sugar and low on nutritional value, a box of microwave popcorn and a four-pack of macaroni and cheese.

He followed her gaze and offered up that charmer of a smile again. "I know. Ridiculous, isn't it? Apparently I have all the culinary taste of a twelve-year-old."

She couldn't help herself, she laughed out loud. "I was thinking more like seven or eight."

"You have to give me a little credit for some maturity! I left out the Cheez Doodles and baseball card bubblegum packs."

Oh, that smile was entirely too tempting. A shiver rippled down her spine, and she wanted to stand there all afternoon basking in its glow. Apparently she wasn't as impervious to sexy cowboys as she had hoped.

"It's usually a fleeting craving," he went on. "By tomorrow I'll likely be back to grown-up, healthy food."

"But today you'll eat like a king. Or at least like the king of Sage Flats Elementary School."

His laughter echoed through the store, sending a warm glow shooting through her as brilliant as any star the Busybees could quilt.

"So how's Hope today?" he asked.

She did her best to push away the unwelcome reaction. "I've been working all day, but my mother says she's been tired but happy."

"Do you think riding helped her?"

"I don't know. Her strength and her balance both seemed better last night when we were doing her exercises."

He smiled, genuine pleasure in the midnight blue of his eyes. "Does that mean you'll be taking her back to the therapy center?"

"At this point, I'm willing to try anything that works. If that means I have to swallow my fear, I guess I'll do it."

The outside door chimed before he could answer. She thought it was Mrs. Salazar leaving with the groceries until she heard a gruff male voice she didn't recognize talking to Michelle.

"I got a truck full of canned goods to deliver. I rang the bell in the back by the stockroom about a half dozen times, but nobody answered."

This time Christa wasn't successful at hiding her groan. Just her luck. Of course the unexpected delivery would arrive this afternoon, the one day when her usually dependable stocker had gone home sick with a cold at lunchtime.

"Excuse me," she said to Jace. "I need to deal with this."

She hurried to the front of the store.

"Hi. I'm the manager on duty. We're shorthanded, but I'll meet you out back to help unload."

"You know I can't unload any of it, much as I'd like to help you. It's company policy. I can only drive up to your bay."

She sighed. "I know. I hope you're not in a big hurry. Our forklift is acting up today."

He shrugged. "You're my last load of the day. I got time."

If only she could say the same. She thought of the paperwork that would be left undone at her desk and how she would have to take it home with her to finish after she worked through Hope's extensive bedtime routine.

She headed toward the door of the stockroom and almost reached it before she realized Jace was following close on her heels.

"Uh, when you're ready, Michelle can ring you up out front."

"Fine," he answered genially even as he continued to follow her.

She stopped, her hand on the swinging door of the stockroom, painfully aware of his heat and strength only a few feet away. He had left his shopping cart behind, she realized.

She frowned. "Mr. McCandless—Jace—what are you doing?"

"Giving you a hand, since that delivery driver appears useless."

She stared. "You don't have to do that."

"I know. But I'm going to."

How could she refuse his help? The idea of unloading a truck full of canned goods—their entire month's supply—by herself and without a forklift was overwhelming.

If Hope's accident had taught her anything, it was the simple, stark truth that she didn't always need to take on the world by herself. Sometimes accepting help graciously was the better choice.

This looked like one of those times. "Oh. Um, thank you, then. It's very nice of you to offer."

He smiled that sexy, dangerous smile. "Let's get to it."

* * *

Jace hefted another heavy box onto the dolly, more loose and relaxed than he had been in six weeks. He didn't know if it was the work or the company.

Good, hard, physical labor was an effective antidote to the restlessness that had been churning through him for far too long. But he also found something soothing about Christa Sullivan.

He couldn't really explain why, he just knew she had this air of quiet strength about her, of calm competence. It eased something wild and restless and aching inside him.

Most women he knew wouldn't be thrilled at having to spend a sweaty hour or two unloading a delivery truck. He had seen that instant of frustrated discouragement when the delivery driver showed up.

But she didn't complain, just knuckled down and got the job done with a surprisingly upbeat attitude. He found it astonishing, especially given what he knew she had to deal with at home.

It humbled him and made him realize just what a self-absorbed, self-pitying jerk he had become since the hotel fire.

"I understand Sully's has been in your family for a few years."

She lifted a box of canned peaches onto a dolly of her own. "My great-grandfather opened it just before World War I, mostly as a general store and gas station for those early automobiles. We've been running it ever since."

"Not you, though. Hank tells me you haven't been here long, that you left a job in some fancy clothing boutique in Texas a year or so ago to come home and give a hand after your dad died."

She gave him a long, measuring look over the top of a stack of boxes. "Hank is just bubbling over with information, isn't he?"

"I asked him about you," he confessed.

"Why?" Genuine surprise flitted across her features.

He shrugged. "Something about you doesn't quite fit Sage Flats. Your clothes, your hair. I can't put my finger on it."

"I was raised here and lived just a few blocks away from Sully's until just a few weeks shy of my eighteenth birthday. And now here I am, back."

"Where were you in between?"

She turned away. "You mean Hank didn't fill your ears with that long, boring story, too?"

"He was a bit vague on details. He just said you took off as soon as you could."

She rolled the hand truck down the ramp. "I can't imagine why you would possibly be interested."

He couldn't have explained it to her, but he found he was very much interested in her answer. He hadn't been able to stop thinking about her since he watched her drive away from the therapy center the afternoon before.

For the first time in weeks his dreams hadn't been haunted by the cries of those he couldn't help. Instead they had featured this woman he found intensely fascinating.

He had taken one of his own horses for a long, bracing trail ride into the mountains after he left the therapy center—the first time he had done that in weeks. As he rode, his mind had drifted over the encounter with Christa and Hope, and he had marveled all over again at the courage and tenacity in both of them.

He didn't have a whole lot of experience when it came to mothers. His own had been a real piece of work, too drugged up to remember she even had a kid most of the time. She'd dragged him from one piece-of-crap crack house to another until his grandmother Junemarie finally tracked him down when he was eight and rescued him.

But if he could have chosen a mother, he would have wanted

someone like Christa, with that same unwavering determination in her eyes to do what was best for her child.

How long had it been since a woman had genuinely intrigued him? Most of them were painfully transparent, usually buckle bunnies who were only interested in him because once upon a time he had been moderately good in the rodeo arena.

But he had the definite impression his rodeo days would actually prove an obstacle to Christa Sullivan.

"Why wouldn't I find your life interesting?" he asked.

"I've seen the tabloids, Mr. McCandless. You're a jet-setting celebrity on a first-name basis with other jet-setting celebrities. You date movie stars and appear in commercials for macho pickup trucks and sexy blue jeans. I, on the other hand, am a thirtysomething single mother who spends my days taking my daughter to doctor appointments and stocking cans of peas and corn and cream-of-chicken soup on the dusty shelves of a tiny grocery store in some backward town in Utah no one has ever heard of. I'm sure you can understand my skepticism that any portion of my scintillating life might be of interest to a man like you."

He laughed out loud at her dry tone, even as some part of him had to wince at her indictment of his life—mostly because it was dead-on. Since his retirement, his life had seemed pretty damn meaningless, something that became starkly obvious while he was escaping for his life through the flaming, hellish hallways of a burning hotel.

He pushed the images aside, vastly preferring to focus on the woman in front of him.

"Believe me, you underestimate yourself, Ms. Sullivan."

She leaned against a stack of boxes, looking dusty and bedraggled and immensely appealing.

"Okay. Fine," she said after a long moment. "You want to know my life story? Here it is. I ran off a few weeks before high school graduation with a rodeo cowboy nearly ten years my senior."

She sighed, already looking as if she regretted saying anything. "We had an exciting, passionate love affair for all of about four months before I found out I was pregnant. He, of course, wanted nothing to do with a ready-made family, so we parted ways in Texas. I was too ashamed to come home and face my parents' disappointment. Though I reconnected with them after Hope was born, I stayed away from Sage Flats until my father died, when my mother begged me to come home and help her with the store."

She climbed up into the truck for another stack of boxes. "You'll have to forgive me if I don't have the fondest spot in my heart for rodeo cowboys with egos bigger than their horses."

He couldn't help himself, he followed her into the truck. "That's all you think of me? Some washed-up rodeo cowboy with a big ego?"

She focused on the sole remaining stack of boxes. "I don't think of you at all other than as a man who helped my daughter with equine therapy as a favor to Hank Stevens."

Something in the sudden evasiveness of her features made him think her answer wasn't completely truthful. He moved closer, until they were only a few feet apart, until he could smell the sweet scent of strawberries that surrounded her.

Her eyes widened slightly, but she didn't back away.

"There's more to me than a washed-up rodeo cowboy or a jet-setting celebrity," he said quietly. "Just as I think you're more than only a single mother coping with an unimaginable tragedy."

Chapter Four

She gazed at him out of those huge green eyes, and their less-than-romantic surroundings seemed to fade. He completely forgot they were standing in the back of a hot, dusty tractor trailer, forgot the boxes of canned goods on the loading dock, forgot everything but the soft, entirely appealing woman in front of him.

Without conscious thought, he took a step forward, his heart leaping in his chest like a bronco bursting through the gate, and he saw color climb her cheekbones, saw her lean toward him slightly, that sweetly upturned mouth parted…

"You folks about done? I'd like to get a move on."

Christa whirled around at the trucker's impatient drawl, then she jerked away from Jace as if he had dumped a whole hand truck full of boxes on her toes.

"Y-yes. We're done. This is the last load. I… I'm sorry it took us so long. The forklift should be fixed next time."

Jace saw her hands tremble a little as she pushed the last load off the truck before he could make his brain work enough to insist on taking it from her. She didn't so much as look at him while she signed for the delivery and saw the driver on his way.

When the truck pulled out of the loading area, she finally turned to Jace, though she focused somewhere over his right shoulder. "Thank you for your help. My stocker can organize all this in the morning."

"You're welcome. I'm glad I was here to help."

She hesitated for a moment, then sighed and finally met his gaze. "As for the other, for what almost happened back there… I won't deny some foolish part of me is…flattered. But I have to be blunt with you. I don't have the time or the energy for a flirtation right now, if that's what you're after."

"And if it's not?"

More color flooded her cheeks, something else he found intriguing about her. He didn't remember the last time he'd met a woman who could still blush.

"Then I'm mortified for misreading the signs and I'll just look around for a convenient hole to disappear into while you go pay for your shopping cart full of junk food."

He laughed and with deceptive casualness he reached a thumb out and brushed away a smudge of dirt on the plane of her cheekbone she must have picked up while they were unloading the boxes.

She trembled slightly but didn't jerk away. All too quickly the smudge was gone and he had no more excuse to touch her. He forced himself to drop his hand back to his side.

He was suddenly not at all convinced a harmless flirtation was what he had in mind when it came to Christa Sullivan.

The prospect should have sent him rushing right out of her little grocery store. Hadn't he spent the better part of his adult life trying to avoid anything deeper than that?

He knew he should have been panicking right about now. Instead he felt the same wild emotions he used to experience on the circuit as he waited in the chutes for the gates to swing wide—a jumbled mix of exhilaration, anticipation and uncertainty.

"You didn't misread any signs," he finally said. "I'm attracted to you, Christa. More attracted than I've been to anyone in longer than I can remember."

Something flickered in her eyes, something hot and intense, before she looked away from him. "Then what I said before still stands. I might…return that attraction. But I don't have time right now for a flirtation or a fling or anything. My life is in crisis. Hope takes every single bit of energy I have, and that's the way it has to be."

Hope.

Damn it. How had he forgotten Hope so quickly?

Christa had responsibilities and pressures he couldn't even begin to imagine. As much as he might want to argue that she ought to at least give things a chance to see what might happen between them, he recognized the impossibility of that.

He had no business coming in and stirring things up for her. It was just one more selfish, irresponsible act in a long string of them.

Hank was absolutely right. If Jace had, indeed, been given a second chance at life after being trapped in that hotel fire that killed two dozen people—and should have killed him—maybe it was time he stopped feeling sorry for himself and started doing something worthwhile to prove Somebody hadn't made a mistake in saving his sorry hide.

And maybe he needed to start by not pursuing Christa Sullivan just because he wanted her, as though he was some kind of greedy kid in a toy store with a fistful of dollars.

"I have to get back to work," she said abruptly. "Thanks again for your help. There's an employee restroom back there if you need to wash up. Michelle can ring you up out front."

"All right. Thanks."

"Enjoy your mac and cheese."

"I'll do that," he answered, though what had seemed so enticing a few hours earlier now seemed like the rest of his life, without much redeeming value at all.

Christa did her absolute best to focus on invoices when she returned to her office, but Jace McCandless proved more of a distraction than she wanted to admit.

The darn glass of her office and the panoramic view it allowed into the grocery store allowed her to watch him undetected as he returned to his cart.

She watched as he selected a gallon of milk, some bananas and a small quart of gourmet ice cream of a flavor she couldn't quite determine from her viewpoint.

The store had become more busy while she had been unloading the truck with Jace. She saw him stop and speak to a few customers—women, mostly, though even from here she could sense a restlessness in him and guessed he was anxious to leave Sully's.

Could she blame him?

She winced when she remembered the awkwardness of their last interaction. The most gorgeous man she'd ever seen in real life had almost kissed her, had told her he found her attractive, and she had jumped into full-blown panic.

She could have at least let herself have a little taste, just so she could remember in her old age that she had once kissed a man like Jace McCandless.

What was his story, anyway?

While they had been unloading that truck, he had talked and joked with her, but she hadn't missed the shadows he hadn't quite managed to hide. Those shadows were none of her business. *He* was none of her business. The orbits of their respective lives had briefly bumped up against each other, but it was just a random fluke and certainly wouldn't happen again. She wouldn't let it happen.

Anyway, he'd purchased the Silver Spur ranch near Junemarie and Hank more than a year ago, and as far as she knew, this was the first time he had spent any significant amount of time there.

No doubt he would be leaving Sage Flats soon and probably wouldn't be back anytime in the near future.

She knew darn well that prospect shouldn't depress her so much.

* * *

The next two days were too hectic for Christa to give Jace McCandless much thought at all. Hope had appointments with her neurologist and her rehab specialist an hour away at the children's hospital in Salt Lake City.

Both doctors seemed heartened by her progress—and both urged Christa to continue with the equine therapy.

"I think it's a great idea," the rehab physician said. "It can only help with her tone and with muscle memory. She loved to ride before the accident. Putting her back up on a horse has to help her body remember how it used to move, which can only help rewire those neural pathways."

Even more beneficial to her than the stretching and physical movement, Dr. Kolford explained, was the emotional lift Hope received from being around the horses and reconnecting to what had been an important part of her life preaccident.

Christa knew all that. In her heart she had seen her daughter's improvement after even just one session and her excitement to try it again. That didn't do much to ease her apprehension or her continuing worry about trying to afford it.

And now she had Jace McCandless to add into the mix. She could only hope he would follow his usual pattern and leave town soon so she wouldn't have to risk encountering him again at Hope's therapy sessions.

The next day, one of the three checkers at the store called in sick and the other two had commitments they couldn't escape, so Christa had to fill in at the cash register most of the day. Two days away from her regular responsibilities at the store left a serious backlog in her workload.

She tried to call home to let her mother know she was running late, but Ellen didn't answer. She left a message on the answering machine, then tried her mother's cell phone and again received no answer.

She set the phone receiver down, fighting down her instinctive unease. Ellen would call her if something was wrong.

They had probably just gone for a walk or something. Sunshine poured through the front window of Sully's, and it looked like a lovely spring day. Hope loved to be out basking in the fresh air.

Christa did, too, come to that. She had a sudden wild urge to take one of her father's two Arabians for a good, hard run after work to shake off the cobwebs—to feel the soft breeze against her skin and the leather reins in her hands and the strength and beauty beneath her.

How long had it been since she had indulged in a few selfish moments for herself? Between work and Hope, she had little time for any of her old pastimes.

Maybe she needed to make time. The rehab physician had taken her aside after Hope's appointment to ask how Christa was doing. Dr. Kolford had urged her to take care of herself first or she would have no reserves left to care for her daughter.

It was good advice in the abstract. But the reality of five months had taught her there was always one more thing she needed to do for her child—one more exercise to get in before bedtime, one more prescription to track down, one more battle to fight with the insurance company.

She sighed and set her paperwork aside. Though she still had much to do, most of it could wait until the next day. Right now Christa needed to be home and get to all those *one-more* things.

When she neared her mother's home, she slowed her SUV at the unfamiliar shiny silver pickup in the driveway.

That wasn't so unusual to find a vehicle she didn't recognize at the house. Between the medical case workers and the therapists and tutors at school, Hope had a wide circle of caregivers and many of them made home visits.

Perhaps that was the reason Ellen hadn't answered either

the home phone or her cell, because she'd been occupied with a visitor.

Christa opened the door, ready to smile and be polite, but inside the house only echoing silence greeted her.

"Mom? Hope?"

No one answered, and she walked from room to room on the main floor and found no sign of them. Since Ellen couldn't take Hope up the stairs, she didn't bother checking there.

This was odd. She could believe Ellen might have pushed Hope outside to enjoy an afternoon walk, but that certainly didn't explain the unfamiliar pickup truck.

Where could they be? she worried. She knew her mother would have called her if Hope had had a bad seizure or something. But what if Ellen wasn't able to use the phone?

She walked outside to look around and thought she just heard the murmur of voices on the wind. Odd. It sounded as if the voices were coming from the horse pasture where her father's beloved pair of Arabians resided.

What on earth would they be doing there? The path between the house and the horse pasture was uneven gravel, far too difficult terrain for Ellen to easily maneuver Hope's wheelchair.

But when she listened, she could distinctly hear voices. Drat her mother. She pushed herself too hard. Even if Hope had begged her grandmother to take her there—which she probably had—Ellen shouldn't have given in.

Christa followed the path, thinking how many times she had walked this same route when she was a girl. She had been just as horse-mad as Hope—which might explain why she'd run off with the first hunky cowboy to come her way.

The evening was warm for April and lovely with spring. Daffodils and tulips swayed in the breeze along the fence line, and the trees in her mother's small fruit orchard burst with color, heavy with lush blossoms.

This was home. In those rough early days on her own in

Texas, she had dreamed of the sweetness of a Utah spring, of lilac bushes and cool mornings and their neighbors' new lambs leaping through the grass.

She remembered Jace McCandless telling her she didn't quite fit here and she knew in this moment she could have offered him a powerful counterargument. Sometimes she wondered if she had ever truly belonged anywhere else.

Following the sound of voices, she rounded the corner of the barn, then stopped abruptly, her instant astonishment quickly giving way to a slow bubble of anger.

She should have known a man like Jace McCandless wouldn't take no for an answer. She had asked him to leave her alone. So what was he doing there? He stood by the corral with Ellen and Hope, looking impossibly gorgeous as he supported Hope, who leaned against the fence railing and fed apples to the horses.

"Hi, Mom," Hope chirped, sounding so much like her old self that Christa blinked and had to fight back tears.

"Hi," she answered.

"Shiloh remembers me."

"I'll bet she does."

With some measure of defiance, she leaned in and kissed her daughter, doing her best to ignore Jace just inches away from the two of them. Darn him anyway for coming around, for making her so painfully aware of the emptiness of her life.

"How did you get down here with that bumpy pathway?"

"Jace." Hope beamed at him.

Of course. Who else?

"We were taking a little walk earlier down the street when Jace happened to drive past," Ellen offered with a smile that seemed just as smitten as her granddaughter's. "He was kind enough to stop and say hello. And before you know it we were inviting him home with us for pie and coffee. We've spent a lovely afternoon together."

"Is that right?" she murmured.

"Oh, yes," Ellen answered, apparently oblivious to the frustration seething under Christa's skin.

"I'm sure you don't mind," her mother went on blithely, "but I've invited him to have dinner with us."

So much for any ideas she might have briefly entertained on the short drive home about spending a quiet evening at home with her mother and daughter. Any pleasure she had found in the lovely spring evening seemed to float away on the breeze.

Her mouth tightened. What was his game? She had quite firmly rejected him the other day. Given that, why on earth would any man still want to hang around with her and her sixty-year-old mother and her brain-injured teenager?

She wanted to tell him to go back to his starlets and his sultry country music stars and leave her and her little family alone. But of course she couldn't. This was her mother's house, and Ellen could invite anyone she darn well pleased to dinner.

"Lovely," Christa murmured instead.

He sent her a swift look as he helped Hope back into her wheelchair, and she could swear she saw him wink, as if he knew exactly the dire thoughts racing through her mind.

She was angry.

All through Ellen's mouthwatering pot roast and creamy mashed potatoes, she concealed it. She was polite to him as she passed the peas or another roll and she even smiled a few times, usually at her daughter but sometimes at Ellen and even once at something he said.

She was cordial and good-humored, but underneath it he sensed the slow burn of her temper, just waiting to flare.

She said nothing through the delectable dessert Ellen produced—a crunchy, golden-crusted peach cobbler that would have brought a lesser man to tears, served with vanilla ice cream.

He finished every scrap on his plate and would have licked

it clean if his grandmother hadn't raised him better. Christa, on the other hand, barely touched hers.

When they all finished, she rose from the table and started clearing away dishes.

"I can get these," Ellen said. "Just relax. You've been working at the store all day."

"And you've been working here all day, which is every bit as hard. You're the one who needs a rest."

"You *both* rest. I'll clean up," Hope interjected with her labored speech before the argument could turn heated.

Both women smiled and Christa hugged her daughter's shoulders. Jace swallowed a lump in his throat at the obvious affection between the three of them.

"Why don't we all do it?" he suggested. "Junemarie used to say something about many hands making light work."

"Good idea," Ellen said.

The four of them quickly cleared the dishes away and loaded them into the dishwasher.

When they finished, Christa wiped her hands on a dish towel. "I need to go feed the horses," she said.

"Oh, we should have taken care of that when we were down there," Ellen said, apology in her eyes. "You've been doing the chore for so long I don't even think about it anymore."

"It's no big deal. It won't take me long."

Jace stood. "I'll come with you."

A small, tight smile crossed her lovely features. "That's really not necessary."

"Many hands make light work, remember?"

She studied him for a long moment, then she shrugged. "Fine. Come on, then."

She had been simmering all through dinner, and he figured it was almost time for her temper to blow. As he was the cause of it, the least he could do was step up and take the sharp edge of her tongue like a man—especially since he knew damn well he deserved it.

They walked in silence until they reached the small, well-kept horse pasture. The Arabians were beautiful, high-spirited animals and they sniffed the air when Christa and Jace approached.

She murmured in a low voice to both of them, and without hesitation both horses trotted to the fence and nudged at her with affection, much as they had done earlier with Hope.

"They're magnificent animals," he said.

"They are. My father loved them. He rode every day of his life, up until he dropped dead of a heart attack. Hope loved to ride them, too, before the accident."

"I guess they're a little high-strung for her now."

She sighed. "You could say that. They're both gentle as can be most of the time. But I would worry about those times they tend to get a little overexcited."

She went about the business of feeding and watering them—something he should have handled for her earlier if he'd been thinking.

He helped as much as she would let him. Finally he decided he might as well jump feetfirst into the fire rather than stand here being scorched by excruciating inches.

"Go ahead. Spill it."

"Spill what?"

"The ire you're itching to pour on me. I know you're not happy I stayed for dinner."

"You're a guest of my mother's," she said promptly. "This is her home and she's certainly free to invite anyone she wants for dinner. Beyond that, Hope is obviously thrilled to spend even a minute with you, so I have no right to be annoyed."

"But you are."

She was quiet for a long moment, her face a pale, lovely

blur in the gathering twilight. "Yes," she finally said, her voice low. "This is…awkward for me."

"I didn't mean for this to happen, if that helps at all. I really was just driving on my way back to the Silver Spur from the feed store and I happened to see Ellen and Hope. I stopped to say hello, and before I quite knew what happened I was pushing Hope's wheelchair while we walked and Ellen and I were talking about the Busybees and they both sort of invited me to stay for dinner."

"You could have said no," Christa pointed out. "It would have been easier all the way around."

"I could have," he agreed. "But I didn't want to."

"Even after the…after the other day? I told you I wasn't interested in anything with you. I haven't changed my mind."

Her words were firm enough, but he thought he heard a slender thread of uncertainty in her voice, just enough to make him wonder if she wasn't as unaffected by him as she wanted him to think.

No. He was probably imagining things. Damn it.

"Lucky for me, my ego is healthy enough to survive a little rejection. It's bigger than my horse, remember?"

"How can I forget?" she muttered.

He laughed, charmed by this lovely woman with more prickles than a whole field of burdock.

"Anyway, my accepting an invitation to dinner from your mother and daughter wasn't about you. Or at least not *completely* about you."

"What was it about?" she asked.

He shrugged. "I enjoyed the afternoon with your mother and Hope. More than any afternoon I've had in a long time. Ellen knows everything there is to know about Sage Flats and the people who live here. She's full of funny stories about the mayor's pigs and Betty Renfrew's hair-color-gone-wrong and the time Tag Jensen was cornered by his prize bull and ended up stuck in a tree all afternoon.

"And Hope," he went on. "She's just…amazing."

She was just about the most courageous person he'd ever met. He smiled, remembering how she had laughed at his jokes and even told some of her own. He was getting better at understanding her labored speech.

"Is it my imagination or is she using her hands better than she did before we went riding?"

Christa nodded. "We've been working on writing her name for a long time now, and she just hasn't quite been able to master it until after we went riding. The day after equine therapy, she wrote it plain as can be—and she's been doing it ever since."

"Writing her name? That seems an odd skill to be affected by riding a horse. I wouldn't think the two would go together."

"Who knows? Maybe some hand-brain connection clicked in while she was holding the reins. I'm not going to question the mechanics of it, I'm only grateful for the result."

"It's an amazing thing Hank is doing with his retirement, isn't it? If not for his granddaughter with Down syndrome, I'm sure he never would have come up with the idea to start the center. And now look what he's accomplishing. It's not every day a guy like me gets to be part of a miracle."

Hank was changing lives, helping children, while Jace had spent the better part of two years wasting every single chance he'd been given with self-indulgence.

She was silent for a few moments, watching the horses enjoy their dinner. When she turned to him, her eyes were softer than they'd been when they left the house. "You're a tough man to stay angry with. How does anyone do it?"

"Lots of practice?"

She laughed out loud, something he sensed she didn't do nearly often enough these days, and a warm sense of accomplishment bubbled up inside him. Maybe his life wasn't completely a waste if he could bring a little laughter into her world.

He wanted more, he suddenly realized as he watched her features relax. She was extraordinarily lovely in the dusky light, her features soft, subdued like a pastel watercolor.

He ached to touch that skin along her jawline, to trace a finger there and feel the softness, then learn the curves and hollows of her smile.

Her gaze collided with his and after a moment, her smile slid away, replaced by something else—wariness, awareness, hunger. He wasn't quite sure.

He only knew he had to kiss her.

Chapter Five

Christa held her breath, her heart racing in her chest like Shiloh on a wide stretch of alpine meadow.

He was going to kiss her. She had seen his gaze flicker to her mouth and saw the sudden heat flare there.

Anticipation swirled inside her, rich and sweet as the finest Belgian chocolate.

He was going to kiss her—and she was going to let him. Just one taste. That's all she wanted, one heady, delicious taste of him that she could savor after he went back to his whirlwind life and she was left here amid the tumult of hers.

It was foolish, she knew. Selfish, even. But didn't she deserve a little respite from her constant stress over Hope? Surely heaven couldn't begrudge her this one indulgence.

She held her breath as he slowly moved closer, his eyes dark as a moonless night. At last—at long, long last—his mouth found hers with an aching, unexpected gentleness.

She shivered and closed her eyes as his heat and strength surrounded her. He smelled a thousand times better up close—of pine and sage and life, like her favorite mountain trail after a spring rain shower.

She was vaguely aware of the sounds of evening around them—crickets chirping somewhere, one of the horses whinnying, the wind sighing in the top of the huge elm tree.

Mostly she was consumed by Jace. The taste of him, the

silk of his hair beneath her fingertips, the leashed strength in his muscled frame.

Oh, heaven.

She leaned into him, wanting this stolen moment to stretch out forever, like a sultry, endless summer afternoon. He deepened the kiss, his tongue tangling with hers, and she lost all reason as heat and hunger churned through her. She wanted to be closer—and closer still.

When he finally drew away from her, they were both breathing hard, and beneath her fingertips she could feel his heartbeat, as urgent and fast as her own.

It took her several moments before she could string any coherent thoughts together and force herself to step away.

"Okay, you've obviously made your point," she finally said, her voice rough.

He waited several beats before answering. "Did I…have a point?"

He looked slightly dazed; his eyes had a vague, unfocused look to them. She sternly told herself not to find that flattering in the least.

"Wasn't this some sort of object lesson? I'm attracted to you. I told you as much the other day. Obviously that hasn't changed, but neither has anything else."

Not exactly true, she admitted. She was now even more attracted to him, and not just on the obvious visceral level. Yes, she responded to him physically, but watching him charm both her daughter and her mother during dinner had stirred something in her heart—something far more dangerous than simple attraction.

She was beginning to discover he wasn't the feckless ex-rodeo star she wanted to think him, concerned with nothing but his image.

Jace was different. He had befriended a girl who could barely communicate and he had been inordinately kind to her mother, listening to her humble stories about Sage Flats as if he found them the most fascinating tales in the world.

Blast him! It had been far easier to tell herself she couldn't possibly be interested in a man like him before he'd shown all these other facets that proved her wrong.

"Okay," he finally answered. "You're attracted to me, but nothing has changed. Good to know."

She sighed, feeling foolish all over again. "I get the impression you're a man who likes to get his own way."

He leaned a hip against the fence post and crossed his arms over his chest. "Guilty. I'll admit it. I do like to get my own way. Sorry. So does that make me particularly unusual among the men you know?"

A half laugh slipped out before she could jerk it back. "No. Of course not. Quite the opposite, in fact. Most men do, I'll give you that. But not only do you like your own way, you also strike me as a man unaccustomed to hearing the word *no.* I think maybe you wanted to show me what I was missing. Why else would you kiss me?"

She had never noticed he had a little indentation on the side of his mouth that quirked when he was amused.

"Why else?" he asked dryly. "And did I?"

"I'm not stupid," she said, though of course it was a blatant lie. Only an idiot would think she could kiss Jace McCandless and be content with one little kiss.

"You're gorgeous, successful, loaded and just about the sexiest man I've ever met," she went on. "Of *course* I know what I'm missing! That doesn't change one thing about what I said the other day—that I'm not interested in some kind of… of fling with you."

He opened his mouth and she braced herself for arguments. Instead he closed it again and gazed out at the horses for a long moment, now just silhouettes in the gathering darkness.

When he finally turned to her and spoke, she had the definite impression he had originally intended to say something else.

"It might surprise you to know that I didn't have any ulterior motive by kissing you. It was one of those just-can't-help-myself moments. I'm not sorry for it, though. Not one damn bit. I should probably confess I would do it again in a heartbeat."

Again she fought down the impulse to be flattered. "All the more reason for me to ask you to leave me and my family alone."

She was such a coward. Could he tell how much the idea of falling for him terrified her? Oh, she hoped not.

"You don't trust yourself very much, do you?"

She flushed. "Wh-what do you mean?"

He shrugged. "I said I would probably try to kiss you again. But if you have such strong objections—as you apparently do—there's no reason you have to let me."

She released a relieved sigh. He didn't suspect exactly how weak she really was inside, how she was just another kiss or two away from falling hard for him, like every other woman he'd ever met.

With supreme effort, she forced herself to give him a cool look. "My life is in chaos right now, Jace. I'm sure this is a shock to that profoundly healthy ego of yours that we've discussed at length, but did it ever occur to you that maybe I have better things to do with my time and energy than spend my limited free time fighting you off?"

He laughed so hard the horses trotted over to investigate. "Fair enough. But what about Ellen and Hope? They've invited me to visit again, and I'd like to come."

"Why?"

He shrugged. "I like being with them. Today was just about the best day I've spent since…well, in a long time."

The wise thing would be to tell him not to come around. It was the easy road, the comfortable one.

But she couldn't deny that Hope seemed to try harder at re-learning skills when Jace was around. If he motivated her to work harder, surely Christa could control herself around him.

"I guess I'm okay with that." Cool evening air swirled around them, and she shivered a little, with the oddest feeling that she had just made a terrible mistake.

She scrambled to regain her footing. "I need to set some conditions, though."

"Such as?"

"If I feel that spending time with you is detrimental for my daughter—hindering her rehab progress in any way—I will insist on no future contact. I want your word that if I believe it's in Hope's best interest, you'll agree to stay away."

"Just on your opinion alone?"

"I'm her mother," she said bluntly. "Right now my opinion is the only one that matters."

"Not Ellen's?"

"I owe my mother more than I can ever repay for all the help she's been the last five months. But I'm still Hope's mother and I'm ultimately the one responsible for her care. I try to listen to Ellen's opinion when it comes to Hope, but in the end I have to trust my own judgment about what's best for my daughter."

It was all she could do, she thought, though sometimes the weight of that task seemed heavier than she could bear.

"All right," he finally said. "If you feel my presence isn't helping Hope, I'll agree to back off."

"Thank you," she murmured, somewhat surprised at how readily he agreed. "We should probably go back to the house or they'll be wondering where we are."

He nodded and followed her back up the rocky pathway toward home.

It looked as if her luck had finally run out—or finally caught up with her, depending on how she wanted to look at things.

Nearly two weeks after their intense kiss and equally intense conversation by the barn, Christa pulled into the driveway of her mother's house beside a familiar gleaming silver pickup truck.

Nerves skittered through her, equal parts excitement and wariness.

She hadn't seen Jace since the evening Ellen had invited him for dinner, though she was grimly aware that had to be more a matter of coincidence than anything else.

Or perhaps he had taken her concerns to heart and done his best to stay out of her way.

She wasn't exactly sure how she felt about that. Had she given him the impression she wanted nothing at all to do with him?

Probably, she admitted. She had been running scared of the fledgling emotion taking root in her heart.

Two weeks away from him had done nothing to yank it out, especially since she couldn't escape him, even when he wasn't physically present.

She sighed, looking at all the evidence of his handiwork around her mother's place. The graceful new redwood ramp he had built off the back porch. The smooth-as-glass new sidewalk he'd poured the week before down to the horse barn so Hope could visit Shiloh and Shane. The new coat of white paint on the fence that made the whole property seem brighter, happier somehow.

She wasn't sure how she felt about all those improvements, either. She supposed in her heart she still hoped the wheelchair and the accommodations necessary for it wouldn't be needed for much longer. At the same time, this was her mother's house. Since Ellen had obviously given permission for the changes, Christa couldn't very well complain.

Besides, universal design elements such as ramps and smooth sidewalks made sense for more than just someone using a wheelchair. Though Christa didn't like to think about it, Ellen wasn't getting any younger, and those same things that made it easier to push a wheelchair also helped ease the way for aging bones and joints.

Jace had settled right into their lives—or at least into Ellen's and Hope's.

Christa hadn't even seen him at Hope's second equine therapy session, since an emergency at the store had demanded her presence and Ellen had ended up taking her.

Hope had spent the entire evening afterward trying to squeeze the words out to tell Christa about how she had ridden by herself and Jace had walked her around on the lead line and how Debbie, the center physical therapist, said next time she might even be able to trot.

Jace had occupied much of Hope's conversation the last two weeks. He seemed to spend every afternoon Christa was working at the house, and one memorable evening when she'd had a chamber of commerce meeting he had invited Ellen and Hope to his ranch, the Silver Spur, for dinner.

He'd taken them both for a tour of his ranch on a horse and old-fashioned buggy he had on the property, and Hope had glowed for days.

Christa sighed, worried all over again that Hope would be devastated when he eventually got bored of the quiet pace of Sage Flats and returned to his real life.

And he would, she knew. Rodeo cowboys always got itchy boots eventually. It was the nature of the beast.

She let out a breath. She couldn't sit out here all night, like the craven coward she was.

Her nerves jumped crazily as she opened her car door and headed for the house.

The last time she had returned from work during his visit, silence had greeted her inside the house. This time she heard raucous country music blaring from inside before she even opened the door.

She recognized the song as a hit from the singer whose name had been linked romantically with his some months ago, and though she had always enjoyed the group's music before, she decided on the spot that the woman had to be a talentless has-been.

She forgot all about some washed-up Nashville honey when she walked into the family room and found the furniture had been pushed against the walls. Her gaze passed briefly over Ellen, sitting at her quilting frame in the corner, before her attention was completely caught by the other two occupants of the room.

Jace stood in the middle of the space, supporting Hope's weight as her daughter swayed to the music, beaming as though she were at the prom on the arm of the high school football star.

The sheer, unaffected joy in her daughter's smile hit her like a fist in the gut. Oh, she had missed that smile. Tears burned behind her eyes and she blinked them away, taking in how well Hope was moving. Her coordination hadn't completely returned, but as they moved to the music, she seemed much more in control of her limbs.

Christa looked at the man who had brought about such amazing progress. He watched Hope with pride and delight and a deep affection, and to her eyes he had never looked as gorgeous.

It's not every day a guy like me gets to be part of a miracle, he had said.

Something bright and hard flashed through her and settled in the vicinity of her heart. She rubbed at her chest, and for one panicked second she wanted to rush back out of the house and slam the door behind her.

Something monumental had just changed, and she wasn't at all sure she was ready to face it.

She didn't want this. He was entwining himself through their lives, and she didn't know how they would ever be able to untangle themselves.

Jace was the first to spot her. He halted, and she saw something leap into his gaze, something hot and welcoming.

She had to swallow hard before she trusted her voice. "You don't have to stop dancing on my account."

At the sound of her voice, Hope turned and grinned at her mother. "Hi, Mom. Jace likes to dance."

Her words were barely slurred, Christa thought, marveling all over again at her progress.

"You both looked great."

"M'feet still don't work right." Frustration filtered through the glow and Christa shook her head.

"That will come, baby. You know it will. Look how far you've come! A few months ago you couldn't stand at all, and now you're dancing!"

Hope didn't look convinced until Jace planted an affectionate kiss on her forehead. "You're the best partner I've had in longer than I can remember."

"My mom's a good dancer, too," Hope said.

Jace slanted a look toward Christa. "Is that right?"

"Oh, definitely," Ellen piped up. "Christa always used to love to dance. You should have seen her waltz around by herself during Saturday-night Lawrence Welk reruns on PBS. She was better than any of the dancers on there."

"Thanks for sharing that, Mom," Christa muttered as Jace laughed.

"I'm sorry I missed that."

"Me, too," Hope said.

Though she grinned at her mother, Christa could see her legs tremble, her muscles still weak. Jace must have sensed it, too. He guided her to her favorite easy chair and helped her transfer into it.

When she was settled, he shoved his hands in his pockets. He seemed extraordinarily masculine surrounded by three women.

"I'll get out of your way," he said, though he didn't look at all as if he wanted to go.

Christa debated with herself for only a moment. She had missed him, she suddenly realized.

"You don't have to." She spoke quickly, before she changed her mind. "Why don't you stay? It's my night to cook and I'm grilling chicken."

She saw her mother look up from her quilting frame, her eyes wide with surprise at the invitation.

"Yes, do, Jace," Ellen urged with a sudden smile.

"Stay." Hope added her voice to the chorus. "Mom's grilled chicken is yum."

Given how much time he spent here when she wasn't home, she might have expected him to jump at the invitation. Instead reluctance flickered in the dark blue depths of his eyes.

She was certain he would refuse, but finally he smiled. "A man would have to be crazy to refuse a chance to share a meal with three such lovely ladies. I'm definitely not crazy. All right."

"Yay!" Hope exclaimed.

"I'll stay on one condition," he continued with a wide smile that made her toes tingle. "You have to let me help."

"Of course." Christa forced a smile, though those nerves were jumping around her insides like an entire cast of Lawrence Welk dancers.

What had she done? An entire evening with Jace McCandless and all these glittering feelings bursting through her.

She had to be crazy.

Chapter Six

Jace leaned against Ellen's deck railing, noting a bit of a wobble. He made a mental note to brace it the next time he was out here.

If there *was* a next time.

He grimaced. He had been trying not to think about it all day, but he knew his time here was limited. The night before, he'd received the latest in an increasingly urgent series of phone calls from his business manager. Tom had been hounding him for three weeks to get off his butt and return to Houston so they could wrap up last-minute details of several business endeavors that were hitting critical mass.

He'd done his best to ignore the man, but he knew he couldn't do it much longer—nor was he at all certain he wanted to.

Maybe a little distance from the Sullivan women would be good for him, would help him scramble back to safer ground.

All of them—Ellen, Hope, Christa—were becoming too tightly wrapped around his heart, and it scared the hell out of him.

He didn't let people inside his life like this. He just didn't.

It wasn't as though he was some kind of hermit. He had friends he cared about—plenty of them—but always from a much safer emotional distance.

Yeah, he knew it was probably another of those grim lessons he'd learned from his mother and the particular hell of spending his formative years with a junkie. But sometimes the patterns of the past were just too damn ingrained not to keep repeating.

Through the window he could see Ellen and Hope watching television. Ellen smoothed a hand over her granddaughter's hair, and something tightened inside him.

He let out a breath, wishing fiercely for a little Jack Daniel's to block all these terrifying emotions. But he hadn't had anything to drink since that evening two weeks earlier when he had kissed Christa. In many ways, that night had been a wake-up call, when he fully realized how very much he hated what he was becoming.

For the first time since the hotel fire he was thinking clearly. He was still haunted by that night and by the cries of those he couldn't get to in time after the flames became too intense, but he finally allowed himself to be comforted by thoughts of the dozen people he *had* been able to save.

He sighed, gazing out at the pretty little valley. As grateful as he was for the change in perspective, that didn't change the essential fact that he would soon have to leave this place and especially this family.

The screen door squeaked open and Christa came out holding a platter. She was so lovely she took his breath away.

He was fairly sure he had known more beautiful women in his life, but he couldn't remember any of them affecting him the way this one did, with her huge green eyes and her soft smile.

He had missed her these last two weeks. He didn't even like thinking about how much. It had been painfully tough to force himself to schedule his visits with Hope and Ellen here at the house for times when he knew Christa would be at work.

"Are the coals ready?" she asked.

He cleared his throat, but his voice still came out gruff. "Uh, yeah. They should be just right."

"Good. I'm starving." She flashed a smile at him.

He watched her bustle around the grill—she checked the coals and moved them around with her tongs, adjusted the rack just so, then finally transferred the chicken breasts to the grill. In only a moment, savory smells emanated across the deck.

He might have expected her to keep her distance. Instead, after she had the chicken grilling, she joined him at the deck railing. Her shoulder just brushed his as they both leaned on it, looking out at Sage Flats and the surrounding area.

"This has to be the prettiest view in the whole valley," he said after a moment.

"I've always thought so."

"Must have been great growing up here."

He didn't miss the way her shoulders suddenly seemed more tense. "Must it?"

He shot her a swift glance. "Look around! It's every kid's dream. Room to explore, horses to ride, that beautiful view out your window. What's not to love?"

She was silent for a long time. "I hated it," she finally murmured. "I couldn't wait to leave."

Before his grandmother rescued him, Jace would have given every single one of his precious few belongings to spend his childhood someplace like this, somewhere he could be safe and warm and loved. He couldn't quite grasp the concept that anyone would throw this away.

"How could you possibly hate it?"

She shrugged. "Lots of reasons. Hick towns and big dreams don't always mesh. I was stupid and thought the real world started just outside the Sage Flats town boundaries. Plus, my mom and I fought all the time. That didn't help anything."

He stared, unable to imagine Ellen fighting with *anyone*. To him, she had always been kind and serene, and he had never once seen her lose patience with her granddaughter, no matter the provocation.

Christa gazed through the window at her mother, still sitting by Hope's side on the couch. Hope rested her head on her grandmother's shoulder, and the older woman seemed perfectly content to let her stay there, though he guessed it couldn't be comfortable.

"Sorry. I'm still trying to process that," he finally said. "What on earth would you have to fight about with Ellen, just about the sweetest person I've ever met?"

If he hadn't been standing so close to Christa, he might have missed the sorrow that flickered in her eyes, then was gone just as quickly.

"Lots of things. My clothes, my hair, my attitude. I couldn't stand her rules or, worse, her expectations. Mostly I was just a stupid, selfish girl who couldn't believe her mother knew anything about the world."

"Sounds like a typical teenager."

"Maybe." She paused and that sorrow and regret flickered again. "Should I tell you the worst thing I've ever done?"

He didn't know why she seemed in the mood for confession—or why he had this urgent need to pull her into his arms and whisper in her ear that everything would be all right.

This tenderness scared the hell out of him, so he covered his reaction with glibness. Anything to wipe that sadness from her features.

"Okay," he drawled, "but I've heard and seen some pretty rotten stuff in my worthless life. I've *done* some pretty rotten stuff. This better be good."

She nudged him with her shoulder, a brief smile playing at her mouth, but it slipped away quickly and she let out a long, sighing breath. "It's not good. It was cruel and heartless. That's all it was. Now that my own daughter is only a few years younger than I was when I left, I can see clearly just how cruel it was."

She turned around and looked through the window into her

family room, at her mother and her daughter sitting together on the couch. "I told you about the worthless cowboy I ran off with. I didn't tell you that I left in so much anger that I didn't bother to contact my parents for a year. No postcard, no letter, no phone call. Nothing. They didn't know where I was or that Kip had dumped me or that I was pregnant or anything. They didn't have any idea whether I was alive or dead. I think I was just so ashamed of the mistakes I had made I was afraid to face them. But, whatever the reason, I put them through hell. No parent deserves that. It's so hard to come back from something like that and establish a healthy relationship."

"But you and Ellen seem to have done just that."

She seemed surprised by his comment, then she smiled again, a little more genuinely this time. "It's taken a lot of work. I finally gathered all my nerve and called the day Hope was born to tell them they had a new granddaughter. Do you know, my dad closed the store for the first time I remember and they both caught the next flight down to Austin. Just like that, they were willing to forgive everything. I understand that kind of love much better now that I have my own child."

The echo of an old ache spasmed through him, but he pushed it away.

"What about you?" she asked. "You said you've done horrible things. What's the worst thing you ever did to your parents?"

Does being born count? It sounded so melodramatic he knew he could never say it aloud without sounding like an idiot. Instead he shrugged. "I didn't know my dad at all. Like your cowboy, he took off before I was born. And my mom wasn't… healthy most of my life."

Whitewashing the stark truth the way he'd done Ellen's fence posts didn't seem right, not when Christa had just confessed her darkest regret.

"She was a drug addict," he said quietly, words he didn't think he had ever willingly told anyone else in his life.

"Oh, Jace."

This was the reason he didn't tell anyone, that mixture of pity and compassion in her eyes. He wasn't good at being on the receiving end of sympathy and he didn't quite know what to do with it.

"We moved around a lot. California, Georgia, New Mexico. I think I figured once that we'd spent time in just about every state in the union except Utah."

He didn't add that he'd often wondered if that explained why the clean, quiet pace here appealed to him so much, why he had been quick to buy property near Hank and Junemarie even though he didn't spend much time in Sage Flats.

"My grandmother was finally able to track me down when I was eight and kept me with her in Nevada. For the most part, anyway. Nancy—my mother—tried to clean up her act a few times and came back for me, but the good intentions never quite stuck. She died when I was twelve and Junemarie got full custody."

"What a blessing you had your grandmother," Christa murmured, her hand covering his on the railing in a comforting kind of gesture.

It warmed him, both her touch and her words. He had often thought the same thing—that without Junemarie's steady influence he probably would have traveled the same road as his mother, a desperate, lost soul always looking for the next fix.

The day he'd realized broncobusting had become like a drug to him—that he was coming to need the exhilaration and the adrenaline and, yeah, even the adulation of the fans—was the day he'd decided it was time to think about retiring.

Another reason he'd stopped drinking—because he'd been coming to need that oblivion too much.

Christa's small hand still covered his on the railing and the connection between them seemed to pulse with life.

He was falling for her.

Falling hard.

The idea intrigued him just as much as it scared the hell out of him. He'd never been in love before. Never even come close. He'd been attracted to other women, of course, but he'd never known this fragile emotion fluttering through his insides.

He wanted desperately to kiss her again. She was so close, so soft, so very, very appealing…

And she had firmly asked him not to a couple of weeks ago.

He let out a breath. But hadn't he told her he would probably try again? Anyway, she wasn't exactly keeping distance between them. She was right next to him—and *she* was the one who had initiated contact. She was practically holding his hand, for pete's sake.

One more kiss, he promised himself. That's all. He would be leaving any day now and this was probably his last chance.

Her gaze met his and he was certain he saw a warm and enticing welcome there. He saw her pupils widen, saw a fragile pulse beating at the curve of her throat, and he leaned forward.

Just before his mouth would have brushed hers, she jerked away.

"I've got to turn the chicken," she managed, though her voice came out breathy and strangled.

"Right. The chicken." He let out a long breath. Probably better this way. He would already miss her entirely too much when he left Sage Flats.

This had to stop.

After dinner, Christa sat at Ellen's quilting frame with her mother, practicing the most basic of stitches—all she dared—while Jace helped Hope work on walking.

It was entirely too domestic a scene, probably the reason for this restlessness she couldn't quite shake.

No. She knew the reason. Because some part of her ached to recapture those moments on the deck when he had nearly kissed her—to rewind and replay and see what might have happened if she hadn't panicked and rushed away.

Impossible. What was the matter with her? She knew what would have happened. He would have kissed her, she would have responded…and she would have fallen even deeper for him.

The whole situation was fraught with emotional pitfalls. She had recognized it from the very beginning, but she was too foolish to put a stop to it.

She wasn't quite sure how it happened, but he had become so tightly stitched into the fabric of their lives that she had no idea how they would yank him out when he left Sage Flats.

And he would. She knew it, could feel his departure looming nearer. Hope would be devastated when he left—and hadn't her daughter been through enough pain?

Christa would be devastated, too.

She pressed a hand to her stomach, beneath the level of the quilting frame, hoping Ellen didn't notice.

Oh, what a mess. She was falling in love with him—his gentleness with Hope, his caring for Ellen, the laughter he had brought into their lives.

She had the oddest feeling they had all been lying dormant for five months, just waiting for him to blow into their lives and shake things up.

"Everything all right?" Ellen asked.

She met her gaze, hoping her perceptive mother couldn't see the wild tumult of emotion in her eyes. "Of course," she lied. "Everything's fine."

"Hope is doing great, isn't she? Jace has been so good for her."

She turned her attention to the pair in the middle of the floor and her hands froze on the quilt top. Jace had let go of Hope's hands and she was taking a few shuffling steps on her own.

Careful! Christa worried, but her daughter looked radiant at taking those few hesitant steps.

"Look! My balance is better," she exclaimed, her words almost perfectly clear.

"You're doing great," Jace encouraged her. "Just a couple more."

She moved toward him, her arms as wide as her smile. She turned her head to make sure Christa and Ellen were watching, and in that instant something happened. Christa wasn't certain whether Hope lost her balance or her legs gave out. Either way, she started to fall and Jace rushed forward to catch her. Their foreheads collided with a loud thud, but he managed to keep her from tumbling to the floor.

"Ow," Jace said with a laugh. "You've got one hard head, young lady. Are you okay?"

She didn't answer, and Christa, already half out of her seat, jumped the rest of the way, her instincts humming.

The instant she had a clear view of Hope in Jace's arms she knew what was happening. Hope's head lolled backward and her arms twitched violently.

The impact of their heads colliding must have triggered one of Hope's seizures. They had become much less frequent since the initial brain injury, but the signs were still unmistakable.

Ellen knew, as well, and both of them rushed into action.

"Lay her on the couch," Christa ordered.

He complied, then stood by while Ellen arranged her limbs safely and Christa tilted her head to make sure she had a clear airway.

"What time did it start?" Christa demanded.

"Eight-oh-six," her mother said promptly. "I'll get the DIASTAT."

"Okay, but let's wait a couple minutes and see if she comes out on her own."

Oh, she hated this. Of all the trials Hope faced since her

accident, the damn seizures were the worst—especially the gnawing fear that Hope would suffer more brain damage after a particularly bad one.

She brushed wispy blond hair out of Hope's eyes, aching inside at all her child had to endure.

"What can I do?" Jace stood beside the couch, his features pale beneath his tan.

"Nothing," she bit out. *Haven't you done enough?* "Just go home."

"I can't leave until I know she'll be okay."

Hope wasn't okay. She hadn't been since that instant last December when their world changed forever.

This was his fault. He was pushing her too hard. Why hadn't he been more careful? He was overstimulating Hope just by his presence, stirring her up, making her take dangerous risks she wasn't ready for.

Christa knew her anger was irrational—the fall had been an accident that could just as easily have happened when Christa or Ellen or one of the other aides was working with Hope. Some part of her knew she was only looking for a convenient excuse to push him away. As far as she was concerned, this definitely fit the bill.

Ellen returned with the DIASTAT before Christa could snap at him to get out of the way and let her take care of her daughter the only way she knew how. Her mother held it out in her hand that only trembled a little, but Christa shook her head.

"I don't think we'll need it. I think she's coming out of it."

"Oh, good!" Ellen breathed.

"What time is it?"

"Eight-twelve," her mother answered promptly.

Six minutes. It wasn't the longest seizure she'd ever had, but, as always, each second seemed an eternity.

"We'd better get her into her bed. She'll be postictal for a while."

"What's that?" Jace asked.

Christa didn't want to take time to answer him, but Ellen did it for her. "It's a postseizure state. Almost semiconscious. Seizures exhaust the system, and Hope usually sleeps for a long time after she has one."

He seemed overwhelmed by the information, but he nodded. "I'll carry her into her bed."

Before Christa could object, he scooped Hope into his arms without effort and carried her through the doorway to her bedroom.

"I can handle things from here," Christa said. After a moment, he nodded and slipped out of the room, and she quickly changed Hope into a nightgown, administered her evening meds through her G-tube and checked her vital signs.

When she returned to the family room, she found Ellen and Jace sitting together on the couch. His eyes were dark, haunted.

"It's absolutely not your fault, my dear," Ellen said in her serene voice, patting his hand. She spied Christa. "Tell him, sweetheart. Jace isn't to blame, is he?"

She was so angry at the world, at fate, at *him*. Though she knew it was harsh of her, she couldn't bring herself to answer, and her silence was condemnation enough.

Ellen frowned at her but said nothing. If possible, Jace looked even more upset.

"I should go."

"Yes. You should."

His mouth tightened, and this time Ellen narrowed her gaze. She opened her mouth, but Christa cut off her reprimand before she could utter it.

"I'll walk you out," she said to Jace in a much gentler voice.

He rose and said goodbye to Ellen, then followed Christa outside. The evening had cooled considerably, typical for spring in the high desert valleys, and she shivered and crossed her arms over her chest.

"You really think the seizure is my fault?"

As much as she would have liked to confirm it, her conscience wouldn't let her, especially when she heard how upset he sounded.

"Maybe a little bit but not completely. Like Ellen said, Hope sometimes has seizures for no reason at all." She paused. "You push her harder than my mother or I do. I'm not sure that's a bad thing. She's made great progress these last few weeks, in large part because of you."

"That's something, I guess."

"Yes."

A cold breeze blew down out of the mountains and she shivered. "When are you leaving Sage Flats?" she finally asked.

Great. More guilt to add to his plate. Jace let out a breath, playing for time. "Why do you ask?"

"I just wondered. You've already been here nearly a month. That's some kind of a record for you, isn't it?"

He grimaced. Yeah, it was. About three weeks longer than he usually stayed. "I didn't realize I had a time limit for staying at my own ranch."

"You don't. Of course you don't."

He sighed, not sure why he was suddenly so reluctant to tell her he had already made the decision to leave. He owed her honesty if nothing else.

"I'm due in Texas in a few days to meet with my business manager to look over some investments."

She nodded, and he had the distinct impression she wasn't at all surprised. Was he sending out some kind of one-boot-out-the-door vibe?

"Are you coming back to Sage Flats?"

"I haven't figured that out yet. I'm sure I'll be back eventually."

She crossed her arms even tighter around herself, a clear message that she wanted him to keep his distance. Better that way, he decided.

The silence stretched between them, tight and awkward now. He opened the door of his truck. Before he could climb inside, she spoke quickly, as if afraid she wouldn't be able to get the words out.

"I think it would be better for Hope if you stayed away between now and when you leave."

Instant objections rose in his throat, even though he'd thought the exact same thing earlier in the evening. He hated the idea now as much as he had then.

The thought of his life without the three Sullivan women in it filled him with dread—Hope, with her endless courage, Ellen's quiet dignity and Christa.

He studied the woman in front of him. As always, her loveliness seemed to take his breath away, seemed to strike some elemental chord deep inside him.

Christa, with her slow smile and her green eyes and the steel core of strength that carried her through adversity.

He was in love with her.

He clenched his hands into fists at his sides, fighting with everything he had against the overwhelming need to pull her into his arms.

He definitely needed to get the hell away from Sage Flats.

"I'm sorry, Jace. I don't want you to think I don't appreciate all you've done. But it's going to be hard enough on Hope when you leave. I have to think about her best interests. I think this way is better."

Better for whom? The absence of the three Sullivan women was going to leave a gaping hole in his life. Maybe she was right, though. Maybe it would be best to leave before he was in this too deep to climb back out.

"All right," he said promptly. "I want to do what's best for Hope."

"She loves you already, Jace. With every day you become more important to her. She's dealt with enough loss in her life. I can't bear to sit by and watch her deal with this, too."

"Can I email her? Call once in a while to see how she's doing?"

She shrugged. "I can't stop you. It might make this a little easier on her."

"I guess this is goodbye, then." His voice sounded ragged, raw, and he was stunned at the ball of emotions lodged in his throat. "Tell Hope and Ellen that for me, will you?"

"Yes," she whispered. He saw in the moonlight the slender tracks of tears on her cheeks. Was she crying for Hope or for herself?

Did it matter?

He started to climb into his pickup, then froze. Before he could talk himself out of it, he climbed back out. In a single quick motion, he pulled her into his arms one last time.

She gasped his name when his mouth descended on hers, but she didn't yank away. Her mouth was soft beneath his, warm and sweet, and a deep wave of longing and regret and tenderness washed over him.

All too soon he knew he had to end it or he would never be able to leave. He wrenched his mouth away and brushed a thumb against one more tear trickling down her cheek.

"Goodbye," he murmured.

This time when he climbed into his truck, he didn't climb out again. He just fired up the engine, backed out of her driveway, then drove away, fighting with everything he had not to look in his rearview mirror at what he was leaving behind.

Chapter Seven

Two days later, Christa still felt as if all the joy and color had been sucked out of her world. The weather perfectly matched her mood, a gray, ugly day full of clouds but no rain.

At least rain might clear her head a little so she didn't feel this constant, grinding pressure, the fear that she'd made a terrible mistake.

She had to stop, had to snap out of this funk. Her work was suffering, she was short with Ellen and Hope and she couldn't seem to focus on anything but the aching emptiness of her life.

To her relief, Hope didn't seem to share her dark mood. At least not right this instant. Christa glanced in the rearview mirror, where Hope was peering out the window, anticipation on her features.

"Do you think Jace will be there?"

If she hadn't been driving, Christa would have closed her eyes and groaned. She had explained to Hope that Jace had to leave and he didn't know when—or if—he would be back. But the reality didn't seem to sink through with her daughter.

"I doubt it. He's probably already on his way to Texas."

One more thing to fill her nights with guilt. Had she done the right thing, trying to protect her daughter from future pain? Or had she pushed him away for purely selfish reasons, so she could insulate her own heart?

"I wonder when he'll be back."

Christa sighed. "I don't know if he will, honey. I talked to you about this, remember?"

Hope made an exasperated face, looking so much like her typical teen self that Christa nearly drove off the road. "Mom, I'm not stupid. I can remember something we talked about yesterday."

"Then you should remember that I said I didn't know if he would be back. He has many business interests away from Sage Flats that demand his attention."

"He'll be back," Hope said with complete assurance, and Christa sighed heavily.

"Maybe. But you have to promise you won't be too disappointed if he's not."

"He has three other houses. Did you know that?"

With the millions of other possible conversation topics, why did they have to continue talking about Jace? "No. I didn't know," Christa answered, racking her brain for a way to change the subject.

"Yep. One in Houston, one in California, on the beach, and another ranch somewhere in Montana."

To her relief, they reached the equine therapy center just then and she didn't have to scramble for a reply.

The next few minutes were busy taking out the wheelchair and transferring Hope, all while fighting a ridiculous flutter of anticipation that he might be inside the arena just like the first time they had come here.

But she was doomed to disappointment. No, it was relief, she told herself quickly after a scan of the building showed no sign of a familiar lean, gorgeous cowboy with blue eyes and a black Stetson.

Instead Hank Stevens greeted them with his usual gruff warmth.

"No Jace?" Hope asked, and Christa saw with a pang that much of the light had left her features.

Hank rested a beefy hand on her shoulder. "No. Sorry, kid. He's catching a flight out tonight and had some things to do on the ranch before he left."

"Oh."

Compassion washed across his grizzled features, and his gaze flicked to Christa, then back to Hope. "You're gonna want to try to find a smile in there again, especially when you see the surprise he left for you."

Some of her excitement returned. "What surprise?"

"You stay here. I'll be right back."

He walked away, only to return a moment later leading a small sorrel mare with black markings.

As he approached, Hope caught her breath and clasped her hands together.

"What's this?" Christa asked, not quite believing what her instincts were already telling her.

"Jace picked out this pretty little mare for our girl here. He must have looked at two dozen horses before he found this one. She's the sweetest-tempered horse I've ever seen, with a smooth, easy gait that will be just perfect for Hope."

"Mine?" Hope's eyes shone with the light of a thousand stars.

"You want her?"

"Yes," she breathed. "Oh, *yes*!"

"Her name's Milagra. Mila. It means *miracle* in Spanish."

He bought Hope a horse? Her own Miracle? Christa stood beside Hope's chair, trying her best to comprehend why he would do such a thing.

He had looked at dozens of horses, Hank said, until he'd found the perfect one. The idea of Jace taking such care and energy for her daughter—a girl she had ordered him to stay away from—sent her reeling, her emotions a wild, jumbled, choking mess inside her.

Oh, heavens. She loved him.

This was no crush, no mere physical attraction.

She was in love with Jace McCandless. And he was going to break her heart.

The rest of the therapy session passed in a blur. She was barely aware of her surroundings, only of the exuberant joy on Hope's features as she rode around the arena on her own horse.

Christa was still in a daze when Hank joined her at the railing.

"She's a real beauty, isn't she?"

She gave him a sidelong look. "The horse or my baby girl?"

Hank guffawed. "Take your pick. They're both winners in my book."

She managed a smile, but it faded quickly. "We can't possibly accept such a gift, Hank. Surely you understand that."

He held up his hands. "You're gonna have to take that up with McCandless. I'm just the middleman. I should tell you, though, he figured you'd say that and he told me to tell you the gift is nonnegotiable and nonreturnable. He suggested you leave her here and board her at our place while Hope still needs the horse therapy—that way your girl will have a warm, secure place to ride all year long until she's ready to take off on her own. He figured it would be safer that way, for a few more months, anyway."

Christa closed her eyes, overwhelmed all over again.

"And don't you worry about the cost of boarding her or the cost of Hope's therapy. You've got enough on your plate. That's all been taken care of."

Jace again. She knew he must have worked things out with Hank. She had ordered him out of their lives, but somehow he had still managed to find a way to have a lasting impact.

She wanted to sit right there in the hay and heaven knows what else and just sob.

"How can I accept such a gift?"

Hank patted her hand, and the compassion in his eyes

brought those tears ever closer to the surface. "It's not for you, is it? It's for Hope."

That seemed to say everything. Yes, his gift had been for Hope. But she remembered that last searing kiss, the tenderness in it she hadn't dared let herself believe, and she knew some part of his gift had been for *her*, as well.

"He's a good man, isn't he?" she murmured, unable to take her eyes from Hope.

Hank was quiet for a moment. "Yeah," he finally said. "His heart's always been in the right place. I think he just lost sight of that for a while. But you and Hope helped him find it again."

He walked away, and she spent the rest of the hour trying to make sense of that. When Hope and Milagra approached the mounting block at the end of the session, Christa hurried to join them.

"I love her, Mom," Hope gushed after she was helped off but before she transferred to her wheelchair. "She's beautiful. The best horse ever!"

To her surprise, Hope threw her arms around her mother and hugged her tight, and Christa returned the embrace, a lump in her throat.

She couldn't help remembering those tension-filled days before Hope's injury, when they seemed to fight about everything—much as Christa had done with her own mother when she had been Hope's age.

She could never look at the accident and its horrific consequences with anything resembling gratitude, but she had to admit many blessings had come into their lives they would have otherwise missed.

Her relationship with Hope had been forever changed. There was a bond between them that would never have been forged without the trials of the last five months.

She could say the same for her relationship with Ellen. Living in her mother's home as an adult had its challenges, but they were vastly outweighed by all they had gained. She had truly come to know her mother and had discovered a hundred things to admire in her—things she had always been too busy and too distracted to notice before.

Hope's accident had taught Christa just how intertwined her life was with so many others. Caregivers, therapists, medical professionals, wonderful neighbors, strangers who had reached out to them.

People like Jace, who had entered their lives completely by chance and had left them forever changed.

Hope was still glowing as Christa pushed her wheelchair out to the Liberty.

"I can transfer by myself," she insisted, something she wouldn't have dared try a few weeks earlier.

After Christa broke apart the wheelchair and loaded it then climbed inside, Hope leaned forward from the backseat.

"Mom, I need to tell Jace thank you. I *have* to. Can we go to his ranch so I can tell him how much I love Mila?"

Christa swallowed hard, dreading the idea of seeing him again as much as she longed for it. She had already said goodbye to him and had thought that was the end of it. Would she have to do it all over again?

Yes. For Hope's sake, she would.

"Of course," she murmured. "He might not be home, but we can try."

"He'll be home," Hope assured her. "I know he will."

But Hope was wrong. Fifteen minutes later they stood on the front porch of his ranch house, a massive, gorgeous log-and-river-rock structure with soaring gables and a stunning view of the mountains.

"That's the third time we've rung the doorbell. I'm sorry, honey. I just don't think he's here."

Hope slumped into one of the half dozen rocking chairs on the porch, tired out since she had walked up the three steps on her own. She stubbornly insisted on walking as much as she could now, to Christa's mingled dismay and pride.

"I thought for sure he would be home."

"We can try to call him later."

"It won't be the same."

Maybe it was better this way, Christa thought, though she knew it was cowardly of her to want to avoid another meeting that would only end in heartbreak.

They sat for a moment in silence to let Hope catch her breath for the walk back down the porch, though Christa couldn't shake the awkward feeling they were trespassing, sitting here on the man's porch when he wasn't home.

"We should probably be going," she finally said. "You have homework, right?"

"I guess."

Hope needed much more help on the way down the steps than she had on the way up. At the bottom she faltered a little and had to hang on to the railing.

"Do you want me to get the wheelchair?"

"No. I can make it. It's not far."

As always, her daughter's determination humbled her. Everything would be okay, she told herself. Hope was as resilient as a tough willow sapling. Just look at her. She was walking again! If she could survive what should have been a fatal accident, surely Christa could endure her broken heart.

They were only a few steps from the Jeep when Hope's features suddenly brightened.

"Mom!" she exclaimed, looking off in the distance. "Look! Is that Jace?"

Her heart seemed to catch, but she followed Hope's gaze to find a rider on a magnificent bay heading toward them at a hard gallop.

The sun had burst through the clouds after they'd arrived

at the ranch and now it caught in his dark hair, and he was staring at them in shock, and she suddenly couldn't breathe.

Her insides clutched in panic and she wanted to rush Hope into the vehicle and drive away again. But then she saw her daughter standing on shaky legs beside her and shame washed through her.

Hope had spent every single day since her accident demonstrating incredible courage and strength. Surely Christa could learn from her example and show a little courage of her own.

She loved Jace McCandless. She couldn't just let him walk out of their lives without a fight.

Jace stared at the two women standing in the spring sunshine.

If he'd still been drinking, he would have figured them for a hallucination, brought on because he hadn't stopped thinking about them since he'd driven away from Ellen's house two days earlier.

He never would have expected to find them waiting for him when he returned from one last ride to work out the kinks before heading to the airport.

But here they were.

He slid from the horse and looped the reins loosely around the top rail of the fence, then started toward them.

To his shock, Hope took several steps toward him, completely unsupported by her mother.

"Look at you!" he exclaimed, meeting her halfway and pulling her into a hug.

"I've been practicing," she said, a definite note of accomplishment in her voice. "My mom's been helping."

"I'm so proud of you, Hope! You're going to be running races in no time."

"As long as they're barrel races."

He laughed and she hugged him, then stepped away, standing on her own.

"Thank you so much for the horse. I love her. She's so perfect. I rode her today all by myself."

Aw, hell. He'd forgotten all about the horse. That must be why they were there. He had really hoped to avoid a scene like this. He slanted a look at Christa and found her watching him out of those huge green eyes that seemed drenched with emotions he couldn't identify.

He wanted to shove his hands in his pockets, but he thought he might need them if Hope started to wobble.

"You're welcome. I hope she'll do until you can ride Shiloh again," he finally said.

"She will. She's perfect. Her gait is so smooth. You should see her!"

He made a noncommittal sound, knowing he never would. He wasn't coming back. He was going to sell the Silver Spur and stay far away from Sage Flats. The alternative was just too painful.

"I have to sit down," Hope said suddenly, and he saw the signs of fatigue in her eyes.

"Are you all right?" Christa asked, stepping forward.

"Just tired."

"You shouldn't wear yourself out just for me," Jace said. "Come on, let's get you inside."

He scooped her up and carried her into his house, setting her on one of the couches adjacent to the big river-rock fireplace that dominated the room.

"Could I have a glass of water?" Hope asked.

"Of course! I'll get you one."

Before he could head to the kitchen, Christa spoke up, addressing him for the first time since he'd ridden up to them. "I'll help you."

He shot her a look of surprise. Yeah, he'd led a pretty worthless life the last two years, but he figured he was probably capable of grabbing a glass of water on his own. Still, he said nothing as she followed him into the empty kitchen, where he found a glass in the cupboard and turned on the filtered-water tap at the sink.

The glass was almost full before she finally spoke. "Jace, I… I don't know what to say to you. You gave her a horse!"

He hadn't expected seeing her again to hurt so much, this steady ache in his chest he could barely breathe around.

"You don't have to say anything. I don't want your gratitude."

She fell silent. "What do you want?" she finally asked.

Your love. Your arms around me. To kiss you again before I die right here in my kitchen for wanting you.

He couldn't say any of those things. Just thinking the words made his throat close up. But something of his feelings must have been reflected in his expression. She stared at him for a long moment, then she gave him a radiant smile.

"Jace," she whispered. Just his name. That was it. Then, before he could respond, she stepped forward and wrapped her arms tightly around his neck. Then, to his shock, she was kissing him with fierce tenderness.

He stood like an idiot for about half a second, then he grabbed her and returned the kiss. Sunshine seemed to pour into the kitchen, bright, vivid light that soaked through him, pushing out all the darkness.

This was what he'd been looking for all these years. This moment, this feeling.

This woman.

"Wow," he managed when he could breathe again. "Want another horse? I've got a dozen out there. Take your pick. Hell, if you kiss me like that again, you can take the whole herd."

She laughed, but her smile slid away quickly. "Don't go, Jace."

Her voice was so low he could barely make out the words and he thought for sure he had misheard. "Sorry—what?"

"Stay. Hope needs you."

She paused, then she shivered a little and met his gaze. The vulnerable expression in her eyes ripped him open like the business end of an angry bull.

"And so do I."

He froze as joy burst through him, wild and radiant.

"Well? Aren't you going to say anything?"

He didn't trust himself to speak, so he pulled her into his arms again as all the disjointed pieces of his life seemed to suddenly fit snugly into place. She settled there with a contented sigh, her mouth softly eager beneath his.

"I love you, Christa," he murmured, brushing the corner of that delectable mouth. "You walked into Hank's therapy arena and you brought the spring sunshine inside with you, and I think I knew in that instant my life would never be the same."

He loved her. She closed her eyes as the sheer wonder of it seeped through her, cleansing and sweet.

"I had a crush on you before I even met you," she answered, "when Hope and I used to watch you on the rodeo circuit. But that was just a two-dimensional image on the TV screen. Then you came into our lives and I fell in love with more than just the image. I fell in love with you. How could I not fall hard for the man who taught my daughter how to dance again?"

His kiss stole her breath but replaced it with more of that sheer, bubbling happiness.

She touched his cheeks, savoring the rasp of his afternoon stubble and the heat of his skin. Her fingers tingled to explore every glorious inch of him, but she couldn't forget her daughter was in the other room.

There would be time. She suddenly knew it with sweet certainty. He might have to go on this business trip, but she knew he'd come back, to Sage Flats and to her.

"Mom? Jace? It's just a lousy drink of water. What's taking so long?"

Christa stiffened as Hope's voice called from the other room, growing louder as she approached. She would have pulled away from him, but Jace's arms tightened around her.

"She's going to know sooner or later," he murmured in her ear. "I'm not letting you go now. Either of you."

Christa turned in his arms to find Hope standing in the doorway, her eyes wide.

"Whoa," she said. Just that.

"I'm crazy about your mother and she feels the same way," Jace said. "You okay with that?"

Hope studied them for a moment, then a sudden, crafty light entered her expression. She looked so much like a typical teenager trying to figure all the angles for her own self-interest that Christa had to fight a smile.

"Does that mean I get to keep the horse?"

Jace laughed, a rich, full sound that seemed to fill the kitchen.

"That's up to your mother."

"I suppose," Christa answered. "I guess a girl can never have too many miracles."

* * * * *